PRAISE FOR CLAIRE COOK'S BOOKS

"Cook creates an impossible-not-to-love cast of imperfect, funny, wistful, and wise characters."
　　　　　—*Publishers Weekly*

"Laugh-out-loud chick-lit confection."
　　　　　—*Good Housekeeping*

"Claire Cook is wicked good."
　　　　　　　—Jacquelyn Mitchard, bestselling author of
　　　　　　　The Deep End of the Ocean

"Reading Claire Cook might be the most fun you have all summer."
　　　　　　　—Elin Hilderbrand, bestselling author of
　　　　　　　Barefoot and *Silver Girl*

"Charming, engagingly quirky, and full of fun, Claire Cook just gets it."
　　　　　　　—Meg Cabot, author of *The Princess Diaries* series
　　　　　　　and *Queen of Babble Gets Hitched*

"Nobody does the easy-breezy beach book with a lighter hand than Claire Cook."
　　　　　—*Hartford Courant*

"A delightful and compelling page-turner . . . [a] feel-good charmer that is seductively engaging and ultimately downright fun."
　　　　　—*Boston Globe*

BEST
STAGED
PLANS

BEST STAGED PLANS

CLAIRE COOK

voice

HYPERION • NEW YORK

The Library of Congress has catalogued the hardcover edition
of this book as follows:

Cook, Claire
  Best staged plans / Claire Cook. — 1st ed.
    p. cm.
  ISBN 978-1-4013-4117-6
  1. Middle-aged women—Fiction. 2. Female friendship—Fiction.
3. Home staging—Fiction. 4. Domestic fiction. I. Title.
  PS3553.O55317B47 2011
  813'.54—dc22

                                                    2010041839

Paperback ISBN 978-1-4013-4185-5

Hyperion books are available for special promotions and premiums.
For details contact the HarperCollins Special Markets Department
in the New York office at 212-207-7528, fax 212-207-7222, or email
spsales@harpercollins.com.

FIRST PAPERBACK EDITION

10 9 8 7 6 5 4 3 2 1

TO MY READERS
IN READERS

(now or before you know it)

AND OUR FARSIGHTED FUTURE

ACKNOWLEDGMENTS

It's a privilege to get to make up stories for a living, and in my paja-mas, no less. A huge, heartfelt thank-you to the readers, booksellers, bloggers, librarians, and members of the media who have made this midlife reinvention of mine possible. I never take it, or you, for granted for a moment.

As I wrote this novel, my Facebook friends and Twitter followers generously revealed the contents of their junk drawers, suggested names for a minor character, and were always available to hang out. Whenever the going got rough, the perfect e-mail from a reader would pop into my in-box. As much as I love the gig, being an author can be isolating, and I thank you all for making it less so.

Many thanks to Ken Harvey for taking time away from his own writing to share some keen insights about this novel. Thanks to Trish Riden, Hayley Stelzer, Amber Fowler, Jill Miner, Eileen Casey, and Carolyn Burns Bass for generously providing pieces of the puzzle—whether they were aware of it or not! Thanks to my in-credible extended family, plus old and new friends, for being there when I needed it.

A great big thank-you to the amazing Elisabeth Dyssegaard, whose reputation as a force is well deserved and whose arrival was pure serendipity, and to her wonderful assistant, Samantha O'Brien. Thanks to the lovely Brenda Copeland for her sharp eye and kind heart, and to her enthusiastic assistant, Kate Griffin. A special shout-out to Ellen Archer for making me feel like I have a friend in high places, and to Barbara Jones and Mindy Stockfield for being so open and encouraging. And a huge, alphabetical thank-you to the rest of the Hyperionites for their talent, support, and tenacity: Anna Campbell, Bryan Christian, Marie Coolman, Molly Frandson, Caroline Grill, Maha Khalil, Kristin Kiser, Laura Klynstra, Joan Lee, Allison McGeehon, Claire McKean, Lindsay Mergens, Karen Minster, Dana Pellegri, Shelley Perron, Mike Rotondo, Sarah Rucker, Shubhani Sarkar, Katherine Tasheff, Megan Vidulich, and Betsy Wilson.

Often the hardest part of all is figuring out which way is up, and I'm forever grateful to my incomparable literary agent, Lisa Bankoff, for never hesitating to point me in the right direction. Many thanks to Lisa's assistant, Dan Kirschen, for his great sense of humor and unparalleled social networking support, and to ICM's Josie Freedman, Liz Farrell, and Lindsey Dodge. A great big transatlantic thank-you to Helen Manders of Curtis Brown Group for handling my translation rights and to Sheila Crowley for jumping in on the UK front.

When it comes to family, I won the lottery. The biggest thanks of all to Jake, Garet, and Kaden.

I've been absolutely terrified every moment of my life—
and I've never let it keep me from doing a
single thing I wanted to do.

—GEORGIA O'KEEFFE

BEST
STAGED
PLANS

CHAPTER 1

OKAY, SO I ACCIDENTALLY WRAPPED MY READING glasses in one of the packages I mailed.

"It could have happened to anyone," I said to my daughter, Shannon.

"Wow, that's pretty lame. Even for you, Mom." The all-knowingness of her three and a half months of marriage reverberated through the phone line.

I ignored it. "If you get them, just mail them back, okay, honey?"

The minute life starts getting easier, your eyes go. So the time you once spent looking after your kids is now spent looking for your reading glasses. I hated that.

"Good one, Sand," my best friend, Denise, said when I called her next. "Remember that time you left Luke at the pediatrician's office in his baby carrier?"

"Your point?" I said.

As if summoned by the decades-old reference, Luke lumbered into the kitchen and poured a cup of coffee. He nodded once, either by way of thanks or a belated good morning, then turned and thudded his way back down to the bat cave.

"Good morning to you, too, honey," I yelled after him.

I was packing up our old life in order to drag my husband kicking and screaming into a new one. The rest of the morning's boxes were still sitting on the kitchen island, so I rifled through them quickly. Foam packing peanuts fluttered to the floor like a dusting of snow. As soon as each box proved itself glasses-free, I tore a strip from a mammoth roll of packing tape and sealed it shut.

It's not like I didn't have other readers. There were at least a dozen pairs scattered throughout the house. Somewhere. But this pair had been my hands-down absolute favorite. Midnight blue with subtle black stripes and a little extra bling from some silver detailing on the sidepieces. The perfect strong rectangular shape to offset my swiftly sagging jawline. Unique in a world of boring drug-store glasses, they were my go-to readers whenever I needed to see anything smaller than a bread box. The only thing about them that drove me crazy was their tendency to fall off my face when I leaned forward.

It turned out to be their fatal flaw.

Once I'd determined that they'd left the premises, I'd retraced my steps to the post office. The man who'd waited on me earlier was a total jerk. So, of course, wouldn't you just know he'd still be working when I walked back in.

A kind of angry arrogance radiated from this guy, maybe fueled by the inadequacy of a spindly gray ponytail that petered out inches after it began. "Anything liquid, fragile, perishable, or potentially hazardous?" he'd always ask in such a bullying tone that he'd man-age to convince me I was a closet pyromaniac and he was the first to catch on.

I thought my best bet was to strategize so I'd get the nice woman at the other end of the counter. I counted the people in the single line, divided by two, and gave up my place to the person behind me.

Somehow I still got the mean guy.

"Anything liquid, fragile, perishable, or potentially hazardous?" he sneered.

"Yeah," I said. "Apparently my life." I laughed my best laugh, the one designed to melt the heart of even a great big bully of a jerk.

His flat eyes scanned me like a bar code. "This. Is. Not. A. Joking.

Matter." He took a slow step back and reached for something under the counter. An alarm? A can of Mace? A double-barreled shotgun?

I held up one hand like it might actually protect me. "Sorry," I said. "Sorry, sorry, sorry. It's just that you're not going to believe what I—"

His hand was still under the counter. The crowded post office had gone quiet. I seemed to have fallen into a *Seinfeld* episode. The guy behind the counter was the post office Nazi. I was Elaine. At least I hoped I was Elaine and not George. Or even Newman. Oh, God, please don't let me be Newman.

"Answer. The. Question."

"No," I said.

One gray eyebrow shot up. "No? You're refusing to answer the question?"

"No," I said. "No is the answer to the potentially hazardous question."

The whole room was staring. I tried to imagine a graceful segue to getting my packages back just long enough for a quick peek inside. No post office rules about how once you send them, neither rain nor snow nor sleet nor reading glasses can impede your packages' journey to their final destination. No extra charge for double mailing. Ponytail Guy would even help me tape my packages back up with federally funded tape.

I shook my head. "Never mind," I said. "Final answer."

ONCE I GOT HOME I made my phone calls. I took a moment to shrug off the post office fiasco and to grieve the at least temporary loss of my favorite reading glasses. Then I moved on.

I turned on the TV to keep me company while I searched for backup cheaters. I found a hot pink pair (what had I been thinking?)

in the junk drawer in the kitchen. They were a bit weak, maybe a 2.25 or 2.50, but they'd do in a pinch. I found two pairs of narrow, full-strength readers, still in their tubular cases, no less, at the bottom of my unbleached canvas grocery bag. One was kind of a dull bronze and the other more of a flat pewter. I wasn't really crazy about either of them.

A little retail therapy seemed like the next logical step, so I sat down at the kitchen island and fired up my laptop. *Best deal on large quantity of funky but not over-the-top bargain-priced reading glasses to replace lost favorites and if at all possible to make midlife woman feel like her pre-vision-impaired hip self again* I typed into the Google search bar. Amazingly, it fit.

I paused, my index finger hovering over Google Search. I moved it incrementally to the right and contemplated the single-result-producing button. I'm Feeling Lucky, it said.

It was more than a slight exaggeration, but I pressed it anyway.

SEND YOUR FRUMPY READERS PACKING! Pitch your boring and outdated drugstore readers and become a fashion-forward reading spectacle! Pack a pair in your purse, tote, car, office, home, and vacation getaway bag, and you'll never be blindsided again. Set includes 8 pairs stylish reading glasses in fashionista colors, along with 1 pair reading sunglasses in root beer with tortoise highlights, plus 9 individual color-coded drawstring pouches and 1 designer polypropylene water-resistant case. That's 19, count 'em, 19 individual pieces for an astonishing $29.95. Retail value $169.99. Styled in the U.S.A./Made in China.

It seemed too good to be true, but who cared. The price was right, and they looked great in the photo, so the worst that could happen was that I'd wear each pair a couple of times and dump them when they fell apart. The truth was that I thought husbands and houses should be built to last forever, but the less sturdy nature of everything else could be a good thing. I mean, who wanted to be married to an outdated set of dishes or a dining room table you were completely over but couldn't afford to unload because you'd spent a veritable fortune on it? Cheaper, easily replaceable items could be the spices of life.

From across the room, the television clicked into my consciousness. I glanced up. A blond reporter who looked about twelve was standing in front of a cookie-cutter house. She was surrounded by an assortment of broken chairs and three Easy-Bake ovens. Two overflowing Dumpsters were parked in the driveway like cars.

She took a quick, shallow breath. "A four-month search for a local woman came to a grisly end this week when her husband spotted her feet poking out from under a floor-to-ceiling pile of filth."

A cat sprang on top of one of the ovens. The reporter jumped. "Police say they searched the house behind me many times, even bringing in cadaver dogs, but they were unable to locate the body among the endless layers of clothing, knickknacks, and rotting food."

I gave my disheveled kitchen a quick glance, assessing the potential challenge to cadaver dogs.

The camera pulled back, and the reporter introduced an expert on hoarding.

"Two to five percent of Americans are chronic hoarders," the expert began. "But that doesn't let the rest of us off the hook. The problem for so many of us . . ."

I waited. The flavor-of-the-month reporter nodded her highlighted head encouragingly. Or maybe just to speed things up so she could breathe again.

". . . is that we're drowning in our stuff. We can't find what we have. So we buy more. We can't remember what we have. So we buy more. We're emotionally attached to what we have, and we can't let it go. And still we buy more. We can't get past all the accumulated stuff in our lives to get to our own next chapters. We're stuck, and until we get rid of all the stuff that's holding us back and stop the endless accumulation of stuff, stuff, and more stuff . . . we'll stay stuck."

"Thanks for sharing," the reporter said. "And now a word from our friends at Big Lots."

I clicked off the TV, but I couldn't shake the image of that poor dead woman with her feet sticking out from under a pile of junk, like some new twist on the Wicked Witch of the East. This was it, the exact message I needed to hear at the exact moment in time I needed to hear it.

I wouldn't just pack up the mess and relocate it. I'd weed out my life. Eradicate. Eliminate. Streamline. Simplify. And once the dust settled, my next chapter would sprout up to greet me like a sunflower on a fierce summer day.

But first I leaned over my laptop and ordered nine new pairs of reading glasses, just so I'd be able to see my way out.

CHAPTER 2

VOLTAIRE SAID THAT ILLUSION IS THE FIRST OF ALL pleasures. As a professional home stager, I'd have to say he was spot-on. Home staging is all about illusion. It's the sleight of hand that infuses an ordinary house with heart, with panache, with *soul*. After the purging and scrubbing, the organizing and arranging, it's the single perfect strand of pearls for that little black dress. It's the art of creating a mood.

The way you live in your house and the way you sell it are two completely different things. Proper home staging will ensure that your home appeals to the greatest number of buyers, thereby selling more quickly, even in a down market.

I loved my work, and I was good at it. I had a string of local Realtors who referred clients to me, backed up by terrific word of mouth that rippled out and brought in the next wave. But I had to admit that I hadn't exactly been walking my talk on the home front. Oh, the complicated and treacherous mysteries of our overloaded lives. Does the land surveyor's family know where its property lines are, and why-oh-why don't the cobbler's kids have any shoes?

OMG, as my daughter would say, I am old enough to remember cobblers.

I'll fast-forward. In college I double-majored in philosophy and art history. With a minor in women's studies, no less. My dorm was perpetually shrouded in pot haze, and when I walked the length of the hallway, my feet stuck to keg leak, which may have contributed to the fact that I never once considered employability as I boogied down my academic path. When reality reared its ugly head at graduation, I decided my only hope was to teach.

I set my sights on elementary art, because I thought the kids would be young enough not to notice that while I could tell them anything they wanted to know about Picasso's blue period, I couldn't draw for beans. I kicked butt when it came to macaroni necklaces though. And tracing chubby little hands to make turkey place mats.

When the budget cuts came, we lost most of our department as well as the art room. I spent a few years rolling an overstuffed art cart from classroom to classroom. I bailed when they added another two schools to my rotation. I still miss the kids. Sometimes I dream that "Tutti Frutti" is blasting on the portable CD player I carted everywhere, and we're all dancing around with a colored marker in each hand, laughing like crazy and drawing the sound of the music on one monstrous strip of shared paper. I was an awesome teacher.

Next I managed an art gallery until it went under, which was absolutely not my fault. I started wallpapering when a contractor friend came out of our bathroom at a party and asked for the phone number of the person who'd done that great wallpaper job in there. When wallpaper went out of style, I hopped to faux finishing.

Faux finishing died a merciful death, and suddenly home staging was all the rage. And the wonderful thing about this crazy world we live in is that you can be anything you want to be if you just jump in with both feet and fake it till you make it.

IT WAS PROBABLY Gertrude Lanabaster's bordello of a bathroom that put me over the edge.

She met me at the door and guided me through an obstacle

course of dusty ceramic figurines and fuzzy African violets perched on tarnished silver tray tables. A philodendron began in a pot in the living room and wound its way up the wall, across the narrow hallway, and into the dining room, guided by green twist ties attached to white cup hooks screwed into the ceiling. The ceilings were popcorn throughout and yellowed like they'd been doused with butter.

By the time we got to the bathroom I had my game plan. "Mrs. Lanabaster—"

"Trudy." She ran her gnarled, gold-ringed fingers over the black lace she was holding. When she smiled, more gold twinkled at her gumline.

"Sandra," I said. "Trudy, staging a home for sale is less about personal taste and more about neutralizing the home so potential buyers can imagine their own possessions there."

"Lovely, dear. Now about my bathroom." She held up the black lace. "I think we've got just enough here for the windows *and* a shower curtain."

I took in the shiny brass fixtures, the strip of Hollywood lights above the ornate gold gilt medicine cabinet. A mildew-spotted Rubenesque nude posed coquettishly on the wall over the toilet tank, peering down at the fluffy zebra-striped toilet seat cover. On top of the tank, the legs of a Barbie-like doll pierced a roll of toilet paper, which was discreetly covered by the crocheted flounce of her skirt. For just a moment I imagined making Knock-off Barbie a jaunty little hat with leftover scraps of the black lace.

I tore myself away and went for the big guns. "You *are* hoping to sell your house, aren't you, Trudy?"

"Mother of God, no. They'll have to carry me out in a box."

I looked through her bifocals and into her eyes, trying to figure out if anyone was home behind them.

"Do you know what a home stager is, Trudy?" I finally asked.

"I do, dear. I've got every single episode of *Designed to Sell* on DVD."

The impact of HGTV on our society simply can't be overstated. Home & Garden TV rocked our world. Everyone from eight to eighty has been sprawled on their couches ever since it first appeared in 1994, addicted as if to porn, literally watching the grass grow, the deck go up, the walls change color. We spend hours and hours sucked in by *House Hunters, Divine Design, Curb Appeal*, and *Color Splash*, becoming armchair experts at everything from electrical wiring to decorating.

I took a stab at it. "So you're saying that even though you're not selling your house, you want me to stage it anyway?"

She held up the lace. "Yes, dear. I want you to stage this bathroom until it's so hot it could fry an egg. And then I'm going to keep it for myself."

WTF, as my kids would say.

Mrs. Lanabaster and I had a blast. I didn't want to overcharge her, so we dragged out her old sewing machine and I got to work right then and there. There was enough crap in her house that in only a couple of hours we had a bathroom bordello that would make any octogenarian with bad taste proud. All it needed was a couple of red bulbs for the strip light.

It wasn't until I was coming out of Home Depot with the bulbs that a shiver came over me. It started between my shoulder blades and ran up the back of my neck. It was easily distinguishable from a hot flash by both temperature and trajectory, since as everybody who's been there knows, hot flashes tended to begin in the face and work their way down.

An epiphany arrived with the chill: If I didn't play my cards right, in a few short decades I could *be* Mrs. Lanabaster.

My husband and I would still be living in the house we'd meant to dump years ago to downsize, before we got too old and it all became too overwhelming. Halfhearted piles of book-filled boxes would be sitting in limbo. The roof would need to be replaced *again*. Even our prized granite kitchen counters would have gone hopelessly out of fashion as we dawdled and dawdled and dawdled some more. A balding Luke would still be down in the bat cave, where half-eaten bowls of ramen noodles would be stacked floor to ceiling. And, best staged plans and all, my doddering old husband and I would have missed that glorious second honeymoon of life, when the kids are gone but not forgotten, and the two of you buy a tiny cottage near a warm beach somewhere just like you'd always planned.

When I finally pulled into our driveway, my husband, Greg, was leaning up against our freshly painted house, stretching his hamstrings in the unseasonably warm weather.

"What a workout," he said.

"What else did you do today?" I said.

He switched legs. "How was your day?"

I walked by him without answering.

Luke was at the kitchen sink, draining a pot of ramen noodles.

"How can you eat those things?" I said.

He poured them into a bowl. "I like them. They remind me of college."

I bit my tongue so I wouldn't yell, *Oh grow up*.

"We used to heat the water on the radiator," Luke said for what might have been the zillionth time. "We'd all gather around and shoot the crap while we waited for it to boil. Actually, it never totally made it to a boil—"

"We need to talk," I said just as Greg took a careful step into the kitchen.

Greg froze. He slid one sneaker backward. It squeaked against the newly refinished floor.

"Don't even think about it," I said.

"*What?*" they both said at once.

I pointed to the dining room, which we only used for holidays and family meetings.

"Somebody please tell me it's Thanksgiving," Luke said. He twirled his noodles around a fork as he walked.

Greg pulled out my chair for me. He leaned over to kiss me on top of the head as I sat down. "Don't try to butter me up," I said.

I waited while Greg walked around the table and took the seat across from me and next to Luke. Then I slapped both palms down on the distressed farm table.

They both jumped a bit. As well they should have.

"The plan," I said. "Remember?"

I could feel them wanting to look at each other.

My husband stretched his sweaty T-shirt away from his body. He hated not being able to change as soon as he got home from a run. "Of course we do, hon," he said.

I looked at Luke. He shrugged. "What he said."

I bit my tongue and counted slowly to ten.

"What's the date today?" I asked when I finished.

Luke checked his cell phone. He started to raise his hand, then remembered his school days were over and self-corrected. "March fifteenth. Whoa, beware the ides of March."

I nodded. "And we were going to have the house on the market when?"

"Sometime in March?" Greg said.

"March first," I said. "And we're not even close to being ready. Do we need to go through our lists again?"

They shook their heads in tandem.

I blew out a frigid gust of air. "Listen. We made a deal. You know what you have to do. You've got two weeks. Either shape up . . ."

I watched them shift in their chairs while I let the tension build.

When I'd decided they'd had enough, I cleared my throat. ". . . or I ship out. And don't think I'm kidding."

CHAPTER 3

SOME PEOPLE WERE BORN FOR EARLY RETIREMENT, and my husband, Greg, was one of them. He'd never looked better. He'd never felt better. His days were a blur of running to the beach, driving to the gym, and playing tennis with a group of guys who were in the same boat. They met up at the town tennis courts every day at four and played for an hour. If it snowed, they brought shovels.

Greg was a civil engineer and had spent most of his career with the same company. When they went under, he never looked back. We moved his 401K into a cash reserve fund until we could figure out what to do with it, and purely by luck, when the market crashed we didn't lose a cent.

He had a small pension waiting down the road for him, and I had an even smaller one from my teaching days. Our two kids were both out of college, at least physically, and our daughter was married. Greg and I would jump on our Social Security the minute we turned sixty-two, since we were both of the get-it-while-you-can philosophy.

But that was the better part of a decade away. Technically, Greg was still consulting, though there was not a lot happening in the building arena these days. I pulled in decent money, so we were holding our own. But while our mortgage was all but paid off, we'd rolled most of two college educations and one wedding into a home equity loan. Every time I looked at the balance, my breath would catch and my heart would add an extra beat.

Our house was our ticket out.

Situated in a resident-only beach town with train service to Boston, the house was a sprawling 1890 Victorian with an attached screened gazebo porch. It was set on a pie slice–shaped acre of lawn that looked like an old New England town common. The lawn was bisected about a third of the way up from the point by a driveway that opened at either end onto charming tree-lined streets. Massive conifers reached for the sky, and perennial gardens curved seductively.

We'd applied for and received official recognition by the historical society. A white oval plaque edged in black arrived by mail and confirmed the date and the home's original owner, John Otis. The fact that his wife's name wasn't on there, too, totally pissed me off. Even though Massachusetts had passed a law in 1854 that stated women could own property separate from their husbands, the reality, confirmed by a careful drive around my plaque-filled town, was that they didn't even co-own the house they lived in *with* their husbands. I thought we could at least give it to Mrs. Otis posthumously, but my arguments didn't fly with the historical society. Principle eventually caved to increased property value, and I nailed the damn plaque over the massive original front door anyway.

Inside the house were maple floors, ten-foot ceilings, and some of the most beautiful decorative moldings I'd ever seen. A wide central hallway led to an elegant mahogany staircase and opened to large, gracious rooms on either side. A mudroom straddled the space between house and garage, and from the mudroom a back staircase led up to separate quarters for the maid and butler. Since neither had come with the house, the kids used it as a playroom. They called it the secret room.

Our current home was a testament to the benefits of sweat equity and naïveté. When our previous house, a one-bath ranch, began triggering at least one family battle a day, we decided to brave

another rung on the property ladder. We hired a Saturday after-
noon sitter for the kids while a Realtor friend showed us a series of
boring garrison Colonials on cul-de-sacs.

"What about that one?" Greg pointed as we drove by a FOR SALE
sign in front of a big white house that was shielded from the road
by a half circle of ancient trees.

"Ha," our Realtor said. "Rent *The Money Pit* first and then we'll
talk."

"How bad can it be?" I said.

The smell inside the house wasn't very encouraging, and we
couldn't turn on the lights because the electricity had been shut
off. The wooden pulpit in the center of the front parlor and the
REPENT sign over the fireplace didn't exactly add to the ambiance.
Royal blue shag carpeting was everywhere, and a massive burgundy
stain halfway up the stairs made it look like someone had died
there. A huge stainless steel commercial refrigerator blocked the
bay window in the dining room. We actually found empty shotgun
shells in the room up over the garage.

"D'ya think I was kidding?" our Realtor said.

On the way out, I couldn't resist opening the mammoth refrigerator for a quick peek. Twenty years later I can still taste the smell
of the rotting chicken inside.

I WAS IN THE MIDDLE OF A DREAM when Greg came back to
the bedroom and woke me. Movie theater–style buttered popcorn
had been popping off Mrs. Lanabaster's ceiling, and the two of us
had been taking turns seeing who could catch more in the Barbie
toilet paper cover's skirt. We were giggling like kids. Mrs. Lanabaster's hand-eye coordination was amazing for her age, but I was holding my own.

"Bummer," I said. "I liked that dream. Could you keep the noise down a little next time?" I opened my eyes and tried to decide whether I had enough energy to make my own bathroom run or whether my bladder could hold its own through another sleep cycle.

The sound of Greg glugging half a bottle of bedside water made the decision for me. He climbed back into bed and yanked most of my covers over to his side. I yanked back, even though I'd been just about to kick them off and head for the bathroom.

"Hey," he whispered. "You awake?"

"Why?"

"You're not going to believe this."

"Your prostate's better?"

"No, there's a girl in our kitchen."

"Seriously?"

"Yeah. They're popping popcorn together. And get this, she's wearing Luke's Dungeons and Dragons T-shirt. And nothing else."

I rolled over in Greg's direction. "You went down there? God, Greg, you didn't." Luke had had a Goth girlfriend his senior year in high school and a gamer girlfriend throughout most of college. From what we could tell, he'd been in a dry spell ever since graduation, possibly connected to the fact that he never left the house.

Greg made a quarter turn toward me. "No, of course not. Jeez, give me some credit, will you? I sat on the stairs and spied on them through the hallway mirror."

"Oh, good." I yawned. "Do you think the kids ever caught on to that? I don't remember it being on Shannon's endless list of the things she got away with while letting us pretend we had the upper hand."

Greg yawned. "I'm pretty sure they used it on us, too. Especially at Christmas. Remember, we caught them? The bicycle year, when the two of us were downstairs swearing at each other. Shannon said Luke thought he heard reindeer and she was just keeping an eye on him to make sure he didn't get trampled."

"I couldn't believe you didn't pay for them to put the bikes together at the store. I was ready to kill you."

"I had it under control," Greg said. "You were just being impatient."

"It was two A.M. We'd told the kids they could get out of bed at six. They were too old to fall for the changing-the-time-on-all-the-clocks trick."

Greg laughed. "That was a good one."

"Shh. What does she look like?"

"Who?"

"The girl. With Luke."

"I don't know. Young. I just hope all that time down in the bat cave hasn't turned him into a vampire." Greg rolled toward me and tried to bite my neck.

I pushed him away. "Ha. He should be that trendy. *Young*—you're so observant. I hope she has her own apartment. And good social skills. And a rich, full-bodied life."

"What's a rich, full-bodied life?"

I rolled over. "I can't remember. Leave me alone. I'm trying to sleep."

Greg draped an arm across me. "He'll be fine."

I didn't say anything.

Greg massaged the knot between my right shoulder and my neck with a practiced hand. "We'll get there, Sandy. We'll get the house sold. We'll find our next place. Try not to get so stressed-out about it."

I let him massage the matching knot on the other side, then I rolled away.

"If I don't get stressed, nothing happens, Greg. Ever."

I kicked my way out of the covers and headed for the bathroom.

CHAPTER 4

M Y NEW CLIENT WAS IN TOTAL DENIAL. SHE WAS also desperate for her house to sell. My mission, should I choose to accept it, would be to connect the dots between the two.

"Mrs. Bentley," I began after we finished a silent walk-through.

I waited for her to tell me to call her Jane. She didn't.

"Okay," I said. "Well, the good news is I can tell you why your house is still on the market after six months."

"Five and a half."

I shrugged. She had icy blue eyes and three distinct vertical lines between them that would have made her look like a bitch even if she wasn't, which she was.

She ran a dry hand through her flat tan hair. Neither of us said anything. I had half an urge to wait her out and make her speak first. But it was a relatively straightforward job and I'd already decided I wanted it, so I cut to the chase.

"Mrs. Bentley, your home is lovely, but it's a bit stuck in the eighties. I'd recommend a combination of updating and staging."

I followed her eyes as they scanned the black tubular dining room furniture, the mint green and pale pink sectional, the matching glass-and-brass coffee and end tables. I wondered if her kids still had their banana hair clips and slap bracelets.

"Slipcovers over the sectional and the dining room chairs," I continued. "We'll change out the tables. I'm thinking dark wood, some eclectic pieces to give the decor depth. I'll poke around and let you know what's out there. We can rent, or you can buy and take it with you."

"Do you have any idea how much I paid for those tables?"

I opened my eyes wide. "Do you have any idea how much I paid for my shoulder pads? And all the hairspray for that big eighties hair?"

She glared at me. It could have been my imagination, but it looked like a fourth frown line was sprouting between her very eyes.

I gave her a moment to fume before I continued. "I mean, look at you. Your hair and makeup are totally up to date. And see how beautifully you're dressed." This was actually a slight exaggeration, but it was for a good cause. "So many of us forget that our homes need to change with the times, too. We've looked at everything in them for so long we can't even see it anymore."

Mrs. Bentley crossed her arms over her chest. "What else?"

"We'll switch out the heavy drapes for bamboo blinds, replace the brass hardware in the kitchen and baths with brushed chrome. Neutral paint on the walls, maybe Benjamin Moore Pismo Dunes. China White trim throughout."

I walked over to one of the three silk ficus trees that had invaded the formal living room. I shook a branch and released a cloud of dust. "We'll get rid of these."

"But—"

I cut her off with a sneeze. I didn't even have to fake it. "Do you have a tissue?"

Mrs. Bentley pointed to the box.

I blew my nose dramatically.

When I finished, I smiled my most dazzling smile. "For all the rest, we'll use items you've already got to make your house pop." I looked around but couldn't find any examples, so I just let it go. "And then we'll have you out the door and into that cute little condo in no time."

Mrs. Bentley just stood there, as if chewing on her lower lip long enough might make me go away.

"How much?" she finally asked, and I knew I had her.

WHEN WE BOUGHT the big white house, the rotting chicken came with it. Greg gave two guys he knew from around town fifty bucks for Saturday night drinking money to take the refrigerator to the town dump.

One of them came back the next day while Greg and I were dragging a filthy hunk of blue shag carpeting down the front steps. He parked his rusty pickup, kicked the truck door open, and slid out until his feet hit the driveway. His hair was sticking up all over the place, and his T-shirt was on inside out. But who was I to criticize, since my family and I didn't look so hot ourselves. Greg and I had each tied a bandanna around our heads and another one over our mouths. The kids were running around their new yard in mismatched, outgrown Garanimals.

We threw the carpet into a rented Dumpster. Our little boom box was sitting on the edge of the driveway, and Cyndi Lauper was belting out "Girls Just Want to Have Fun." It was Shannon's favorite, so we had to listen to it at least eighteen times a day. I squatted down to lower the volume.

"Hey, man, how did it go at the landfill?" Greg yelled.

The guy pressed the heels of his hands over his eyes. "Whoa, keep it down, will ya? We really tied one on last night."

"Glad we could contribute to the cause," Greg said.

The guy nodded. "Yeah, so, nobody told us about the law that ya have to take the doors off the fridge before they let ya dump it."

Greg and I looked at each other. "We didn't know," Greg said.

The guy uncovered his eyes. "It was friggin' hell, but we finally got the friggin' doors off." He turned his bloodshot eyes to me. "Pardon my French."

"Not a problem," I said.

He scratched his belly with one hand. "Then I puked all over the chicken."

"Eww," I said.

He coughed, then reached for a cigarette. "Friggin' chicken smelled so bad everybody started jumpin' back into their cars and drivin' away before they even finished unloadin' their trash."

Greg apologized, gave him another twenty we couldn't afford, and thanked him again.

He blew a cloud of smoke in our direction and grinned. "Anytime."

Even with the refrigerator and the chicken gone, the house was in rough shape. It had been on the market for two years when we made our ridiculously low offer. We should have been scared away when the owners just said yes, but we couldn't believe our good luck. This was the kind of house rich people lived in.

The couple we bought it from had been using it as a ministry for wayward boys. That explained the pulpit, and possibly even the shotgun shells. The owners had tried to get tax-exempt status as a church in Massachusetts, and when they couldn't, they'd decided to move to Vermont.

Our Realtor assured us that the house would be empty and clean before the final walk-through prior to the closing. We never even got a final walk-through. When we showed up, the sellers simply refused to let us in the door.

The Realtor called a lawyer. The lawyer called the sellers. The lawyer called our Realtor back.

The Realtor turned to us. "Crazy people can get away with a lot of things," she said. "Do you want the house or not?"

Everything we owned had already been loaded into a moving van. We'd just closed on the sale of our three-bedroom ranch an hour before. It was the way we had to do it. Without the money from the first house, we couldn't buy the second.

"How bad can it be?" I said.

We went to our second closing of the day. After a lot of arguing, and a minisermon by the minister, the Realtor got us a six-hundred-dollar escrow to cover the cost of cleaning and removing anything that hadn't already been removed by the sellers. Twenty years ago, that was a lot of money.

But not enough. The movers managed to cram everything we owned into the garage. We piled ourselves into Greg's mother's rumpus room until we could make our new home livable, all four of us sleeping on one big mattress on the floor.

Each night we had a painfully repetitive dinner conversation with my mother-in-law. No matter how we tried to redirect the conversation—current events, local gossip—she always brought it back to two topics: the kids not eating their vegetables and the kids not sitting still at the table.

"When you were their age, Gregory, we could take the four of you anywhere. You'd sit at the table like little angels."

"Ma," Greg would say, "what are you smoking?"

"Don't smoke, Grammy," Shannon would say.

"Don't you remember, Ma? We used to slide down the banister in our cowboy boots, and jump on those big dusty drapes at Grammy and Grandpa's house and try to swing across the room on them? Grandpa would chase us around, yelling, 'I'll get you little bastards,' and Grammy would back him up with a frying pan."

Luke would look up from furtively rolling his grandmother's salty canned peas one by one off the tray of his high chair. "Bastards," he'd say.

"See what you just taught him," Greg's mother would say. "My children never swore."

"Damn right we didn't," Greg would say.

Everybody but my mother-in-law would crack up. And the next night, we'd do it all over again.

After dinner, Greg would head back over to the new house to get a little more work done. I'd give the kids their baths and put them to bed. Then I'd hide out in the rumpus room until Greg came back, a prisoner in someone else's home.

One night, just for something to do, I looked up *rumpus* in an ancient dictionary I found on the knotty pine bookshelves. Noisy clamor. Disruptive commotion. Confused disturbance. Din; tumult; stir; fuss.

We'd entered our rumpus years.

CHAPTER 5

I UNSCREWED THE LAST KITCHEN CABINET DOOR AND stood back to take it all in. If eyes were the windows to your soul, then doorless kitchen cabinets were the portholes to your life. The last two decades lay before me, totally exposed.

The white bowls with the turquoise and chocolate stripes that we'd bought at the Dansk factory outlet on a trip to Kittery, Maine, were so old they were back in style again. I lifted them up and sponged the shelf clean, then arranged them into a snazzy little triangle.

Way in the back of a cabinet, I found a box of artificial sweetener packets, circa 1990-ish. I'd bought it for a diabetic neighbor of the same decade who used to stop by for coffee, and no one else had ever touched it. I hadn't thought of this neighbor in years, and hadn't even been all that crazy about her, but I had a sudden urge to track her down and send the rest of the box off to her. I pitched it instead.

I packed up a collection of Danish modern stainless serving trays to send to Shannon. They'd go perfectly with the sleek, contemporary look she was shooting for in her new house. They'd been wedding presents, but I had no urge to ever serve another appetizer again. If I changed my mind, I'd find something else to put them on.

I'd spent the better part of my life accumulating things, and now I couldn't let them go fast enough.

I worked my way through another cabinet, dividing the stuff into boxes labeled SHANNON, LUKE, DONATE, PITCH, and PACK. I returned just a few items to the cabinets—things we couldn't live without and things that would show nicely when a prospective buyer inevitably peeked inside.

I dropped twenty-nine perfectly good, if slightly crusty, cabinet knobs into a plastic Stop & Shop bag and tied it in a double knot. They weren't awful, but new knobs bring instant sparkle to a kitchen, and I'd already found some great replacements. I dropped the bag into the DONATE box. Who knew, my old knobs could be somebody's big find at the Vietnam veterans' charity thrift shop.

I took a deep breath and kept going. Mismatched soupspoons. Three teapots. Dog dishes that had outlived our much-loved series of family dogs. A melon baller. Two ice cream scoops. A bread maker. A waffle maker. A hot dog steamer. A George Foreman grill.

I was a long way from a guest appearance on *Hoarding: Buried Alive*, but I could relate to the emotional lure of things. It required vigilance to keep them from taking over your life. Those ice cream scoops might remind me of hazy, lazy summer afternoons, all four of us just back from the beach, when the kids were at their cutest and mint chocolate chip or cookie dough was the most earth-shattering decision of the day.

But I could let go of the scoops and still keep the memories. Sometimes I even advised my clients to take a photo of an object before getting rid of it. I crisscrossed the two scratched plastic ice cream scoops—one turquoise, one pink—on the counter and ran upstairs to grab my camera.

I knew the drill. When deciding whether to let something go, there are two important questions to ask: *Have I used it in the last year? In the unlikely event that I ever need it again, could I replace it?*

I rummaged through another cabinet. My mother's prized collection of Tupperware, including a cake carrier and a deviled egg tray. A stuffed Betty Crocker doll from my grandmother that I'd tucked in with the cookbooks. The Reddy Kilowatt pin I'd earned at my first cooking class when I was six.

We had a theme: *ridiculous things you are emotionally attached to.* The trick was to whittle down the collection as much as possible. I pulled out another box and labeled it CRAZY. Anything I could fit in here I could keep. I hadn't baked in years, and Shannon would only laugh at me if I shipped it to her, so I dumped the Tupperware into the DONATE box. If there was a heaven, my mother was now one pissed-off angel. I tucked the doll and the pin into the CRAZY box.

I pulled out the junk drawer and set it on the counter. I reached into the tangled mess, pitching the dried-out markers, the twisted paper clips, the keyless key chains.

"Little Jack Horner" flashed randomly through my mind as I reached in again, but instead of a plum I pulled out my old mood ring from high school. I couldn't imagine how it had ended up in the junk drawer. I sat down in a chair, stretched the adjustable silver band out as far as it would go, and forced the ring over my knuckle and onto my finger.

"Aww," I said out loud.

Back in high school my friends and I had taken our mood rings seriously. We checked in with them all day long to tell us what we were feeling. *Am I in a good mood today? Do I have a crush on Michael Sylvester?*

We trusted our mood rings the way we'd trusted our Ouija boards and Magic 8 Balls in junior high. But mood rings were far more sophisticated. There was even actual science behind them. The clear glass stone in the center of the mood ring was filled with liquid crystals that were extremely sensitive to heat. The crystals twisted their position in response to your body temperature. The position of the crystals determined the wavelengths of the light that were absorbed. When those wavelengths were reflected back, the stone appeared to change colors.

If the clear stone of your mood ring turned blue while you were wearing it, that meant you were happy. Purple meant passionate. Green indicated calm. Amber signified uncertainty. Black said you were seriously stressed.

Funny that I could still remember all this in such detail, but ask me to figure out a basic algebraic equation, or to conjugate the simplest Spanish verb, and I drew a complete blank.

Luke thudded into the kitchen and grabbed the last of the cabinet doors. He and Greg were arranging them on twenty-nine empty liquor boxes they'd picked up at the package store and spread across the side lawn. The plan was to scrub down the cabinets and drawer fronts and then freshen them up with a coat of white spray paint.

Never spend the money to replace your kitchen cabinets before you sell. Just spruce them up. It's simply not worth the cash outlay, and you can't predict the cabinet taste of the next owners. For all you know, you could spend tens of thousands of dollars just to have the new residents rip them right out.

"How's it going?" I asked.

Luke grunted. His eyes squinted against the unfamiliar morning light.

I grabbed some cleaning supplies and followed him outside. "How's it going?" I asked again.

"Great," Greg said. He took two of the cabinet doors from Luke and balanced them on matching Stolichnaya boxes. I hoped the people driving by our house didn't think we'd actually consumed all this liquor.

"Good," I said. I held up a spray bottle. "Okay, don't forget, start with this Simple Green. If that doesn't work, go right to the trisodium phosphate and bleach."

"So much for the environment, huh, Mom?" Luke said.

"I'll make it up to the environment," I said. "As soon as we get rid of this house."

Greg checked his watch discreetly. "Got it. We'll jump right in as soon as we take a little break."

"Yeah," Luke said. "I've got a couple clients I need to check in with."

I noticed that Greg was wearing his newest running shoes. The bottom edge of a sweat-wicking running shirt peeked out from under his ratty old T-shirt. Luke was already hunched over his iPhone, texting.

Luke worked from home as a bug tester for several small video game companies. As near as I could tell, his goal was to work exactly enough hours to pay the tiny portion of the college loans that were in his name as well as the meager rent we were charging him for his own good.

I'd suggested that since all he did with the rest of his time was play video games anyway, he might as well rack up some hours and save for his own apartment or even a down payment on a town house. He'd nodded pleasantly. It was impossible to tell whether he was working or playing, since the electronic sounds reverberating up from the bat cave were identical. I figured there was at least a fifty-fifty chance he was simply humoring me.

Luke was smart and sweet and even handsome, with Greg's shiny brown eyes and athletic build. Somewhere underneath the oddly groomed facial hair, the heavy boots, and the wardrobe of geek T-shirts and pants made shapeless by dozens of pockets was a star waiting to be born. My hope was that pulling the bat cave out from under him would speed up the birth process.

"Listen, you two," I said. "It's a one-day job. You've got to get the cabinets washed, wiped down, and then sprayed with two light coats of paint before the temperature drops below fifty degrees.

And you have to finish early enough that they'll dry and you can get them back into the house before dark. Then after dinner, if all three of us work together, we should be able to screw them back up tonight. We can save the new knobs for tomorrow."

Luke's phone beeped. "New level hot off the presses," he said as he headed for the bat cave.

I looked at Greg.

"Don't worry," my husband said. "Just leave it to me. I've got it under control."

"If I had a nickel for every time I've heard that one," I said as I walked away.

I went right back to sorting through the cabinets so I wouldn't lose my momentum. I got rid of boxes and boxes of tea—chai, chamomile, peppermint, Red Zinger. I dumped a package of coffee filters from the second-to-last coffeemaker we had before the one we had now. I threw out a drawerful of old maps that had become obsolete with the invention of MapQuest, along with the instruction manuals for two toasters and a microwave we no longer owned.

The box for Shannon was full, so I took a break to write her a little note. I tucked it inside and taped up the box.

I peeked out the kitchen window to check on the cabinet progress.

Two of the liquor boxes had tipped over and thrown their cabinet doors to the damp March ground. The Simple Green was exactly where I'd left it, and the roll of paper towels didn't look any smaller.

Greg and Luke were MIA.

I didn't really need to check in with my mood ring to know what I was feeling, but I looked down anyway. A furious black stone stared back at me.

CHAPTER 6

I COULDN'T REMEMBER IF SHANNON HAD EVER VOICED an opinion about the trays I was planning to mail off to her today. I was pretty sure she'd like them, but if there was one thing I'd learned as the mother of a daughter it was that you never, ever knew.

I pulled up her name on my speed dial.

"Hey," she said on the first ring.

"Hi, sweetie. Do you want those Danish modern stainless trays? You know, the ones Dad and I got for our wedding?"

I could hear the wheels of her brain turning from Atlanta. "I don't know. Would you want me to have them if I were a client? Or is it purely sentimental, and you just don't want to be the one to dump them?"

Shannon had been asking questions like this since preschool, so I was used to it by now.

"Yes or no," I said.

"Okay, yes. Thanks. Listen, I can't talk. Later."

"You're welcome," I said, even though my firstborn was long gone.

Denise called before I even had a chance to put my BlackBerry down. She skipped right over *hello*. "Who's your BFF?"

"Uh, give me a minute. It's right on the tip of my tongue. Carol Flanagan?" I switched the BlackBerry over to my other hand, opened the refrigerator, and started making a grocery list.

"Oh, please. That little trollop? She slept her way through the entire boys' debate club junior year."

I shook my head. "They were probably just really convincing. So what's up? You're not calling to cancel on me, are you?"

"No, I'm calling to tell you how lucky you are to have me and how excited you'll be when I tell you what I just did for you."

"Milk," I said.

"What?"

"Oh, sorry, I was writing." I opened a carton of eggs for a head count.

"Begging won't get you anywhere," Denise said. "You're just going to have to wait till lunch to find out."

"Yogurt," I said. "Hey, do you think that probiotic stuff is for real, or is it just a load of crap?"

OUR CURRENT HOUSE was only a hop, skip, and a jump to the post office, but our letter carrier's route started at the farthest point and worked its way back. It drove me absolutely nuts that I could watch the post office jeep drive by our house with our mail in the morning, but I couldn't get my hands on it until sometime between 4:00 and 5:00 P.M.

Over the years I'd tried flagging down a series of letter carriers, with and without bribes ranging from doughnuts to lemon pound cake I'd pretended to bake myself. They all took the food but said regulations prevented them from giving me my mail. Who makes these regulations, and wouldn't their time be better spent on things that make sense?

Eventually I gave up and rented a post office box with guaranteed delivery by 10:00 A.M. It seemed a small price to pay for my sanity, and I enjoyed the short walk. I'd pop in and out the side door to a room with floor-to-ceiling mailboxes and unlock an ancient box numbered 609 with a big brass key. There was a sorting counter and a recycling bin, so I could even get rid of my junk mail before I headed home.

Even though I'd solved the issue of getting my mail, there was another problem I couldn't touch. The post office was a design disaster. I'd actually brought this up once, casually, to the postmaster, and she'd simply asked me if there was anything else she could help me with today. As a home stager, I felt an almost physical pain that I could see the post office's shining potential but couldn't do a thing about it.

I imagined people in other professions had their version of my pain. A personal trainer confronted with underdeveloped quadriceps or a flabby set of abs. A landscape designer gazing at a field of weeds. A plastic surgeon assaulted by the sight of Heidi Montag's nightmare breasts.

Staging is all about highlighting strengths and downplaying weaknesses. Sure, it'll help you sell your house, but maximizing your environment will also help you live your best life. I mean, who wants to see the ugly stuff?

Everything about the post office was wrong, from the stark entry to the cold gray institutional walls. Window boxes filled with cheerful annuals would work wonders, as would sunny yellow paint on the interior walls. Even the fonts on the signs behind the registers were unwelcoming. I mean, it's enough that you have to charge an arm and a leg for postage. At least use friendly fonts—rounded with serifs—to announce the bad news. Georgia is a good choice for a friendly but professional serif font.

And clutter, don't get me started on clutter. The overflowing gray metal wastebaskets. The pile of Express labels toppling over into the Priority labels' territory. I mean, what would it take to find some cute wicker baskets? And the wall art, ugh. Those yellowed wanted posters with the curled edges weren't doing anything for anyone. Seascapes by local artists in bright contemporary frames would make all the difference.

I rested the package for Shannon on the sorting counter while I separated the bills from the supermarket flyers. Then I dumped the latter, since I was too responsible to dump the former.

I pushed open the door to the main post office and took my place in the long single line. A young woman in front of me, not much older than Shannon, was holding a baby over her shoulder. She had put the large package she was mailing down on the floor and was kicking it along in front of her as the line moved incrementally forward. The baby was fussing, and the woman was bouncing gently to settle it down. I caught myself bouncing my own body in time with the woman's, as if it might help.

When the line moved again, I gave the package a little kick for her.

"Thanks," she said. Her light blue eyes had dark circles under them, and the cloth diaper spread over her shoulder gave off the sharp, sour smell of infant spit-up.

"It'll get easier," I said.

"It better," she said.

Shannon was a planner. One day on the phone she'd said babies were on their five-year agenda. A part of me thought Greg and I were far too young for even long-range conceptual grandchildren, and another part thought we'd better have fun fast because we'd get sucked right in as soon as the first one was born.

I had a sudden urge to sidle up to the woman in front of me. *Psst*, I'd say. *You'll never stop worrying about that baby you're holding. Ever. No matter how old it gets. Warning, warning: Your life as you knew it is officially over.*

It was probably not what she needed to hear right now, so I kept my mouth shut. When her turn came, I carried the box over to the counter for her, then walked back to the front of the line.

"Next," Ponytail Guy said.

"Shit" slipped out of my mouth. The woman behind me giggled.

I turned to her. "Go ahead. I'm not in a rush."

"No way," she whispered. "He's all yours."

I stepped forward and placed Shannon's package on the counter.

"Anything liquid, fragile, perishable, or potentially hazardous?"

I looked up.

I blinked my eyes.

I shook my head and blinked again.

I squinted.

Ponytail Guy was wearing my glasses.

Just to be sure, I took a moment to put on a pair of my backup cheaters.

Magnified, my favorite glasses were unmistakable. Midnight blue with subtle black stripes and a little extra bling from some silver detailing on the sidepieces. That perfect strong rectangular shape.

Oh, I'd missed them so.

Ponytail Guy glared at me, my readers perched low on his nose. "Answer. The. Question."

"Excuse me," I said. "But did you find those glasses in the Lost and Found?"

Ponytail Guy took a step back and reached a hand under the counter.

"No," I said quickly. "Nothing liquid, fragile, perishable, or the rest-of-it-able."

His hand came back into view. "Express Mail?" he sneered.

"Priority," I said. "Listen, it's just that I left them here—"

"Delivery confirmation?"

"No. And they're my favorite reading glasses. I'm really attached—"

"Insurance?"

"No. I mean, I can understand that the Lost and Found is a great perk and anything in there would be fair game after, say, thirty days, but it was just last week."

I sniffed, as if I might start to cry at any moment. If I was faking, it wasn't by much. "And I really miss them."

Ponytail Guy tilted his chin up and looked right through my glasses and me. "Cash or credit?"

I reached into my wallet and pulled out my credit card. I leaned in close when I handed it to him.

"You can do better than that," I whispered. "They actually look kind of girly on you."

CHAPTER 7

Denise was sitting at our usual table at our favorite restaurant.

"Okay, out with it," I said. "You look like the proverbial cat that swallowed a canary. Or at least a big yellow Peeps. Hey, did I tell you Luke made Peeps sushi for dessert last week? We told him he had to start contributing. He used Peeps instead of raw fish, Rice Krispies Treats for the rice, Fruit Roll-Ups for the seaweed. Greg and I still can't decide whether it was cute or twisted."

"Lovely," Denise said. "So, guess."

A waiter came by with menus, and I reached for my readers. "Don't make me guess. You know I hate to guess."

Denise reached for hers. "Fine," she said. "Don't guess. I should warn you, I spent the whole morning trying to decide which client to shoot first."

"All of them," I said. "Shoot them all, and I'll take off with you. They'll never find us in Bali."

"Paris," Denise said.

"Whatever," I said. "Before we leave I just need to run in and shoot the mean guy at the post office who stole my reading glasses."

"The guy with that pitiful gray ponytail? I hate that guy. Yes, let's definitely shoot him, too."

Denise was a lawyer who specialized in family law and estate planning, and in our defense, when we talked about shooting people we only meant paintballs. Denise and I had hung around

together a little bit in high school. One day a decade and change
later, we ran into each other in an aerobics class a couple of states
away and had been best friends ever since. We were so different
I'm not sure we would have even liked each other if we'd been meeting for the first time. But she'd seen me in braces and kneesocks,
and I knew what she'd looked like before she got blond and thin.
Somehow that felt like family.

Denise had money. I had kids. I'd been with Greg forever. She'd
been married twice and was now dating a guy who was anywhere
from five to ten years younger than she was, depending on how she
was telling it that day.

To each of us, the grass often seemed greener under the other
one's life, and half of the fun of our friendship was the vicarious
thrill of hearing about the things we didn't get.

I took a sip of my iced coffee. "Yes, we'll definitely shoot him,
too, but we're going to have to aim carefully so we don't damage my
glasses."

Denise added three lemon slices to her iced tea, sampled it,
then added a fourth. "We'll steal them back first. Then we'll shoot
him. Okay, enough about you."

"Wait. It's still my turn." I dangled my hand above the table.
"Look what I just found."

Denise grabbed my hand. "Wow, I wonder what happened to
my mood ring. God, when was that? Junior year?"

"Sophomore, I think."

"Jeez, that stone is *black*."

I looked down. "Maybe it's a hormonal thing."

Denise was already sliding the ring off my finger. She tightened
the adjustable band to make sure I knew her finger was smaller than
mine. Or maybe just to reassure herself that she was still skinny.
She slipped it on.

"Okay, I'm done," I said. "Your turn. How's the boy toy?"

Denise ran a manicured hand through her perfectly tousled blond hair. "*Josh* is fine."

She smiled her canary/Peeps smile again.

"What?" I said.

"Okay, close enough. Josh just bought a boutique hotel in Atlanta at a short sale. He wants to know if you'll do the staging."

"*He* wants to know?"

"Well, maybe I thought it might be a good excuse for you to spend some time with Shannon." Denise grinned like we were still in high school. "Because that's the kind of friend I am."

She extended her hand. My mood ring was glowing a bright happy blue on her ring finger.

FIVE MINUTES WITH MRS. BENTLEY and I was ready to jump on the next plane to Atlanta and get to work on that hotel. At least she'd taken her house off the market long enough to get it staged. The FOR SALE sign had been in the wrong place anyway. When you're selling your house, *always* place the sign on the right side of the front door when you're facing the house. As anybody who knows anything about feng shui will tell you, chi naturally moves to the right, or the more active side of space, the yang side.

I felt about feng shui exactly the way I did about astrology and religion: I used the parts I liked and ignored the rest. When my online horoscope predicted a good day, I was in; otherwise, I just pressed Delete. I thought Buddhism did a good job with meditation, Judaism led the pack with the Sabbath, Catholicism had ceremonial flair and knew how to lay a great guilt trip, and nondenominational was the path of least resistance for just about everything else.

Not entering your house through the front door was another major feng shui faux pas. Both Mrs. Bentley and her husband always drove into the attached garage and entered the house that way.

"You're both going to have to start using the front door at least once a day until we get this house sold," I said.

"That's ludicrous," Mrs. Bentley said. "I don't like coming in that way."

"Sorry," I said, "but we need a positive flow of energy coming through the front door."

The wrinkles between Mrs. Bentley's eyes were working over-time. "And we have to open the door to let it in?"

"Exactly. And your front door also governs your life path. If you enter through the garage, you lose sight of your purpose, which is selling the house."

Mrs. Bentley bit her lower lip.

"It's really just common sense," I said. "We need to make the front entryway irresistible so it will attract buyers into the house. We'll add big pots of flowers on either side of the front steps, and we'll paint the front door Million Dollar Red."

"That part I like," Mrs. Bentley said.

I'd already hired painters to transform Mrs. Bentley's dusty rose walls with Benjamin Moore's Pismo Dunes, and the house had jumped two and a half decades by the second coat. We were going for neutral but not sterile, a chic, transitional palette—essentially a blend of modern and traditional colors and furniture.

Pismo Dunes is one of my all-time favorite wall colors, but you have to be careful that it's Benjamin Moore. Behr also makes a Pismo Dunes. Great paint, wrong color.

Now the painters were working on the crisp China White trim, and I was trying to nudge Mrs. Bentley onward without getting in their way.

I nodded at the three prints hanging on her living room wall. "And now it's time to put these out of their misery."

She tucked her tan hair behind her ears and adjusted her earrings. "You're absolutely sure they're out?" she asked, as if there might have been a style revolution since I'd mentioned them the last time I was here.

"Way out," I said. "And I don't think they'll ever be back in. Honestly, I can say with complete confidence that cabbage rose print trios in brass frames have had their time in the sun. But the stock is heavy and the size is good—and it'll save us a ton of money."

She gave me a hurt look, as if she were a cabbage rose and taking my pronouncement personally.

I was already carrying them out to her yard. "We'll spray the frames a flat black. We'll cover the prints in one of our accent colors, probably Nantucket Fog, then tape off some bold, contemporary lines over that and paint on the other accents, Saybrook Sage and Brewster Gray. Then we'll tape on a big fern leaf from your garden. We'll stipple our wall color right over the fern with an almost dry brush to connect them, and also to draw the eye to that beautiful backyard of yours. We'll peel off the fern—and *voilà!*"

I almost said *woilà*, the way so many of those designers on TV did, just to be funny. I mean, who is in charge at those shows? Before you knew it, *woilà* would be listed in the dictionary, along with *Realator* and *duck tape*. But Mrs. Bentley hadn't demonstrated any noticeable sense of humor, so I decided not to get into it.

Mrs. Bentley followed me outside. "I still can't see it. And I simply don't understand the difference between having cabbage roses and ferns on your wall."

"Trust me," I said. The truth was I wouldn't be sure until we tried it whether it was going to work or not, but it was only paint. Paint is the quickest, easiest fix and also gives you the best bang for your design buck. And if it doesn't work out, you can simply go over your mistakes with another coat.

Unlike the mistakes in the rest of your life.

CHAPTER 8

THE OAK FRONT DOOR WAS ORIGINAL TO THE HOUSE and staggeringly beautiful. It was four feet wide and almost eight feet high, with carved panels and a large rectangular insert of beveled glass. The heavy brass knocker had deepened almost to bronze, as had the elongated doorknob with clamshell detailing.

Every time we turned the knob and pushed the door inward, it creaked with the weight of a century of openings.

Greg and I had opened the door at least a dozen times by now, but we still couldn't get over it. "Wow," one or both of us would have to say.

Shannon always wanted to lead the pack. "Me first," she'd yell as she pushed her baby brother out of her way.

We bought a box of disposable latex gloves and filled the rented Dumpster with all the junk the former owners and the wayward boys had left behind. Then we bought a new broom and a jumbo bottle of Spic and Span. We opened all the windows that would open and started sweeping and scrubbing. Every single surface was covered with dust and grime and cobwebs. But it was ours.

When we needed a break from the mess inside, we worked on the mess outside. Greg and I mowed the lawn, dividing the five hours it took with our old mower between us equally, while the non-mower kept an eye on the kids.

We borrowed a power washer from a friend. "Uh-oh," Greg yelled over the torrential noise of the spray. A shingle teetered sideways, then slid down the side of the house and landed in an overgrown rhododendron. We nailed the shingle back on and gave the power washer back. We had enough going on without borrowing trouble.

We weeded the gardens. We learned to recognize poison ivy in itchy hindsight and found out that vinegar calmed the rash as well as anything. It also had the added bonus of neutralizing the lingering smells back inside the house.

We taught Shannon and Luke how to peel the velvet-flocked wallpaper off the dining room walls in long vertical strips. They wrapped them around their shoulders like capes and played Xena the Warrior Princess versus Michelangelo the Teenage Mutant Ninja Turtle. When they got bored, they climbed the steep steps up to the secret room hand over hand like a ladder.

"Look what we found!" Shannon yelled one day as they clunked their way back down the stairs.

Shannon handed me two empty bottles of Boone's Farm apple wine.

Luke held out a well-worn copy of the February 1988 issue of *Playboy*. "Read me 'tory," he said.

"Oh, those wayward boys," Greg said, grabbing it from Luke.

"I'll take that," I said, grabbing it from Greg.

A week or two somehow turned into six. Things were getting tenser by the minute at Greg's mother's house, so we decided to focus on finishing the master bedroom and move all four of us into that. It was a huge room, almost as big as the rumpus room. It had the added bonus of an attached sitting room, so we'd be able to put the kids on their own mattresses in there.

The big drum sander we rented to refinish the floor had a tendency to eat its expensive sandpaper. It also liked to take off as if it were possessed. If we overcompensated and held it in one place for a moment too long, it made angry gouges in the wood. When one of us would melt down in frustration, the other one would jump in, and eventually Greg and I managed to get the floor sanded. We moved on to two coats of Minwax stain, followed by three coats of satin gloss polyurethane.

We painted the ceiling and walls a soft pearl white, and the trim a shinier, brighter white. We wanted simplicity, tranquility, a sanctuary. We needed a room that looked undeniably clean.

We moved our stuff in and celebrated our first night in our new home, sitting in a circle on the shiny wood floor with a large cheese pizza in the middle. We toasted with cheap champagne and juice boxes.

"To our great big beautiful new house," I said.

Shannon started to cry. "I want my old house back," she sobbed.

Luke crawled into Shannon's lap and started to cry, sounding exactly like Shannon. "Me want Grammy's house," he sobbed.

After the first night, Greg and I hung an old white sheet between the bedroom and the sitting area with masking tape. When the kids were fast asleep, if we were really, really quiet, we could even make love again.

THE CABINET DOORS AND DRAWER FRONTS were stacked neatly against one wall of the kitchen, as fresh and white as twenty-nine slices of Wonder bread. Carrot and ginger soup simmered on the stove. A baguette nestled in a white paper bag stretched across a clean counter.

For a split second I wondered if I'd somehow walked into the wrong house.

I pulled the trash compactor open. Two empty cartons of Trader Joe's carrot and ginger soup sat on top, along with the crumpled plastic from a bag of shredded carrots and the papery skins of several cloves of garlic.

I lifted the lid off the pan and gave the soup a stir with a wooden spoon. I tasted it. I added a generous shake of dried ginger. I tasted again and added some crushed red pepper flakes.

A meal hadn't been cooked from scratch in this kitchen in ages. We were all about assembling now, adding spices and fresh ingredients to premade, healthy, if slightly boring items. Brown rice, black beans, and chipotle salsa mixed with shredded meat from a cooked rotisserie chicken. Frozen turkey meatballs baked and added to whole grain pasta and organic marinara sauce. Hummus and tabbouleh with chopped romaine and shredded veggies on high-fiber roll-ups. Grilled wild salmon arranged on a bed of organic baby lettuce mix.

I was just as over cooking as I was over this house. But I'd taught my family to assemble well, and if they got hungry enough, they actually would.

I opened the fridge, took out a clear plastic box to rinse the mixed greens inside, then put it back and shut the door. The trick was not to jump in. Greg had an annoying tendency to start meals, only to back off the moment I got involved.

I decided to inspect the cabinet doors instead. I put on a pair of readers and bent down to pick one up.

It was stuck.

"Don't even tell me," I said out loud.

I wiggled the cabinet door back and forth. When it broke free, it pulled a jagged strip of paint from the next cabinet door with it.

"What is wrong with this picture?" I yelled.

I thought it was an excellent question, but my words merely echoed from the deep recesses of a kitchen full of doorless cabinets.

I turned off the carrot soup. It was only a clever decoy to divert my attention from the fact that my husband was off playing tennis with his lunatic friends, even though the weather had turned cold again and everyone in their right mind knew that normal people do not play outdoor tennis in New England in March. They sell their house and go play tennis in a warmer climate.

By the time Greg got home and turned off the stove himself, the carrots would be mushy. By the time we got this stupid house sold, we'd both be too old to play tennis. Our carrot ginger soup would have to be strained so we wouldn't choke on it.

I opened the cellar door to yell down to Luke in the bat cave, since Greg was just responsible enough to have left him in charge of the soup. Then I pulled it closed again, wiggling the handle until the century-old couplings clicked back into place. I mean, what was the point?

I'd just take the botched cabinets out to the side yard and start sanding, one cabinet at a time. And then I'd paint the cabinets myself, because at least that way I could make sure they were painted the right way.

I'd pretend I was my own client. I'd finish painting and stage this house until it was ready to sell itself. The offers would come flying in, and we'd go flying out.

"Mmm, smells good," Greg said as the kitchen door closed behind him.

I glared at him over the cabinet door I'd managed to unstick. "You're going to have to start using the front door," I said. "We need all the chi we can get around here."

He put his cold hands on my shoulders and gave me a sweaty kiss over the ruined cabinet door. His eyes were bright and his cheeks were pink, and if I didn't have to do everything all by myself, I'd probably look that good, too.

He beamed at the door between us. "Not bad, huh? The Lukester and I took care of those puppies in record time."

The good news was at least we were past the real puppy stage of our lives, because if we had one I sure as hell knew who'd be taking care of it. I pushed past Greg and stomped through the mudroom and out to the garage. Twenty-nine empty liquor boxes were scattered everywhere, like the remnants of one seriously wild party nobody had even bothered to invite me to.

I grabbed a sheet of sandpaper and carried the cabinet door out to the side yard.

"What time do you want to eat?" Greg yelled from the doorway.

I ignored him and started sanding. And sanding. As if I could somehow sand my way through all the layers of paint on this old wooden cabinet door and into the next part of my life.

Greg and I had been married to each other for more years than we'd been single. It was amazing that couples like us even bothered to fight at all. I mean, pick a marriage, any marriage, and basically it's the same five fights over and over again. You might as well just number them.

"Three," the wife would yell.

"Let me explain," her husband would say.

"Four," the husband would accuse.

"I did not," his wife would argue.

Back in high school, if my friends and I didn't want to do something, we used to have an expression: "Let's not and say we did."

That's exactly how I felt about having the same old getting-the-work-done-on-the-house fight yet again. It's not that I was dodging the confrontation. It's just that I'd been there so many times, I knew exactly how it would go—who would say what, how it would end—and the thought of doing it again bored me to tears. So, let's not and say we did. I'd rather have a root canal. I'd rather repaint the cabinets.

"Soup's on!" Greg yelled from the house.

I kept sanding.

The storm door slammed shut. Greg strolled out, wearing sweats and a hooded sweatshirt.

He stopped in the middle of the driveway. "I wasn't sure if you heard me."

I kept sanding. "I heard you."

"Did we miss a spot?"

"The paint wasn't dry. The doors are all stuck together."

When Greg let out a puff of air, you could see his breath. "So, what, now you're going to play the martyr instead of asking us to fix them?"

I stopped sanding. I crossed my arms over my chest. "I am *not* playing the martyr. I am trying to get the cabinets unstuck, sanded, and painted in this lifetime."

Greg shivered. "Come on, it's freezing out here."

"Right. Funny how it's never too cold for tennis, but when there's work to be done, it's suddenly freezing out."

Greg shook his head. "Why do you always have to do that?"

Two! I wanted to yell.

"Do what?" I said instead.

"Why do you always begrudge me the things I enjoy? I could be out drinking or gambling or screwing around. . . ."

"How about this," I said. "Help me get the house on the market and I'll buy you a girlfriend to celebrate."

Greg took a few steps in the direction of the house, then stopped and turned around again. "The thing I don't understand is, what's the big rush?"

One! I could have yelled. It was like I was Drew Barrymore, only older, and instead of *50 First Dates*, I was stuck having the same day over again, day after day, week after week, as the female lead in *50 First Fights*.

I had my lines down cold. I opened my eyes wide to show my incredulity. "*Rush?*" I said. I shook my long-suffering head. "It's been practically forever."

"I think we're making good progress." Greg had his lines down, too.

In most fights, one of you gets to win. But in a marriage, you can't even savor the thrill of victory. By definition, you're supposed to be on the same side, which really takes the fun out of trying to beat an adversary into submission. The best you could hope for was to make the fight go away.

"Listen," I said, taking a stab at some improv. "I know it's a lot of work, a lot of stuff, a lot of memories. Sometimes it feels overwhelming to me, too. But the sooner we finish, the sooner we can get on to the next part of our life."

Greg looked at me. "What I want to know is what's so wrong with this part of our life."

After Greg disappeared into the house, I stood outside for a long time. I wasn't even sanding anymore. I watched the fiery orange sunset drop and turn the night from dusk to dark. A scattering of stars began to twinkle, and the full March moon peeked through the tall evergreens flanking the edge of the driveway. I'd read that because it heralded the time to start tapping maple trees for syrup, it was sometimes called the full sap moon.

And if I let my husband confuse me, then I'd be a full sap, too.

CHAPTER 9

"**B**UT I *LIKE* IT IN THE BEDROOM," MRS. BENTLEY SAID. "Sorry," I said. "An elliptical machine in your bedroom isn't going to get this house sold. It's bad feng shui. The only working out going on in here should be of the romantic variety."

Mrs. Bentley's cold hard stare made me think that not a lot of hot sex was happening in her bedroom.

But who was I to talk? Resentment between Greg and me was growing like spit in a petri dish. Before we knew it, we'd be sleeping in separate beds, and couple time would mean watching the same show on televisions in different rooms. Luke would feel the vibes and start cooking his ramen noodles on the radiator down in the bat cave.

Even when they were little, both kids could smell a fight between us, no matter how calm we pretended to be. Luke would climb under the kitchen table with one of his plastic dinosaurs and pull his blankie over his head.

Shannon was more direct. She'd stamp her foot. "Go hug Mommy," she'd say to Greg.

"Mommy doesn't want to be hugged right now," I'd say. "Even though she loves Daddy very much, sometimes she gets mad at him, and that's okay."

Shannon would give Greg a push. "Hug her anyway."

Greg and I both grew up in households where outbursts of rage were followed by long stretches—weeks, even months—of frigid silence, and then suddenly everything was all right again. Nobody ever explained to us how people got from one stage to the other. So we spent our first years together figuring it out on our own.

If something bothered me, I'd get it out right away and move on. Greg, on the other hand, let the little things go. Then some random day one of those same little things would set him off, and he'd present me with a detailed list of every other little thing he'd pretended to let go in the last, say, three months.

Fused together, the list seemed unreasonably long in my opinion, and Greg's laid-back attitude up to that point felt like an elaborate entrapment scam. So I would click into high-drama mode, pack a suitcase, and announce that life was too short to put up with this shit and thanks for the memories but I was out of here.

Greg would wait until I was almost to the door. He'd apologize. I'd apologize. We'd have great sex and put the suitcase away.

About three years or so into this pattern, I'd just finished an ovation-worthy speech and was flamboyantly pulling my suitcase out from under our bed.

Greg watched quietly. Finally he said, "Aren't you still packed from last time?"

I looked up at him.

He raised his eyebrows.

We both totally cracked up.

Right after that, we ditched the birth control and I got pregnant with Shannon. And as much as I'd never completely lost the knack I'd inherited for high drama, and Greg could still be a virtuoso of silence, we tried to set a better example for our kids.

We also vowed early on to always present a united front and never to talk about each other to our children. When Luke was younger and I told him it was time for bed, he knew better than to run to his dad to try to get a reprieve. And when Greg was driving me crazy, I knew better than to bad-mouth him to Shannon.

I shook my head to bring myself back to Mrs. Bentley's bedroom. I borrowed the painters to help me carry the heavy elliptical downstairs.

Mrs. Bentley's basement was a total blast from the past—flecked acoustical ceiling tiles, orange shag carpeting. The Big Bird yellow of the Parsons tables popped against a brown-and-avocado-plaid sofa and armchair set. Above the couch a groovy chrome-framed Peter Max poster looked down on the plaid sofa as if to say *this room isn't big enough for both of us*. A dark wood built-in bar dotted with bright yellow ashtrays took over one entire wall of the room.

When I was growing up, we'd had a bar just like this in our basement. It was my father's pride and joy. I'd had my first Shirley Temple there, with two extra maraschino cherries, sitting on one of the padded vinyl barstools that spun all the way around. My sister and brother and I would crack open peanuts and were actually allowed to throw the shells on the cement floor. Then one day the rules mysteriously changed, and we got a linoleum floor and had to start putting the peanut shells in wooden bar bowls instead.

The next owner could turn this space into an Irish pub, or an old western-style saloon, or even a billiards room. But it was more likely that the basement would be gutted and turned into a media room, complete with theater-style seating and surround sound. If the old wooden bar were lucky enough to survive at all, it would become a movie concession stand.

If Denise's boyfriend ever got around to actually calling me about that boutique hotel in Atlanta, I might try something elaborate like that, but for this job I was going for a quick fix. I'd turn this basement into an exercise room.

A big part of what home stagers do is create fantasy space. We'd already gotten rid of all the rest of the furniture in the room except for one overstuffed chair. The painters and I placed the elliptical in full view of the television. I threw a white terry cloth robe over the chair and arranged Mrs. Bentley's exercise videos—mostly unopened, I noticed—on the bookshelf. I spread out an exercise mat on the freshly cleaned carpeting midway between the elliptical and the TV. I crisscrossed two shiny purple weights on top of the mat and placed a royal blue exercise ball beside it.

Next, I took down all the dusty old liquor bottles from the open shelves in the bar and boxed them up. Mrs. Bentley and her husband would have to either rent a storage unit or drink up all that booze fast. I lugged the boxes out to the garage. I rolled up five plush white towels and arranged them on the shelves where the liquor bottles had been. I placed some fancy, overpriced bottles of water on the bar.

The moment potential buyers enter a house, they make a judgment, either conscious or unconscious, based on the smell. They make a second olfactory assessment as they head down the basement stairs. Fortunately, Mrs. Bentley's basement didn't have even a trace of mustiness, so all I had to do was bring in some candles.

I arranged three grapefruit candles in round metal tins across the length of the bar like bowls of cocktail peanuts. The citrusy smell would bring a clean crispness to the space, and the grapefruit might send a subliminal message to potential owners that they were losing weight already just by standing here. This was the exercise room that might finally get them into shape.

Now that all the work was done, Mrs. Bentley meandered into the room. You just never knew with clients. Sometimes they were such hard workers, if only inspired by the thought of cutting down my final bill, that I'd be tempted to hire them to work for me. Other times they treated me like I was the hired help, which I supposed, technically, I was.

Mrs. Bentley didn't say a word as she looked her staged basement up and down. I tried to read her expression, but it was hard to gauge. I wasn't going to lose any sleep over it. Once her house sold, she'd come around and tell all her friends about me. Or she wouldn't. Either way, I'd have my check and be out of there.

There was always a chance she'd eventually be so impressed that she'd want to hire me to help her get her next place set up. Even though I marketed myself as someone who staged to sell, it was a natural offshoot, so I did it all the time.

All I knew was that Mrs. Bentley and her husband had already bought a condo and that they were paying two mortgages.

I faked a big smile. "So, what do you think?"

She shrugged. Clients, especially women, often got really territorial about the homes they were trying to get rid of. Any change I made felt like a personal attack on their taste, or lack thereof. It's crazy. If you want to sell your house, you have to keep your eye on the prize and let that kind of thing go.

I kept smiling. "I don't think I've even asked you where you're heading next. Is your new condo local?"

Mrs. Bentley ran a hand through her hair. "Minneapolis."

"Wow," I said. "Minneapolis. Great place to get out of the winter."

She still didn't say anything.

"Ha," I said. "Actually, I love Minneapolis. Such warm, friendly people. Fabulous arts scene. And those skyways are genius. Why are you moving there?"

Mrs. Bentley shrugged. "Our kids live there. They love it."

As a civil engineer, Greg had spent far too much time working outside during the cold New England winters, so we'd always talked about heading to some warm southern beach one day. Maybe Siesta Key. Or St. Simons or Tybee Island. Or even Amelia Island. Fairhope, Alabama?

Or maybe we'd follow one of our kids so we'd be around when the grandkids came, and they'd be nearby to house-sit for us when we traveled. But what if we got to Atlanta, and then Shannon and her husband packed up and moved somewhere else? And then again, while I knew booting Luke out of the bat cave would be the best thing that ever happened to him, he didn't seem to have any noticeable plans for his next horizon. He might need us to stay in the area, at least temporarily, to keep an eye on him from an easily commutable distance.

We could always put our things in storage and just rent for a while. Somewhere. Or we could even rent a tour bus instead of a house and take the next stage of our life on the road.

Greg and I had had the *where next* conversation over and over again, in ever-widening circles. Maybe we had to let go of one place for the next one to call out to us.

Or maybe we wouldn't really be able to let go of the house we were in until we knew where we were headed.

And then again, perhaps we just had a bad case of analysis paralysis.

CHAPTER 10

T HAT FIRST WINTER IN OUR NEW OLD HOUSE I ALMOST
got pregnant again. Two kids were the trend back then. I'd like
to think we were above being influenced by that sort of thing, but
I've wondered since what would have happened if we'd had our
children a few years later instead, when the pendulum started
swinging back in the big family direction.

In any case, Greg and I had agreed that two children, a girl and a
boy, no less, made our family perfectly complete. We each had one
hand for each kid. When we were both around, we could trade off and
give them lots of one-on-one attention. What could be better? I went
back on the pill after Luke was born, and Greg promised to get a va-
sectomy as soon as things settled down and we had some extra money.

I kept my birth control pills in the cabinet closest to the kitchen
sink, where we also kept our One A Day vitamins and the kids'
Flintstone chewables. Like any habit, taking a pill at the same time
each day reinforces the behavior, and I was religious about it. I believed, and still do, that we choose our lives by our attention to the
little things.

My system was that before I went to bed, I'd put everyone's vitamins on the kitchen table next to their juice glasses and take my
birth control pill at the same time. I'd leave the rectangular top of
the pink plastic case up, and I'd place the vitamin bottles right on
top of the pills so I couldn't miss them.

We drank our morning orange juice from Welch's grape jelly juice glasses. We'd collected the complete set of the dinosaur glasses at the supermarket, but Luke would only drink from the gray ptero-dactyl. Shannon preferred her glass to match her vitamins, so she used a Pebbles' Baby Sitters glass from the 1960s we'd found at a yard sale. I still had my red and blue Betty and Veronica Give a Party glass from high school, and we finally talked Greg's mother into letting go of an original 1953 Howdy Doody glass from her collection of family heirlooms, so Greg could have his own special Welch's grape jelly juice glass, too.

One night when I set out our glasses and went to take my birth control pill for Day 12, I noticed Day 13 was missing. It had been a long week, so I just figured I'd taken the wrong pill the night before. I took Day 12 and forgot about it.

The next night, Day 17 was missing.

"We need to talk," I said to Greg.

He looked up from adding wood to the old Vermont Castings stove the minister and the wayward boys had left behind. After we'd emptied our savings account to fill the 275-gallon tank with oil and to have the furnace cleaned, the furnace had fired up, coughed, and then turned off forever. We didn't have enough money to buy a cord of wood at that point, let alone a new furnace. So we took the kids for daily walks in the woods instead, scrounging what we could and piling it into the back of our minivan. At least we weren't chopping up the furniture. Yet.

The stove door let out a rusty creak when Greg closed it. "Just let me get my boots off." He walked by me in the direction of the mudroom.

This seemed unreasonable, given the circumstances. "If you want to have another baby, you should just come out and say it," I said to his back.

Greg turned around. He had a soot smear on his right cheek from the stove and matching dark circles under his eyes. "*What* are you talking about?"

"I mean, I saw a *Jerry Springer* show like this. The husband poked a little hole in his wife's diaphragm with a diaper pin and then pretended to be surprised when she got pregnant. I just didn't think you were capable of doing anything this sneaky, *Greg.*"

Greg caught the back of one boot with the toe of the other and tried to wiggle it off. "I'm so tired right now I'm not even capable of following you, *Sandy.*"

We looked at each other.

"You're not sabotaging my birth control pills?" I said.

"What the fuck are you talking about?" he said.

It was Greg's idea to put a mousetrap in the pill cabinet. The pill-popping mouse was apprehended by the next morning. I stayed in the bathroom so I didn't have to look while Greg threw it into the wooded area at the far end of the backyard.

"Where's the trap?" I asked when Greg came back in.

"With the mouse."

I filled two mugs with coffee. "I have to admit I wondered why you'd chew a hole through the top of the plastic instead of just pushing the pill out through the foil in the back."

Greg didn't say anything.

"Sorry," I said.

He washed his hands in the kitchen sink.

When he finished, I handed him a towel. "Why do you think it went after my pills and not the vitamins? Maybe it was a girl mouse?"

"More like those childproof caps don't just work on children." Greg took a long sip of coffee. "So, you don't think you could be, do you? You know, pregnant?"

It was my idea not to have sex until after I got my next period. We put our energy into ripping down the rancid-grease-soaked kitchen ceiling instead. Mouse droppings rained down on our bandanna-covered heads, along with a handful of mouse skeletons.

"Gross," I said. "This is almost as disgusting as that chicken."

Shannon was already eyeing the skeletons. "Cool," she said. "Can I take one to school for science?"

We finally agreed, but I put it in a Baggie and made her promise not to take it out. "I know," she said. "You have to be careful of bubonic plague."

"Me take mousetrap to Show and Tell," Luke growled. Luke had been growling a lot lately. One day Shannon overheard us whispering to each other about whether or not we should have him evaluated for developmental delays. "He's not delayed," she said. "He's just being Animal on *Muppet Babies*."

We nixed the mousetrap and gave Luke a Baggie-wrapped mouse skeleton to take instead, and tried not to think about how it would fly at preschool.

When we finished demolishing the ceiling, we knocked down two old pantries, which opened up the kitchen to the dead front parlor where the pulpit had been. Suddenly our house had flow. Instead of having to go back out to the center hallway to reach each room, the kids could jog laps from the kitchen to the old parlor/new great room to the living room to the dining room and back to the kitchen again.

When the pantries came down we uncovered a big freestanding chimney. One day down the road when we had some money we'd hire someone to build a big granite island around it. Until then, we backed Shannon and Luke up against it and marked and dated their heights with a fat piece of chalk.

We knew we'd survived the winter when it warmed up enough to stop foraging for wood. A week later a new challenge reared its head. Some people move into a neighborhood only to be surprised by theft or gangs or an explosion of homelessness. We found out we were on the St. Patrick's Day parade route.

None of us were parade people. We'd taken the kids to watch one once, because it seemed like one of those things you just did when you had kids. Luke covered his ears with his hands when the marching band went by.

"You shouldn't walk and play at the same time," Shannon said. "You could choke on your instrument."

"Yeah," Greg said. "I swallowed a tuba once when I was your age."

"Da-ad," Shannon and Luke said at the same time.

"This is boring," Shannon said a minute later.

"Me go home," Luke growled. He sat down in the midst of a sea of legs. I scooped him up before he could get trampled.

"How about an ice-cream cone instead?" Greg said, and we ditched the parade.

It was impossible to ditch the one in our new front yard. The first people dressed in all green arrived a full two hours before the parade started. They pulled their cars right onto our property, gouging the soft spring soil all around the edge of our pie slice–shaped front lawn.

Greg opened the front door and looked out. "Holy shit," he said. "There are people setting up chairs on our property."

I tied an old terry cloth bathrobe over the T-shirt I'd slept in and joined Greg at the door. A couple pushed two redheaded kids in a tandem stroller through our driveway. A third redhead followed on a tricycle. People were marching onto our front lawn from every direction, like armies of green-clad ants.

"What are we going to do?" I said.

Greg shook his head. "Sell popcorn?"

Halfway down the long triangle of lawn, a family started setting up a hibachi. Two burly men in leprechaun hats and T-shirts that read GANG GREEN placed a huge green and white cooler on the ground nearby.

"Could they possibly think this is town property?" Greg asked.

"Maybe we should call the police," I said.

Greg pointed. A cruiser was parked on the edge of our lawn, too. Two cops sat on the hood.

We watched in silence as hundreds of people filled every inch of our front yard.

Shannon squeezed into the space between us. "Are we Irish?" she asked.

"Yes," Greg said. "And proud of it. But these idiots can kiss my sweet Blarney Stone."

I elbowed him.

"How many percent Irish?" Shannon asked.

"About fifty percent," I said. "Just not the parade half, honey."

"I can't watch this," Greg said. "Let's get out of here."

But it was too late. Cars had parked across both ends of our driveway and blocked in our minivan. We were St. Paddy's Day prisoners in our own home. Our feeble protest was to sit in the living room with the kids and ignore the sound of the bagpipes and the *clip-clop* of horse hooves as we played game after game of Hungry Hungry Hippos and Operation.

Every year after that we got out early. And the next morning we'd head out to the front yard to clean up the empty beer bottles and candy wrappers, and once a scattering of green foil–wrapped condoms stamped with shamrocks. It was just the downside of owning a house in the area south of Boston known as the Irish Riviera.

CHAPTER 11

"SHOULD WE WAKE UP CELLAR DWELLER AND SEE IF he wants to escape with us?" Greg asked.

"Nah. He'll probably sleep through the whole thing and think he was dreaming about bagpipes. I can't believe we have to do this again. We swore we'd be out of here before the next St. Patrick's Day parade."

Greg grabbed his keys off the hook on the back of the mudroom door. "Well, look on the bright side—this place will probably be a lot more saleable after the parade is over."

I gulped down the rest of my coffee and put the mug in the dishwasher. "I don't know. I think it's all perspective. If you love a parade, the location is a huge Erin Go Bragh perk. And think about how many hundreds of people would have seen the FOR SALE sign out there today." I sighed. "If only there was one."

Greg placed his mug beside mine in the dishwasher. "Don't start, okay? I have a surprise for you."

He reached into his pocket and handed me an envelope. Inside were two tickets. I don't know what I was expecting, maybe tickets to a jazz brunch or a midmorning movie matinee. I reached for a pair of cheaters on the kitchen counter so I could read them.

FLY SOUTH REAL ESTATE SHOW

Keep on truckin', Boomers . . . South, that is. Ditch your winter coats and those high taxes and discover beautiful, affordable new frontiers for the next phase of your life. Make new friends and invite the old to join you.

"Wow," I said. "Thank you. How on board of you."

Greg kissed me on the forehead. "I have my moments."

An hour later we were standing in line to pick up our show packets in a dingy hallway adjacent to a ballroom in a decrepit hotel on the outskirts of Boston.

A bubbly gray-haired woman checked off our names on the list. "Don't forget to wear your name tags," she said. "They're all you need to make new friends."

"I kept waiting for her to sing the Girl Scout theme song," I said as we walked away. "You know that one about make new friends and keep the old, la la la la and something about gold."

"Sorry," Greg said. "The Girl Scouts wouldn't let me in. Too much testosterone."

"That was my first thought when I met you, too," I said. "But I adjusted."

I checked out the other couples as we milled around. I thought we looked younger than most of them, but maybe they all thought they looked younger, too.

"Whoa," I whispered to Greg. "Would you look at those mom jeans."

Greg flicked his head. "On her?"

I held up one hand to block the finger I was pointing with. "No, on *him*."

"Is that a toupee?" Greg said.

I followed his gaze. "Ya think?"

Hundreds of booths had been set up along little fake avenues marked by green street signs winding around a big central stage area.

We stopped to read some signs, which were printed in oversize Boomer-friendly letters.

"Cute," I said. "We're at the intersection of Penny Lane and Abbey Road."

Greg opened up the show map. "I'd say we want to head in the direction of Bleecker Street."

"Ooh, ooh. Who sang that?"

"Simon and Garfunkel." Greg ran his finger over the map. "'Positively Fourth Street' was Dylan, 'Cyprus Avenue' was Van Morrison. Let's see . . . 'Blue Avenue' was Roy Orbison. 'Love Street'—"

"The Doors," I said. "'Cotton Avenue' was Joni Mitchell and 'Main Street Saturday Night' was Carole King. Boy, they're really pushing the Boomer button, aren't they? I wonder if you get a *Timeless Tunes of the 1960s and 1970s* CD when you put a deposit down on a house."

"They probably give you an eight-track tape," Greg said.

We took a right on Abbey Road. "Lots of whiteheads here," Greg said as we threaded our way through the crowds.

I decided not to point out that salt was winning out over pepper in Greg's hair. It looked good on him, and I hated that I couldn't just let mine go, too. But while I believed in gray hair politically, I had to admit it was the rare woman who didn't look older as a graynette. I'd been dyeing my hair for so long I couldn't even remember how long ago I'd started anymore. A part of me really, really wanted to know what my hair would look like au naturel. Would I have my paternal grandmother's gorgeous white waves? And what if Mother Nature had graced me with salt-and-pepper hair so fabulous it would outshine the color I paid for every five weeks? But somehow I just didn't think I'd turn out to be one of those rare women. My drab gray locks would simply make me look washed-out, invisible, *old*.

We stopped at a huge poster of a mountain-backed lake surrounded by lush greenery and a walking trail. Cute little docks dotted the front of every adorable house. It looked a bit Stepford Wife-ish, but it's not like I'd have to wear a ruffled apron or anything. And I was more than ready to trade the charm of our 1890s Victorian for walk-in closets and dual vanities.

I reached for a brochure.

"How close is the nearest airport?" Greg asked the guy behind the booth.

The guy reached for a brochure, too. "About four hours, but it says right here it's an easy ride."

Greg looped an arm around my shoulders. "Is there a major fitness center?"

The guy kept reading. "It's in the planning stages, but it looks like there's plenty of fishing in the meantime."

Greg leaned in for the kill. "Trader Joe's?"

"Don't count on it," the guy said. He looked over his shoulder. "Don't hold your breath for any Starbucks either."

We circled the conference room in silence. "You totally set me up," I finally said.

Greg put his arm around my shoulders again. "No, I didn't. Come on, we can just catch the Walk Till You Drop seminar."

We slid into our seats as the PowerPoint presentation was starting.

"Savannah," a white-haired man said as a picture of the city lit up the screen, "is our number one pick for most walkable Boomer-friendly southern city. Plenty of sights to entertain you while you walk, plus lots of great water features, including the Savannah River, the ocean, and let's not forget the spectacular fountains in the beautiful parks."

Everybody nodded and a few people made notes.

Our white-haired guide clicked a tiny remote. "New Orleans," he said, "is our number two Walk Till You Drop city. Eminently walkable, and if you get tired, you can jump on a trolley in the

French Quarter and take it right to the Garden District in Savannah."

"New Orleans," I mouthed.

He clicked another slide. "Asheville is third on our list. Beautiful mountain views, rugged hiking trails, a great walkable downtown area. Just walking through the Biltmore Estate alone will give you a workout if you decide to settle in Savannah."

"Asheville," somebody yelled.

"Good choice," our guide said. "I can't recommend it highly enough. Everybody who moves to Asheville falls in love with Savannah."

"Terrifying," I whispered to Greg as we tiptoed away. "That could be us in a few years."

Greg grinned. "Well, at least we wouldn't have to move. We could just stay right here . . . in Savannah."

"Cute."

"Come on, let's go somewhere romantic and grab a sandwich and a green beer."

I checked my watch. The marching band would be warming up, and the rest of the town would be firing up their hibachis on our lawn.

We decided to skip the green beer, since any pub in the Boston area would be a mob scene this weekend. We drove to the North End instead.

"But we always go there," I said when Greg suggested our favorite Italian restaurant. "It's not like there's a shortage of great restaurants in the North End."

Greg pulled into the small lot we always parked in. "It's just that I can taste that broccoli appetizer already. And you know how you love that pumpkin tortellini."

I hated that my mouth actually watered in Pavlovian betrayal. "Fine," I said.

"To us," Greg said a few minutes later as he clinked his glass of Chianti to mine.

"To us," I said. "Same old boring, never try anything new, us."

Greg wiggled his eyebrows in a bad Groucho Marx imitation. "Why mess with the rest when you've already got the best?"

I looked around the tiny dining room with the open kitchen. A candle wedged in an empty bottle of Chianti lit our wobbly wooden table. It was hard to tell who was older, the rickety brown chairs we were sitting in or us.

I reached into my shoulder bag and dumped the pile of brochures we'd collected at the Fly South show on the center of the table.

Greg flipped two over. "I've got a pair of North Carolinas."

I reached into the pack. "I'll see your two North Carolinas and raise you one Tennessee."

Greg turned over another brochure. "I'm going to have to up the ante and throw in a Florida."

I slapped a brochure on top of the pile. "I think Georgia might be the tiebreaker."

Greg took another sip of his wine. "You always had the worst poker face."

"Gee, thanks." I took another sip of mine. "And when did we ever play poker?"

"I mean I could always tell whether you had a good hand or not. Old Maid, Go Fish, Fireball Island."

"Fireball Island," I said.

"The game where you had to try to recover the giant ruby and take it to the dock while avoiding the fireballs that shot out of the giant idol? Wow, remember how much Luke loved Fireball Island?"

I ran my finger around the lip of the wineglass. Shannon had been just as devoted to Mouse Trap, so we used to have to alternate games.

"Get the cheese, but don't get trapped," Greg said.

I shook my head. "We don't even need to talk anymore. We can just read each other's minds as they atrophy."

Greg reached for my hand. "Of course we do. Talking to you is the best part of my day."

"After tennis," I said.

Greg grinned. "Okay, maybe it's a tie."

"Here's the thing," I said. "I don't want to spend the rest of our lives remembering. I want to make new memories."

"I hear you," Greg said. "I'm just not sure it's all about the house."

"Okay, so what's it about?"

Greg leaned forward. "I think we need another dog. Or maybe a cat. But definitely a new pet. Something to bring in some fresh life."

Once for a school project, Luke had drawn a timeline of our family pets: Tigger, the sweet shelter cat we'd adopted to keep the mice in our new house at bay, and who lived to be a whopping twenty-two years old. Deaf and senile, she meowed at the top of her lungs all night long, night after night, until she forgot she was nocturnal and started doing it all day, too. Then she somehow managed to sneak out, only to get her neck broken in our driveway in broad daylight by something she no longer recognized as a dog.

Dash and Ashley, our much-loved but too-often-neglected Lab-cross shelter dogs who kept each other company when we were too stressed-out with our kids' crazy schedules to give them the attention they deserved. Dash died at thirteen, and Ashley died of a broken heart a few months later.

Indiana Jones, the adorable two-year-old psychotic female beagle we adopted next from a family who couldn't keep her. She chewed the shingles off the house and made a break for freedom the minute anyone left the door open longer than a nanosecond. Right before the four of us left for a funeral one day, I went back into the house to grab some tissues. She darted out between my legs and raced across the driveway and into the road. The big green landscape truck never even saw her coming, and she exploded on contact, splattering the street with black, white, and red pieces of Indie. A passing fire truck circled back and washed off the street, and a kind firefighter with kids of his own wrapped what he could in an old blanket so we could bury her.

Rainbow and Star, the sweet rabbits we loved almost as much as they loved each other. And Comet, Luke's pet rat the rest of us were so sure we'd hate, but who turned out to be one of the smartest, most affectionate pets of all, like a little dog, really. He died a horrible, painful death as a tumor grew on his neck, finally cutting off his oxygen supply during a crazy winter's nor'easter, when the power went out and all we could do was take turns sitting vigil with him by candlelight until the sad, sad end.

They were all buried out behind the garage, along with some mouse skeletons and an occasional bird, marked by beach stones and seashells and little wooden signs carved with their names. Luke had even given up his childhood blankie to bury Comet the rat in, and he'd made us videotape the candlelit burial service. We'd found it a few years ago at Christmas, and the four of us had watched it and cried like babies.

My eyes filled with tears as I looked at Greg.

"No," I said. "I just can't do it again. I want fun new experiences where nobody dies for a long, long time."

CHAPTER 12

I TOOK A DETOUR ON MY WALK TO THE POST OFFICE, looping through the tiny web of downtown streets and around to the harbor. Even though full-blown spring was in the air today, on the roller-coaster ride that was New England weather, tomorrow might be another story. Still, it wouldn't be long before the sun-bleached docks piled behind the harbormaster's office would be back in the water and filled with boats.

Seagulls swooped and screeched overhead, waiting impatiently for the summer tourists to come back and feed them the crusts of their fat deli sandwiches, along with ketchup-soaked French fries from their take-out orders of fish-and-chips.

I unwrapped an old, half-eaten Kashi bar I found in my jacket pocket, leaned over the seawall railing, and tossed it up in the air. A gull nabbed it before it hit the water.

"You're welcome," I yelled.

I had to admit that this really was the perfect little beach town, which was a great thing unless you were ready to leave it. I wondered if people who lived in ugly places just packed up the minute they could and hightailed it out of town. Or maybe they loved their ugly little towns just as much as I'd loved this one.

I wondered if I'd ever really have the guts to go.

Greg and I could always come back and splurge on a rental house right on the beach for a week every summer. Or maybe we'd just go off and have a few adventures, and then come back and buy a little condo.

Word was out. Two new seagulls landed on the park bench behind me.

"Sorry," I said. "I ate the rest of it. Dark Chocolate Coconut is my favorite."

One of the gulls squawked.

"I know," I said. "It was rude of me. Next time I'll bring more."

They eyed me for a moment, then turned their attention to the ocean.

"Pretty place, isn't it?" I said.

We watched the tiny whitecaps rolling in with the tide and listened to the water splashing against the rocks below. Out of the corner of my eye, I saw a woman walking in our direction.

I turned to the seagulls. "You gulls get around. I mean, if you weren't here, where would you rather be?"

The woman caught my eye, then turned and started walking quickly in the opposite direction.

"Ha," I said. "Like she's never talked to a seagull."

The gulls screeched and soared up over the water.

"Have a nice day," I yelled.

By the time I got to the post office, I was feeling better than I'd felt in a while. The ocean will do that for you. I opened my box and started sorting through the junk mail.

A bright yellow package notification was wedged between an ad for a dating service and one for long-term care insurance. I dumped everything but the package slip and our ridiculously high health insurance bill, and pushed open the door to the main part of the post office.

When I finally made my way to the front of the line, I couldn't believe I actually got the nice woman for a change. Maybe the trick was not trying to strategize but to trust fate to nudge things in the right direction.

"How are you today?" I said as I handed her the yellow slip of paper.

The woman gave me a big smile. "Just fine, hon, how 'bout you?"

"Great," I said.

I looked over at Ponytail Guy. My good mood plummeted at the sight of him glaring away at some poor guy through my favorite glasses.

The nice woman handed me a rectangular package. I put on a pair of inferior readers to check the label.

"Cool," I said. I looked up at the woman. "You don't have a knife, do you?"

Ponytail Guy took a step back and reached under the counter.

"Relax," I said. "I'm not even your customer." I turned to the woman. "Never mind, I'll use my fingernail."

I headed over to the table at the back of the room and managed to get the package containing my new readers opened. It was like being an aging kid in a reading glasses shop. I pulled pair after pair from their soft drawstring bags, each one cuter than the one before.

"Wow," a woman in line said. "Where did you get all those?"

"Don't make me feel guilty," I said. "After this, I'm not buying anything."

I gave her the Web address where I'd ordered them, then went back to my glasses. I finally decided I could sacrifice the root beer pair with the tortoise highlights. I sealed the box back up so I could pretend I had something to mail.

"Anything liquid, fragile, perishable, hazardous, or combustible?" Ponytail Guy asked when I'd worked my way to the front of the line again.

"No." I rested my package on the counter but didn't let go.

Ponytail Guy grabbed the box and pulled. "Express Mail?"

I pulled back. I held up the root beer readers with the hand not holding the box. "Listen," I said as fast as I could, "I just want my glasses back. These are much better. Trust me, you'll be a total date magnet."

"Answer. The. Question." He took a step back and reached under the counter.

My eyes teared up. "Please?"

When he glared at me over my beautiful glasses, a part of me wanted to just let him push the damn alarm. At least that way I could have my day in court and maybe get my glasses back.

The bigger part of me was old enough to know better. "Never mind," I said.

BY THE TIME my reading glasses and I got home, I needed a good stiff drink. Since it was still morning, I decided to finally de-clutter my junk drawer instead. Most people don't realize that de-cluttering a drawer can be a calming, zenlike experience.

There is no more important drawer in your house to stage than your junk drawer. It's a fact of life that prospective buyers always snoop. They simply love opening your closet to watch a mountain of shoes and three curling irons come tumbling out. It makes them feel so much better about their own pack-rat habits.

So, under the pretext of finding out whether you have self-closing, spring-loaded sliding drawers in your kitchen, house hunters can't resist poking around until they find the obligatory junk drawer. Imagine their shock when they don't find tangled string, two pairs of broken scissors, twenty-three pens, and a coupon that expired in 2003—the kinds of things in their own junk drawer at home.

Instead they find clean white organizers. One contains stamps, two kinds of tape, and a shiny new pair of scissors. A fresh memo pad and two new pens are nestled in another. The third one holds a clearly labeled extra key for every item you currently own that needs a key.

It's genius. Potential buyers are so blown away that even your *junk drawer* is immaculate, they'll fall in love with your house on the spot. This is a home that has been cared for. Clean people, living the kind of life they aspire to, live here. If they bought your house, this could be their junk drawer. This could be their *life*.

The sad truth is that most people's junk drawers have a long way to go. Just off the top of my head, these are the kinds of things my clients didn't know enough to pitch:

- troll-head pencil with pink hair
- wooden nickels from long-defunct Wisconsin dairy
- unopened Mr. Potato Head from Burger King
- five chargers for cell phones client no longer owned
- Butterfinger Easter eggs from previous Easter (in February)
- vinyl adhesive to fix pool floats for nonexistent pool
- antique friction primer in sardine can–like tin packed with gunpowder to light Civil War cannon (If someone ever gave the owner a cannon, it would undoubtedly have come in handy.)
- Buddha key chain holding catnip mouse
- two dozen packages of carrot seeds that expired in 1997
- red telephone cord and no red telephone
- puzzle piece in shape of Iowa (Client's kids were twenty-two and twenty-five and she was still hoping to find the rest of the puzzle.)
- three emergency rain ponchos (I mean, really, what family needs more than two?)

- gold wedding ring from client's husband's first marriage
  (Junk drawer was the least of this client's problems.)

I'm not pointing fingers here. The first thing I pulled out of our junk drawer was a key to our old red minivan, the one we'd sold almost a decade ago.

I rubbed the key between my thumb and forefinger, and it all came back: buckling Shannon and Luke into their bulky car seats. The big-kid booster seats that followed. The huge relief of getting rid of the seats, only to find myself announcing every time we climbed in that we weren't going anywhere until everybody's seat belts were buckled, and that means you, Luke. Then the endless fights over who got the front seat, and later, a mother's worst nightmare, having to let my babies, first Shannon and then Luke, get behind the wheel.

The key was still attached to a key chain that said WORLD'S BEST MOM. The kids had given it to me for Mother's Day a couple of decades ago.

I tossed it into the CRAZY box. I couldn't help myself.

CHAPTER 13

EVERYBODY CALLS ME SANDY, AND IT DRIVES ME nuts. Over the years, I've also been called Sand and Andi, and even SandraDee and, briefly, LookatMe. But Sandy is the nickname I can't seem to brush off, and it always makes me feel like I've just come home from the beach and need a good shower. Sometimes it seems like I've spent my whole life in the mysteriously unattainable pursuit of the more dignified Sandra.

"Hey, Sandra," Denise's boyfriend said when he finally called. Actually, it sounded more like *Sahndrah*, but it was still better than *Sandy*. "How the hell are you?"

Josh and I had met exactly once, when he'd come by for a drink while Denise and I were having dinner at a restaurant near his office. Since then, Denise and I had both mentioned the four of us getting together, but not in any detailed way that might actually result in it happening.

Their relationship was still new. It was always more fun when just Denise and I went out. And Greg had already spent time with Denise's two husbands as well as several of the more fleeting men in her life, so in his mind, he'd paid his dues and then some.

"If you really want me to, I'll go," he'd say. "It's just that I always worry I'm going to call one of them by the wrong name."

"Imagine how Denise feels," I'd crack.

Greg would shake his head. He wouldn't admit it, but he didn't quite approve of Denise. He wanted her to pick somebody and stick with him.

"There's nothing wrong with any of these guys, you know," he'd said once as we came home from a night out with Denise and a guy she'd just started seeing. "It's Denise."

I thought that was at least half true, and I knew Denise did, too, but I certainly wasn't going to admit it. "Maybe her goal is not to be in a relationship," I said. "Maybe her goal is to lead an interesting life."

Greg held the door connecting the mudroom to the kitchen open for me. "And the two are mutually exclusive?"

I turned in the doorway and struck a pose. "Make the rest of my night interesting, and I'll let you know."

Greg put his arms around me.

"Gross," Shannon said. She walked by us and opened the refrigerator. "Get a room."

I looked at the cell phone in my hand and remembered Josh. "Fine, thanks," I said. "How the hell are *you?*"

"So, are you in?" Josh said. "Denise said you sounded really interested."

"Interested."

"Hotel? Atlanta? Staging? Did I get you at a bad time? Do you want to call me back?"

It's not that I'd forgotten about it. It's not that staging a hotel didn't sound like a fun job, and it's not like I wouldn't normally jump all over any excuse to spend some time with my daughter. But without me around to crack the whip, it was hard to imagine that this house would ever get on the market.

"No, no," I said. "Now's a great time." I grabbed a Care Bears memo pad and one of Greg's old mechanical pencils from the junk drawer. I chose a fiery red pair from my new box of readers. "Can you tell me a little bit more about the job? And the timeline?"

Always be careful when working with friends, or friends of friends, or men your best friend is dating. Pin down the details. If I decided to do this, I'd send Josh an e-mail going over everything we'd discussed, just to make sure we were on the same page, and so we'd both have it in writing.

"Sure. It's an old hotel in midtown Atlanta that went under. Bank owned. I jumped through hoops for so long I'd almost forgotten about it, and then the bank finally caved on the price. It was a total steal."

I could hear the thrill of the chase in his voice. "What's it look like?" I asked.

"I haven't seen it yet."

"What?"

He laughed. "I'm an investor. The bank agreed to an inspection, and the place is solid. At the price I paid that's all I needed to know. I'd like to turn it into a pretty package and get it up and running. Then I'll keep an eye out for the right buyer."

"How many rooms?"

He laughed again. "You had to ask that, didn't you? Listen, if you're interested, I'll send you everything I've got. Spend what you need to and not a cent more. Keep track of the hours, and I'll pay your going rate. I'll have a plane ticket sent to you, send a car to pick you up at the airport. You can stay at the hotel. At least, I think you can."

He sounded about twelve. What kind of grown-up bought a hotel without seeing it first?

"I'd stay with my daughter," I said, as if that were the only decision to be made here.

"Fine," he said. "Just rent a car and send me the receipt."

"When would you need me to start?"

"The sooner the better."

Mrs. Bentley's house was almost a wrap. I had just given bids to three potential clients and was waiting to hear back. There was no reason I couldn't sneak in a quick trip to Atlanta. If the project turned out to be too big, maybe I could find someone to take it over.

I cleared my throat. "Let me check my schedule and get back to you, okay?"

"Sure. Take your time. Just call me by noon tomorrow. I want to get this baby moving."

After we said good-bye, I tried to get back into sorting through my junk drawer, but I was too distracted. Staging Josh's latest acquisition was probably a great opportunity, but the timing was off. And Denise's most recent boyfriend didn't sound like the kind of guy I could talk into waiting. I mean, *take your time but call me by high noon tomorrow?*

I decided to check up on Greg and Luke, who were sanding the cabinet doors out in the garage. I couldn't wait to get those doors back up again. The kitchen looked like a great big toothless mouth without them.

Crazy laughter greeted me when I stepped into the mudroom. I opened the door to the garage. Toys were scattered all over the floor, and my husband and son were both holding joysticks and leaning over a yellow plastic boxing ring set up on an old card table in the middle of the garage. A red and a blue plastic boxing doll were punching away at each other.

"I'll knock your block off, Red Rocker," Greg yelled, even though he was only about a foot away from Luke.

"In your dreams, Blue Bomber," Luke yelled back. "Take that, you wuss."

One of the robots made a *whaaaaaa* sound. The blue doll's head fell off and rolled across the boxing ring.

"Score!" Luke put his joystick down and ran a victory lap around the rickety old card table.

"Two out of three," Greg said. He put his joystick down and jogged in place, punching his fists like Sylvester Stallone in one of those *Rocky* movies.

I cleared my throat.

Greg looked up but didn't break his stride. "Hi, hon," he said. "We found Rock 'Em Sock 'Em Robots in a box up under the eaves. I always wondered what happened to it."

Luke flashed me a big smile and picked up his joystick again. "We're lucky all the moisture out here didn't do any damage. Seriously, we have to be more careful around here, Mom. Rock 'Em Sock 'Em Robots is a classic."

"Yeah," Greg said. He reached into the ring and put Blue Bomber's head back on.

Luke got into position and leaned forward. "Hungry Hungry Hippos is next. Or do you want to play the winner of this one?"

"I'll knock your block off," Greg said.

"Don't count on it," I said.

"Oh," Luke said, "if you talk to Shannon before I do, tell her we found her old Bedazzler. She is gonna freakin' flip out."

"How are the cabinets coming along?" I asked sweetly.

"Great," Greg and Luke said at the same time.

"Owe me a Coke," they both said together. They laughed uproariously.

"We're making good progress," Greg said.

"Totally," Luke said. "We're like just taking a short break."

"Hey," Greg said. "We were thinking we should order pizza for dinner and sit around and play Candy Land. You know, like we used to on Friday nights?"

Luke grinned. "I was just telling Dad how we did this retro board game thing up at school. We'd put like a pile of actual candy on the

Candy Land board, and whoever made it to the end first would get the whole stash."

"Sweet," Greg said.

They both cracked up.

I didn't even bother to make a high-drama speech. I just went to find my suitcase.

CHAPTER 14

WHEREVER YOU'RE HEADED AND WHATEVER THE reason, the best way to pack your suitcase is to roll your clothes. Not only will your clothing arrive virtually wrinkle-free, but the rolling method will also allow you to pack the most clothes in the smallest possible space. This is particularly beneficial when you have absolutely no idea how long you'll be gone.

Place each shirt facedown and fold the arms back neatly, then fold lengthwise. Beginning at the bottom, roll tightly until you reach the top, creating a sausagelike cylinder. Place the cylinder in your suitcase vertically, that is, standing on end. Repeat with the rest of your clothes, jamming them in as tightly as possible. (Fold your pants in half vertically, then fold again and roll, etc.) When you finish, your suitcase will look something like a freshly opened carton of clothing cigarettes.

Because your rolling has created a bend radius instead of a sharp crease, you'll have barely a wrinkle when you unpack. Always unpack as soon as possible after arriving at your destination. Just shake out each item—and *woila*! (Don't forget, it's really *voilà*.) Hang any ever-so-slightly wrinkled items in the bathroom while you shower to steam them to perfection.

Trust me, you'll be totally amazed at how much more you can fit into your suitcase this way. Enough to stay away for as long as you need to.

While you're packing, get rid of that overpriced little travel iron you simply had to have that barely works anyway. Ditto for the itsy-bitsy teeny-weeny blow-dryer that doesn't have enough watts to scatter a dried dandelion head. Face the fact that even if they were marginally useful when you bought them, they're completely obsolete now. Your hotel will have life-size versions of both, and so will your host. If not, you should reconsider your accommodations.

Donate them if you can, or give them away. At the very least recycle them. But let them go. They're weighing you down. They're holding you back. They're keeping you from a smooth ride to your next destination.

After I finished packing, I gave my suitcase a quick spray of Lysol Crisp Linen, a great travel scent, and zipped it up. Maybe everything had a best-by date, but it was just harder to read it with relationships that had lasted so long neither of you quite knew where either of you began or ended anymore.

Maybe Greg and I simply didn't want the same next chapter. Maybe I'd rent a little apartment in Atlanta and leave the house and the projects and the bills to him. I'd read about women who'd just walked off in the middle of the night without so much as a toothbrush. Okay, often abuse or alcohol or drugs or gambling or infidelity or closet homosexuality were underlying factors, but did you always need a big ticket item? Couldn't you just agree to disagree about what you wanted next in life, wish each other well, maybe give each other a high five for lasting this long, and promise to do lunch?

I could almost picture it. And then one day when things had sorted themselves out, I'd fly in for the weekend and pack up just a box or two to take with me. No hard feelings, but would you mind if I took that handblown glass vase we bought on our honeymoon, the one with flecks of blue so brilliant you'd swear you were looking at a cross section of the Caribbean?

The old cut-glass bedroom doorknob creaked when it turned, the way it always did.

"How about one plain cheese pizza and one Spinoccoli?" Greg said as the door opened.

He looked at the suitcase on the bed. "Luke said he'll fly if we buy."

I realized I was still holding the Lysol. I put it on the bedside table and yanked the suitcase down to the floor. "Whatever," I said.

Greg pulled the door closed behind him. "What's up?"

"I took a job in Atlanta."

"You took a job in Atlanta."

Whenever Greg repeated something, it meant he was buying time. Or waiting for me to provide him with more information. I didn't say anything.

He pulled his sweaty T-shirt over his head. I watched. I loved the long lines of his torso and the ropy muscles of his forearms. I almost never even noticed them anymore. It was sad the way familiarity made you stop seeing someone after a while.

Greg wiped his face with the T-shirt and then threw it on top of the wicker basket where he kept his dirty clothes until he had enough for a load of wash. I'd stopped doing everybody else's laundry a long time ago. We were all three roommates, really, Greg and Luke and I. Each with our own life, or lack thereof, and our own laundry schedule.

He pulled on a threadbare white T-shirt with faded green letters that said LENNON & SONS ROOFING, from a softball team he'd played on at least a decade and a half ago.

He sat down on the bed and started untying his sneakers.

"What kind of job?" he finally asked.

"Denise's boyfriend just bought a hotel and wants me to stage it."

He looked up. "Shouldn't we discuss it first?"

I shrugged. "I'm kind of over discussing things. I need them to happen."

Greg was still holding on to his laces. He looked like a little kid learning how to tie.

I couldn't help smiling. "Remember that lacing board we found for Luke when he was so stressed about tying he would only wear his Velcro sneakers?"

Greg grinned. "Luke and I found it today. Tucked under Hungry Hungry Hippos. I told him he could keep it, okay?"

"Of course. I'm trying to picture it. . . . Four different kinds of shoes, painted on a board with laces, right?"

"Yeah." Greg kicked off one sneaker and started working on the other. "Football, skiing, jogging—"

"And hiking," I said.

We smiled at each other.

"Remember that song from preschool he taught us?" I said. "To 'Splish Splash'?"

"Criss cross and go under the path," Greg sang. "Then you got to pull it real tight."

"Loop one, make the other a tail," I sang.

"And soon you'll be tying it just right," we sang together.

"Boy, we can't sing," I said. "We didn't have a musical gene between us to pass down to those poor kids."

"They got a lot of other stuff," Greg said. "And Luke ties like a pro now."

"Ha," I said.

We looked at each other.

"I don't get it," Greg said. "I thought you were all fired up to get the house on the market."

"I don't want to do it all."

"You're not doing it all."

"I'm sick of being the enforcer."

"Maybe it would be easier to get into it if we knew where we were going."

"I know where I'm going. Atlanta."

Greg looked at my suitcase. "I don't want to fight."

I picked up the can of Lysol. "And I don't want to talk. There's nothing new to say."

"There's nothing wrong," Greg said as I pushed the door open. "Unless you want there to be."

CHAPTER 15

THE FIRST NOTES OF "MISS OTIS REGRETS" TRILLED from my BlackBerry. It's a song about a woman who takes a gun from her gown and shoots her lover down, and Denise had approved this message for her personalized ring.

If you haven't assigned a special song for each person on your speed dial, take a moment to do it now. You'll never again have to dig through your purse before you decide whether to answer or ignore a call.

I have to say it was a soothing, zenlike experience to match up everyone in my life with a song from *Bette Midler's Greatest Hits: Experience the Divine*. I gave Greg "Do You Want to Dance?" and Luke "Boogie Woogie Bugle Boy." "Chapel of Love" was a natural for Shannon. Denise was the only one who got a vote. I'd originally been planning to use "Friends," but she thought "Miss Otis Regrets" would be edgier.

"Hey," I said.

"I knew you'd do it," Denise said.

"Yeah," I said. "No pressure on your end."

"Oh, please. If you didn't want a free trip to see Shannon, you would have said no. I'm still waiting for you to say thank you, by the way."

"I'm saving it for after I see the hotel. I can't believe I'm flying out this morning. I don't even want to think about how much that plane ticket cost."

"That's my Josh. He doesn't like to wait for anything."

"Did you tell him to call me *Sahndra?*"

Denise's laugh was rich and melodic, the way it always sounded when she was in love.

Greg had insisted on driving me to the airport. I'd finished up at Mrs. Bentley's house last night, and I was just taking an early morning walk to the post office to clear my head and mail a couple of bills before we took off.

"Sorry about lunch," I said. "We'll do it the minute I get back."

The main post office was still closed, but the room that housed the boxes opened earlier and closed later. I dropped my envelopes into the mailbox outside, then went in through the side door.

"Don't worry about it," Denise said. "I'll just have to shoot my clients without you."

Denise and I rarely overshared details of our personal lives. I think we were both smart enough to know that the spaces in long-term friendships are as important as the intimacy. It seemed to me that women are particularly vulnerable to friendships that flare up and burn out quickly.

But sometimes you just needed to try out the sound of something.

"Who knows," I said, "I just might stay. Greg and I aren't getting along so well."

Denise laughed.

"I'm serious."

"I know you think you're serious, but you're not serious."

"How can you tell? Hang on for a sec." I walked across the squeaky linoleum-tiled floor and opened box 609. I wiggled out the incredible amount of junk mail that had accumulated since just yesterday. With all the free opportunities for online spam, why would anyone still want to pay to have it printed? I sorted through to make sure I wasn't missing anything exciting, like a bill, then dumped the whole mess into the recycling bin.

There was a big CLOSED sign on the glass door to the main post office. Behind it, a woman walked by carrying a clear plastic bin filled with mail and then disappeared from view.

I don't know what made me do it, but I reached for the door handle and pulled.

It opened.

"Are you still there?" Denise said into my ear.

"Shh," I whispered. I wasn't quite sure what I was going to do, but if someone nice came out, maybe I'd say I lost my reading glasses and ask to see the Lost and Found. I mean, who knew, maybe Ponytail Guy put them back at the end of the day.

There was no one in sight.

I took a step into the room.

I couldn't believe it. There, sitting right on top of the postage scale, were my favorite reading glasses.

"Sandy, what's going on?"

"I think I'm going to steal my reading glasses back," I whispered.

"Ha," she whispered. "Do it."

"What happens if I get caught?"

"Did they cost less than two hundred and fifty dollars?"

"Ha," I said. "Way less."

"Then, worst-case scenario, it's only petty larceny."

I took another step forward. "What's best-case scenario?"

"Uh, you get away with it?"

Behind some partitions I heard a woman laugh.

I tiptoed forward. Randomly, I flashed back to all the Nancy Drew mysteries I'd read as a kid. I pictured myself in black and white, moving stealthily and sleuthfully with a flashlight clasped firmly in one hand. I was channeling Nancy in *The Secret of the Original Cheaters*. Or maybe it was *The Mystery of the Traveling Reading Glasses*.

I reached out a shaky hand and grabbed my readers.

Ponytail Guy came around the corner.

My heart skipped a beat, then started thumping wildly.

"Stop," he said, even though I wasn't moving.

I looked at him.

His eyes met mine. They were cold and hooded, almost reptilian.

He took a slow step back.

I turned and shoved the glass door open.

Just as I reached the second door, the alarm went off.

"Uh-oh," Denise said into my ear.

I ran. I ran as hard and as fast as I could, squeezing my Black-Berry and post office box key together with one hand, and care-fully holding my long-lost reading glasses in the other. All I wanted was to put some distance between that ridiculously loud alarm and me.

Three cars drove by without stopping to make a citizen's arrest. When I ran past a guy walking his dog, neither of them made a peep. Maybe I was blending into suburbia and looked like just another morning jogger, though I'd made the unfortunate choice of wearing ballet flats so I wouldn't have to change my shoes before I left for the airport.

I stopped and ducked behind a tree to get a pebble out of my shoe.

"Uh-oh?" I repeated. I panted while I tried to catch my breath. "That's the best you can do? What kind of lawyer says 'uh-oh'?"

"Calm down and tell me what's happening."

Just as I peeked around the tree trunk, the *whoop-whoop* of the alarm cut off abruptly. A dog barked from inside someone's house, as if to say thank you. Everything was so suddenly quiet that I no-ticed the sun was shining. A patch of snowdrops was blooming in front of the tree next to mine. The world was a beautiful place when you were free.

"Nothing," I whispered. "Nothing's happening. I think I made a clean getaway. Do you believe Ponytail Guy actually pulled the alarm? I mean, how twisted can you get?"

"It's all about power," Denise said. "Guys with small ponytails just can't get enough of it."

"What do I do next? I've never been a thief before."

Denise laughed. "Relax. Go to Atlanta and forget all about it. If anything happens, I'll take care of it. Listen, I have to go. I've got a meeting in five."

"What if—"

I heard a click, and my best friend was history.

CHAPTER 16

I KNOCKED ON THE DOOR OF THE BAT CAVE.
Luke opened it a crack. I could hear the splash of the shower
running in the little bathroom over the blare of the Syfy channel
playing on the huge flat-screen TV he'd bought with his first paycheck.

Just in case my plane crashed, I decided to skip the conserva-
tion lecture so it wouldn't be the last thing he remembered about
me. "Just give me a good-bye hug, honey. I'm on my way to Atlanta."

He didn't move. "Okay, bye, Mom."

My mother used to say she had eyes in the back of her head.
Maybe I had X-ray vision.

"What's going on?" I said.

"Nothing," Luke said.

I waited.

"Raven is taking a shower."

I took a moment to ponder whether a girlfriend in the shower
was better than no girlfriend at all.

"Raven," I said finally. "That would be the girlfriend we haven't
met yet?"

"Mom," he said.

"Just tell me you're using birth control," I said.

"Mom, you put condoms in my stocking at Christmas when I
was sixteen."

"You're not still using them, are you?"

"Mo-*om*."

If you added up all the words Eskimos had for *snow* and Zulus had for *green*, and then doubled it, you'd have roughly the same number of inflections Luke had for the single word Mom. *Mom, you're embarrassing me. Mom, you're in my space. Mom, I'm fine. Mom, I get it.* It was a language all its own.

My concern for my son was possibly a little bit meddle-y, but not unwarranted. Luke was brilliant, but he sometimes missed a clue or two. Lukisms were told and retold in our family until they reached the level of urban legend. Or at least suburban legend.

One day in preschool he wanted to know how come his classmate got to be a doctor and he didn't. "She's not a doctor, honey," I said. "She's adopted."

Another year he came home from school singing, "Put another dime in the juice box, baby."

"Up and at 'em," Greg said one morning when he was waking him for school. "Who's Adam?" Luke said.

In high school Luke would stay up all night reading a book and then remember that he had a biology exam second period.

The first time we let him drive one of our cars to college, he filled it with diesel fuel.

I knew he'd find his way, but there seemed to be a slight disconnect between Luke and the rest of the world. It was a mother's job to worry about these things.

I gave him a mom hug. "Be careful out there," I said.

IN THE UNLIKELY EVENT that they came to arrest me while I was gone, I filled Greg in on my post office caper on the way to the airport.

He put his blinker on and pulled onto the highway. "Well, I wouldn't worry about it too much. And look at it this way, at least it got you out running."

"Why do you always do that?" I turned in my seat to make sure no one was going to hit us when we merged, as if seeing it about to happen might somehow prevent it.

"Do what?" Greg hit the accelerator and veered into a ridiculously small gap between two cars. I would have waited for a noticeable break in the traffic. I mean, what was the hurry? We had plenty of time.

"Miss the point," I said.

Greg turned to look at me. "I didn't miss the point. I was trying to bring a little levity to the situation."

"Watch the road," I said.

We drove for a while in silence.

"So," Greg said. "Tell Shannon I love her. And tell"—he cleared his throat dramatically—"Chance—"

I burst out laughing. "How the hell did we end up with a son-in-law named *Chance*?"

"Our daughter picked him. And he's a nice guy."

"I agree. But that ma'am stuff totally freaks me out."

Greg laughed. "How about when you told him not to call you ma'am, and he started calling you Mom instead?"

I shook my head. "I think it was the champagne talking. But, still, I mean, *Mom*? It was maybe the third time we'd met. What's that saying about how in the South everyone is your best friend for that day, and in the North it takes five years before they'll talk to you on the street, but once they do, you're friends for life."

Greg reached over and turned the radio off. "He really loves her. It's all over him. He's a lucky guy, and he knows it."

I patted Greg's thigh. "No bias there."

He put his hand on my hand.

"God," I said. "How about that engagement party?"

Greg shook his head. "And that shower thing. I mean, what is it with those people and their zoot suits?"

"Shannon was into it," I said. "Any excuse to buy a new dress."

"By the time the actual wedding rolled around, I was thinking it was going to be a letdown after all the hoopla."

"I know." I reached into my bag and triple-checked that I had my driver's license and e-ticket. "I still kind of wish we'd been able to talk her into having the wedding up here. I mean, from the moment we bought our house, I could picture it. Big white tent on the side yard, ceremony under the wisteria arbor. All that planting and weeding for all those years, you'd think we could have at least gotten a wedding out of the deal."

Greg took his hand off mine and pulled into the HOV lane. Once we had a concrete barrier on either side to protect us from all the crazy Boston drivers, I relaxed a little.

"They wanted to have it in Atlanta," Greg said. "It was their wedding."

"It was our dime," I said.

Greg put his hand back on mine. "That was one big dime. How about when Shannon e-mailed us those articles and told us our wedding budget was below the national average? I'll tell you, that daughter of ours is one good negotiator."

I shook my head. If I had one brilliant piece of advice for parents whose daughter is getting married, it would be to offer to contribute a specific amount of money to the cause. Then tell the happy couple they can keep whatever they don't spend. The early months of planning had been fraught with arguments about how much Shannon could pay for her dress and whether they could fly in a live band. Yes, a live band. The minute we told Shannon she could keep the change, *poof*, the fights went away.

"You mean, we can spend the money on *anything?*" she'd asked. "What if we decide to elope?"

"Great," I'd said. "We'll meet you there."

We pulled into the drop-off area in front of the Delta terminal. Greg put the car into park and popped the latch on the trunk. He put his hand on the door handle.

"I still don't get it," he said. "You have plenty of work up here. And Denise's boyfriend could turn out to be a total nut job. It wouldn't be the first time."

"I can't have this conversation again." The *click* my door handle made sounded like punctuation.

Greg's knuckles turned white when he squeezed the steering wheel. "Fine. Well, have a good trip. Wish I were going with you."

I blew out a puff of air. "Once we sell the house, we can go anywhere we want to go. And the only way we're going to sell it is if you get your rear in gear."

"I thought you didn't want to talk about it," Greg said.

We looked at each other.

He leaned over and kissed me. "Call me when you get there."

In the gray light of Logan, crow's-feet crisscrossed the corners of his eyes and tiny cords of loose skin draped his neck like a garland. Looking at my husband was like watching my life flash by.

"I don't think so." I closed my eyes. "You call me, Greg. But not until the house is ready."

CHAPTER 17

"MOMMY," A GIRL'S VOICE YELLED AS I STEPPED INTO the baggage terminal.

I turned. A toddler reached her arms up to her twenty-something mother.

"I saw that," a voice said behind me.

I turned around again and fast-forwarded two and a half decades. Shannon gave me a big hug and a kiss on the cheek. She smelled like some new exotic version of my old daughter.

"Just wait," I said. "It'll happen to you one day. Some primitive part of me still thinks every crying baby is somehow my responsibility."

Shannon tucked her sleek bobbed hair behind her ears. "Good to know. Chance and I will be sure to put that little nugget to use down the road."

I kept my arm around her as we walked over to wait for my suitcase. "Just give Dad and me a year or two to have some fun first. As soon as we unload the house, that is."

Shannon slid out from under my arm and pulled her iPhone from an impossibly small bag. Her fingers danced across the screen. "How's that going?" she asked without looking up.

"Ha," I said.

She scrolled through the urgent messages that had piled up since she last checked, probably thirty seconds ago. I unearthed my clunky BlackBerry from my shoulder bag and turned it on, just so I wouldn't look like a total dinosaur.

Shannon was a CPA. I knew that part because Greg and I had financed it. She traveled around the country doing audits for one of those national finance companies everyone has heard of but no one quite knows what they do. She threw around phrases involving millions of dollars like it was Monopoly money.

The company paid for her continuing education credits, which were mysteriously called CPEs instead of CECs, which would make a lot more sense, if you asked me. They also took care of her membership in the AICPA, which I had to admit I always got confused with the ASPCA. Shannon's explanations went in one ear and out the other, though I wasn't sure if that was my math phobia or the fact that I was becoming increasingly allergic to acronyms.

I mean, WTF, you could spend your whole day deciphering acronyms. I knew early on Denise was my BFF, but by the time I figured out that LMAO was laughing my ass off, I wasn't. ROTFL-MAO? When was the last time you were actually rolling on the floor laughing your ass off, I mean, *really*? And I'm not sure I could have a true friendship with anyone who underscores every funny comment with LOL. It's ridiculous. If you have to cue someone to laugh out loud, you're simply not being funny enough.

"OMG," Shannon said to the text she was reading. "Could you give me like three minutes to hang out with my *mother*?"

This was the way things always went with Shannon. Blink and she was gone.

I grabbed my suitcase from the luggage carousel. "Do what you need to do, honey. Just drop me off at the car rental place and I can meet you at the house later."

Shannon tucked her phone back into her tiny purse. "Okay, you can take my GPS."

SHANNON HAD BEEN ADAMANT about picking me up. She'd also insisted that I rent a car not at the airport, but at the rental car company closest to the house she and Chance had recently bought. I went along with this because she was my daughter and Atlanta was her territory, but as was so often the case in my life, it would have been a lot easier to do it my way.

Their new house was OTP, or Outside the Perimeter, which in Atlanta-speak means outside the circle of Interstate 285. For Shannon and Chance, trading their Virginia Highland apartment for the suburbs north of the city meant happy home ownership, a great school system for their penciled-in children, and room to spread out.

For me today, it meant climbing into my rental car and driving back into the city again.

I unearthed my recently recovered reading glasses from the bottom of my bag. I held them up and watched the silver metal on the sidepieces twinkle in the hot Atlanta sun. I gave them a quick kiss, then put them on so I could read the address Denise's boyfriend had e-mailed me.

I punched the hotel's address into Shannon's GPS, then stuck it on the windshield of my rental car. I rolled slowly through the lot while it searched for its coordinates.

I should have loved the drivers in Atlanta, but the truth was, they made me nervous. Boston drivers are aggressive and nuts. Atlanta drivers are just plain nuts. Given that Atlanta is one of the traffic capitals of the world, it's ridiculous the way they take their sweet time getting where they're going. I mean, do they actually *want* to stay on the highway in their fancy SUVs all day?

A woman stopped her car and waved me on to the road in front of her.

"What are you, crazy?" I said out loud.

She smiled and waved again.

I followed the sign for Route 400 South and merged onto the highway.

"Drive point eight miles, then turn right onto Route 400 South," Shannon's GPS said in a fake woman's voice.

"*Hello*," I said. "I'm already here." Apparently, even GPS machines were slower in the South. I put on my blinker and moved into the middle lane. I'd just take a quick look around when I got to the hotel, maybe make a few notes. Then I'd call Shannon and see if I could pick up something for dinner on the way home.

"In five hundred feet, turn right onto Route 400 South," the GPS said.

"LOL," I said.

"Please turn right," the GPS said.

"Please shut up," I said.

I'd seen Shannon's new house only once, when Greg and I flew down to check it out after their offer had been accepted but while they still had time to pull out, contingent on the home inspection. The neighborhood was lovely, with ivy-edged sidewalks, mature landscaping, and green manicured lawns. It encompassed a mixed bag of houses that spanned the decades, refreshing in an area where so much was new and cookie-cutter. The house they'd chosen was a 1970s contemporary in desperate need of TLC. I was proud of Shannon for seeing its potential. When you're house hunting, especially the first time around, always buy the worst house in the best neighborhood you can afford.

"Please make a legal U-turn as soon as possible," the GPS said.

"Please calm down," I said. "I'll let you know when I need you."

A strange man passed by in the lane to my right and smiled over at me. Possibly because I appeared to be talking to myself. Possibly because he was a lunatic. I resisted the urge to out myself as a northerner by giving him the finger.

Shannon liked to do things her way, but I couldn't wait to get in there, see what they'd done so far, and help out with a project or two while I was here. In some crazy 1970s Swiss chalet–inspired fantasy, possibly fueled by too many drugs in the '60s, the master bedroom actually had shutters that opened onto a tiny balcony overlooking the living room. I mean, what was that architect thinking? All I could picture were kids hurling each other over the edge one not-too-distant day. I was pretty sure removing the balcony and covering the opening with drywall would be something the three of us, plus maybe one or two of Chance's burly groomsmen, could handle. Then we'd have to figure out what to do with that big expanse of blank wall.

I passed a woman putting on mascara in her rearview mirror. While I certainly agreed that none of us should be texting or talking on our cell phones while we drive, where was the public outcry about women putting on their makeup while cruising along the highway at breakneck speed?

"Reverse direction at the earliest opportunity," the GPS said.

"Keep it up and I'll make my daughter return you," I said.

"Recalculating," the GPS said.

"You and me both, honey. Wait till you get to be my age. And I thought it would be all smooth sailing by now. Ha."

"Rerouting. Please stand by."

The traffic slowed to a crawl. Maybe the GPS actually knew something I didn't. It was an interesting thought. Because if it were true, then I wouldn't have to be in charge. That would be such a nice change. I mean, I was good at being in charge, but sometimes I just wanted somebody else to take a turn. And to know that if I turned over the reins, someone, or I guess in this case, some*thing,* else would pick up the slack. Sometimes you just didn't want to be everybody's mother.

I leaned over and turned up the volume. "Okay, girlfriend, give it to me."

"Drive three point three miles, then take ramp on right."

"Affirmative," I said. "GPS is my new BFF."

I put my blinker on to start gradually merging over to the right. Greg would have waited until the last possible moment, but this was the GPS's and my show now.

The traffic inched along and then came to a complete stop.

"Drive three point three miles, then take ramp on right," the GPS said.

"You're repeating yourself," I said.

The GPS was silent.

Four lanes of traffic sat on the highway like beached whales, not moving an inch. I put the car into park and polished my much-loved reading glasses.

"Make a legal U-turn as soon as possible," the GPS said.

"Make up your mind," I said.

We sat forever and then some more. I put on my cheaters and called Denise just to make sure a warrant for my arrest hadn't been issued, but she didn't pick up. I thought about calling home, but what was the point of an ultimatum if you didn't stick to it? I sorted the receipts I was collecting for Josh, arranging them neatly in the clear plastic folder with the Velcro seal I'd brought along.

"Drive three point three miles, then take ramp on right," the GPS said.

I ignored it. We sat some more. And some more. My stomach growled and reminded me of the lunch Shannon and I hadn't managed to go out for. I drank some bottled water and rooted unsuccessfully in my shoulder bag for a snack. I always traveled with emergency provisions—mini packages of raw nuts, baby carrots, Kashi bars. My post office heist must have thrown me off my game. They were probably still sitting on my kitchen counter. I hoped Greg and Luke had the sense to eat the carrots before they got moldy.

"Drive three point three miles, then take ramp on right," the GPS said.

I reached over and yanked the cord out of the cigarette lighter. "That's it," I said. "That's all you get. I'm sick and tired of giving everybody second chances."

A minute later I saw a zebra galloping down the middle of the highway against the piled-up traffic.

I took off my reading glasses and looked again.

A formation of police motorcycles followed the zebra.

"I guess we're not in Boston anymore," I said to the GPS. When the GPS didn't answer, I almost plugged it back in again. I kind of missed having someone to talk to.

All around me car doors were opening.

"WTF," I said. I climbed out, too.

"Are you believin' in that?" the guy next to me said.

"Did y'all see what I just saw?" a woman in heels and a sundress said.

"I got it on video with my cell phone," another woman said. "I already sent it off to CNN."

"Must have escaped on the way to Philips Arena," a guy said. "The wife and kids and I have tickets to the Ringling Brothers circus there tonight."

"Talk about taking your act on the road," the woman in the sundress said. Everybody laughed like they'd known one another for years.

Two women a few vehicles down opened up the tailgate of their SUV. "Tired old soggy sandwiches aren't going to do the folks at work any good by the time we get 'em there," one of them yelled. "Help yourselves, y'all!"

CHAPTER 18

EVEN THE GPS WAS TIRED BY THE TIME I PLUGGED IT back in and we finally found the hotel. We would have simply turned around and gone back toward Shannon's house, but we were more than halfway there when the traffic stopped. Two hours later when it finally started moving again, one of us really had to go to the bathroom.

I lucked out and found a parking place right on the street. I double-checked the address on my BlackBerry. The place looked great, exactly what you would imagine if you did a picture search for BOUTIQUE HOTEL. It looked almost like a large brick town house, with a cute arched front entryway and a brick patio surrounded by a waist-high black wrought iron fence.

Already I could imagine a striped rounded awning over the door, the perfect hip come-hither statement. Awnings have been around since ancient Egypt and Syria, but they hit their stride in the United States when the advent of the steamship forced canvas mills and sailmakers to look for new options. I loved the way they'd been reinventing themselves ever since, calling out shelter and tradition from doorways, windows, and decks. I'd order a classic bubble dome awning in a nice Sunbrella stripe, maybe Hartwell Lagoon or even Gaston Seaglass.

Then I'd hit some flea markets for mismatched bistro tables and chairs. We'd have a nightly wine reception with a local musician playing loudly enough to create some buzz.

I'd done my research, so I knew that boutique hotels had made their splashy entrance in the late 1980s, complete with ultramodern decor, dance music playing in the lobby, and hip people greeting guests as they arrived. Almost by definition, they'd been small and unique and funky.

More recently, boutique hotels had begun to flounder as major chains jumped into the act, spending lots of money to give their hotels a faux boutique vibe. Apparently, if it looked like a boutique hotel and quacked like a boutique hotel, most people were happy to pretend that a five-hundred-room generic hotel with leopard skin chairs in the lobby *was* a boutique hotel.

I hid the GPS in the glove compartment and fished for the key Josh had FedExed me. I checked the number again, since the hotel didn't appear to have a sign. Maybe the bank had let the old owners take it with them.

Dead flowers crumbled in huge terra-cotta pots on either side of a horizontally striped glass-and-teak door. I slid the key into the lock and turned. I pushed the door. It didn't budge. I wiggled the key around and gave the door a little kick.

It opened suddenly, and I hopped forward with one leg up.

"Hey," Josh said. "Watch the merchandise."

I stood there for a moment like an aging chorus dancer before I remembered to put my leg down.

"Did I know you were going to be here?" I asked.

Josh grinned a boyish grin and opened the door wide. "If you did, that would have been one of us."

I walked past him and into the hotel, because it seemed like the only available option.

The place was a mess. Three barrels of trash were lined up on the bamboo floor just inside the door, and wires dangled from a hole in the ceiling where a chandelier should have been. The reception counter was covered with more trash, and an ancient fax machine teetered dangerously close to the edge. To the left was a bar area with a stool-less cement bar, a few bottles, and not much else.

Josh followed my gaze. "At least they left us some booze."

A bottle of Kahlúa sat on the bar next to a glass with a chocolate puddle's worth of liquor in it. A stack of papers was piled beside the glass.

"Kahlúa?" I said.

He ran his fingers through his carefully gelled hair. "It was that or peach schnapps."

"They took the barstools with them?" I said.

He nodded. "The stools, some of the tables and chairs, the sheets, the towels, even some of the sinks."

"The sinks," I said. "Are they allowed to do that?"

Josh shook his head. "I've got a guy looking into it, but I'm pretty sure I bought this place as is." He picked up his Kahlúa glass. "Can I buy you a drink?"

"No thanks," I said.

His face fell, like someone had just told him there wasn't a Santa Claus.

"Okay, just a tiny one," I said. "But what I really need is a restroom."

Josh shook his head. "Good luck."

I found one just beyond the little lobby. I had to open the door to be sure, since the previous owners had taken the MEN and WOMEN signs with them, leaving ugly screw holes in the dark wood doors. Once inside, I was pleasantly surprised to find it had toilet paper. And soap in the dispenser. There were even two rippled glass sinks sitting up on the counter, making them vessel sinks in design lingo. One was a little bit lopsided, so maybe they'd tried to hijack the sinks, too, but had run out of time. I couldn't even imagine how awful it would be to have put your heart and soul into a business, only to lose it to the bank. I'd probably have taken the toilet paper, too.

Josh was holding his phone when I walked back into the bar. When he saw me, he pushed a button and put the phone away. He was young, but he did have manners. Maybe Denise had picked a winner this time.

He drizzled some Kahlúa into an oversize brandy snifter and handed it to me. He poured himself a refill.

He tapped his snifter to mine. "To one of the stupider moves I've made in a while."

"You mean Denise?" I said.

His eyebrows went up.

"Sorry," I said. "I forgot she wasn't here. That's just kind of the way we talk to each other. You know, sort of juvenile and imma-ture. Not that I think there's anything wrong with being young," I added quickly.

His eyebrows were still up.

"Sorry," I said. "I don't even know why I said that. Was that De-nise you were just calling when I walked in?"

He nodded.

"Call her. I don't mind."

Josh took a sip of his Kahlúa. "She didn't pick up. She must have been in a meeting or something."

"She'll call back," I said.

"Thanks for the reassurance."

"Oh, God," I said. "Sorry. I didn't mean it that way."

Josh took another sip of Kahlúa.

"So," I said. "Did you hear about the zebra on the highway?"

"No, but I have a great one about three llamas who walk into a bar. You go first."

I shook my head. "Never mind."

"Wait. You were serious?"

I swirled the Kahlúa around in my snifter. "This isn't going too well, is it?"

Josh laughed. "Okay, let's start again. A zebra, you say?"

I smiled. "Yes, a zebra. An actual zebra. I think it escaped on the way to the circus."

When Josh smiled, he looked a little bit like Johnny Depp around the mouth. Just for a second, and then he went right back to being noncelebrity Josh. But it was there: that glimmer of bad boy daring.

"Now that's something you don't hear about every day," he said.

I gave my Kahlúa another swirl and put it down on the bar. "They caught the zebra safe and sound, so that's good. Anyway, everybody started tailgating on the highway during the chase."

I reached into my shoulder bag and put a page of notes and three business cards on the bar between us. "And I got some great referrals—carpenters, electricians, plumbers."

Josh picked up one of the cards and turned it over. "We're gonna need 'em."

I reached for my Kahlúa and took a tiny sip. Coffee, alcohol, and sugar mainlined their way to my stomach and fought to take over my brain. The undertones of vanilla and caramel were soothing, like adult Easter candy.

"Chocolate," I said.

Josh picked up his glass. "Nah. It's just so sweet it makes you think so."

"No, No. The hotel. We could call it Chocolate. Ooh, or how about Hot Chocolate?"

"I don't know. In this climate wouldn't something like Iced Tea make more sense?"

"They call it Hotlanta, don't they? Oh, wait, my daughter told me Hotlanta is out. She said there's even a local radio campaign to make people stop saying it. But that doesn't mean we can't still use Hot Chocolate."

Josh took another sip of his Kahlúa. "Okay, what else?"

"We target solo women business travelers."

"Can't argue with that," Josh said. "Just don't tell Denise."

We looked at each other.

"That was stupid," Josh said.

"I did it first," I said. "So now we're even. Anyway, high-speed Internet, overstuffed chairs with cute little portable laptop stations on casters, great security, chocolate soap, chocolate candles."

"Chocolate candles? Are they edible?"

"No, they just smell like it. The smell of chocolate creates a warm fuzzy feeling for most people and puts them into a relaxed state."

Josh nodded. "Will we have chocolate that you eat, too? Or is that a guy thing?"

"Of course we will. I was thinking an all-chocolate menu, or almost all-chocolate. Every kind imaginable, from totally decadent to low-cal spa twists. Chocolate chip pancakes—"

"Whoa, you're killing me." He checked his cell phone. "Hey, do you want to go grab something for dinner?"

"Thanks," I said, "but my daughter's expecting me. I should take off now anyway. I'll see you here tomorrow?"

Josh was still looking at his phone. "Actually, I'm booked for the weekend. So why don't you hang out with your daughter, and we can meet back here bright and early on Monday."

CHAPTER 19

I DIDN'T EVEN BOTHER TO OFFER TO PICK UP DINNER before I jumped back on the highway. I was too exhausted. Not mom-with-a-new-baby-sleep-deprived exhausted, just it-had-been-a-long-day tired.

By this point in my life I'd collected a whole set of touchstones like this. Sure, my sprained ankle hurt, but compared to twenty-six hours of unmedicated labor, how bad was it really? And yes, it was an unfortunate haircut, but not nearly as awful as that asymmetrical cut with the perm on the long side only back in the 1980s.

I was hungry, too. Not fasting-before-a-colonoscopy hungry, but still. By the time I finally got off the highway again, I could have eaten a horse. Or at least a chocolate zebra. I would have even settled for a bowl of cereal.

Even the blossoms of the cherry trees made me think of food. Spring was in full bloom in Atlanta. It was like fast-forwarding a couple of months from New England.

"Continue point eight miles," the GPS said.

"Thank you," I said.

"In five hundred feet, your destination will be on your right."

The GPS was turning out to be everything a BFF should be—calm and supportive, someone who had your back 100 percent of the time. I had to admit Denise was more fun, but she was also way too busy to plug into my lighter and drive around with me.

"Thank you again," I said. "I don't know what I'd do without you."

The GPS let out a little burst of static that sounded almost like I'd embarrassed it. "You have reached your final destination."

"I wish," I said. "But it'll be a nice break while I'm recalculating."

Chance opened the side door as soon as he heard the car.

"Mom," he yelled.

"Here we go," I whispered to the GPS as I unplugged it.

I walked by a pot of lush pansies and into the arms of my son-in-law.

Shannon came out and linked her arm through Chance's as I was backing out of his bear hug. "Just in time for dinner," she said.

"Sorry," I said. "I meant to call to see if I could pick up something."

Chance held out his other elbow in my direction. I pretended I didn't see it. He was tall and blond and handsome, and really, really nice, but I still didn't get it.

A Crock-Pot was simmering on the counter. The table in the little dining area was set for three. With cloth napkins, no less.

When Shannon took the top off the Crock-Pot, my stomach growled in appreciation.

"Is that beef stew?" I asked.

"It is," Shannon said. "Just the way you used to make it when I was a kid."

"You still remember that?" I'd thrown out my harvest gold Crock-Pot years ago.

"Of course I do. Remember, you gave me the recipe over the phone that time?" Shannon grabbed an actual apron off a hook on the kitchen wall and looped it over her neck.

"Is that an apron?" I asked.

Shannon picked up a wooden spoon and stirred the stew. "Chance likes the way it looks on me."

I turned to Chance. "Who is this woman and what have you done with my daughter?"

He let out a big chuckle. "Can I get you a glass of wine, Mom?"

"Sure, son," I said. Nobody laughed.

Shannon scooped up a spoonful of stew and held it out for Chance to taste. The apron made my daughter look like she'd just stepped off the set of *Ozzie & Harriet* or *Leave It to Beaver*. Or even *Desperate Housewives*.

Just in case Shannon had any plans to put that spoon back into the stew, I found a fresh one and started stirring. I wasn't sure if it was Chance's germs or his cooties I was worried about.

"Perfection," Chance proclaimed.

"Me or the stew?" my darling daughter said.

By way of answer, he dipped her like a ballroom dancer and gave her a kiss. I focused on the stew.

"Why don't you two go chat, and I'll call you when dinner's ready," Shannon said when she came up for air.

I reached for the baguette on the counter. "We wouldn't think of it, would we, Chance?"

He poured two glasses of red wine and popped open a beer for himself.

"I'll leave you little ladies to it then," he said as he headed for the living room. A minute later we heard what sounded like a fishing show blasting from the TV.

I picked up a knife. Since filleting my son-in-law didn't seem like a real option, I started slicing the baguette.

Shannon put her wineglass down on the counter. "I'll be right back," she said. "I just have to go iron Chance's shirt for tomorrow. He likes a nice crisp shirt. Extra starch."

I tightened my grip on the knife and gave the cutting board a quick stab. "Shannon Elizabeth," I said. "Didn't I teach you anything?"

My beautiful daughter looked at me with wide eyes. "What do you mean?"

I probably should have stopped to think before I opened my mouth, but in my defense, it had been a long day and I was tired. "There's no excuse for you," I said. "Women have fought and sacrificed and even died to give you the equality you're so casually throwing away. It's your life, but if you were going to turn into some twisted version of an apron-wearing 1950s housewife, you might have at least given us a heads-up before your father and I threw away a fortune on your education."

From the living room, Chance let out a startlingly loud burp.

Shannon didn't seem to notice. She put her hands on her hips. "What's wrong with aprons? It seems to me that women have earned the right to choose."

"Choose *aprons?*" I asked. Clearly her father and I had taken a wrong turn somewhere. I wondered if it was too late to reconsider an occasional spanking. Maybe our parenting had been too perfect. Maybe we hadn't given her enough to rebel against.

"Choose *aprons?*" I repeated. I could literally feel the blood pounding in my ears. Mother Has Massive Stroke while Confronting Aproned Daughter, the headlines would read.

Chance and his beer bottle strolled back into the kitchen. He was actually whistling "Whistle while You Work."

I glared at him. "You," I said.

Shannon reached over and gave him a high five. Chance put his arm around her.

They both grinned at me.

"What?" I said.

Shannon yanked off her apron and threw it on the counter.

"Gotcha," she said.

"LAUGH IF YOU WILL," I said, "but you are sooooo written out of the will. Dad and I are leaving everything to Luke."

It felt strange to mention Greg. I couldn't remember when I'd last gone almost a full day without talking to him, and I kind of missed him. I wondered if I'd start looking for ways to casually sneak his name into the conversation, like a high school girl with a crush or a woman having a secret affair, just so I could feel connected to him.

"Oh, well. It was totally worth it," my darling daughter said. "See," she said to Chance. "I told you how easy it was to push her buttons."

I tried to ignore her by picturing Greg and Luke covered in sweat and thrashing away at all the work that needed to be done before we could put the house on the market, taking a break only to check the list I'd put on the refrigerator three months ago. It was a stretch.

I reached for my wine. "Oh, puh-lease," I said. "What buttons? So where did you get that awful apron anyway?"

Shannon smiled sweetly. "Chance's mother."

"Oops," I said. "Hey, did you hear about the zebra on the high-way?"

They both nodded. "Welcome to Georgia," Chance said. I wondered if he was talking about zebras or aprons.

I decided to recalculate, just like the GPS would have done. I was simply going to ignore my daughter until she started behaving again, forget all about the house, and focus on the hotel. After dinner I'd go through the business cards I'd collected on the highway during the zebra incident and start making phone calls. I'd also gotten the name and number of a guy who had a crew that did odd jobs. I couldn't imagine one odder than the hotel Denise's boy-friend had just bought.

"Great stew, babe," Chance said.

"Thanks, babe," Shannon said.

The way they called each other *babe* made me think of the old Sonny and Cher song. I pictured them singing "I Got You Babe," Chance with a mustache and bell-bottoms and matching vest, and Shannon a head taller with her bobbed hair grown down to her waist. Great, now I wouldn't be able to get the song out of my head.

I really didn't have anything against Chance, per se, and I had to admit Shannon had never looked happier. Even a mother could see how much they loved each other. Chance would probably grow on me. I just needed time to adjust, and if he'd back off with the Mom thing, it might happen a lot sooner.

I devoured some stew and thought about all the times the four of us had sat around our kitchen table eating this meal. Stew was such a great place to sneak in the vegetables that Shannon and Luke would otherwise resist. Luke would make a little hollow in a thick slice of crusty Italian bread, spoon it full of stew, and try to eat it like an open-faced stew boat. It was messy, but creative, just like him. It was funny how your taste buds brought back memories.

I took another bite. "Delicious," I said. "There's something different, though. What did you add?"

"A bottle of Guinness stout," Shannon said. "From Chance's side of the family."

"Well, that certainly balances out the apron," I said. "So, what are your plans for the weekend anyway? Don't let me get in the way. I have plenty to do."

Shannon and Chance looked at each other. I had a sudden feeling they were going to tell me Shannon was pregnant, in which case she'd be in big trouble for both the wine and that Guinness in the stew.

"I've got the whole weekend to spend with you," Shannon said. "I was thinking you could come with me to Zumba in the morning, and then we'd go shopping and get pedicures."

"Great," I said. It was our mother/daughter tradition that whenever Shannon and I saw each other we shopped and had pedicures. Zumba was a new twist, but I could work with it. I felt totally cutting edge that I actually knew it was a Latin-inspired fitness dance craze, and I wouldn't have to embarrass myself by asking Shannon to define Zumba.

Shannon and Chance looked at each other again.

"What?" I said.

"I fly to Boston on Monday," Shannon said. "I just got a promotion, and I have to do this training thing."

"That's wonderful, honey," I said. "Congratulations. Will you have enough time to visit Dad and Luke while you're there, or will you have to fly back Monday night?"

"Actually," Shannon said, "I'll be there for almost a month. And I'm staying with Dad and Luke."

"Oh," I said.

"I know," Shannon said. "I totally lucked out. It could have been Houston, and then I would have had to use my hotel allowance on an actual hotel. Not that I won't take Dad and Luke out for dinner or something to say thanks."

The reality of my situation was just starting to sink in.

I looked at Chance.

He smiled. "Our house is your house, Mom."

CHAPTER 20

THE GUEST ROOM WAS THE ONLY DOWNSTAIRS BED-
room in my daughter's new house. Under most circumstances
this would be an ideal setup, providing plenty of privacy for guests
and owners alike to rest comfortably. But home-alone-in-your-
daughter's-house-with-your-son-in-law fell outside the *most circumstances* category and squarely into *other*. Once Shannon left on
Monday, it would take a lot more than a downstairs guest room to
make me feel comfortable here. At least a few more floors, and pref-
erably a separate guesthouse.

Shannon, and to be fair, possibly Chance, had done a nice job
on the room. The walls were painted a restful sage green. The twin
beds were small but comfortable. When you're putting a guest
room together, never ever give your guests the worst mattresses in
the house. Unless, of course, you don't want your guests to stay for
more than a night. If I walked in and found an old rickety mattress
in place of this one once my daughter was gone, a variation on that
old short sheet trick from summer camp, I'd know.

The top two drawers of the old wooden dresser were empty, and
the closet had a welcoming expanse of vacant space, too. There was
a cozy chair in the corner, which I recognized from Shannon's college apartment, and a good reading lamp. There was even a bottle
of water and a tiny vase filled with fresh pansies on the bedside table.

Either I'd brought up a spectacular daughter, or she was feeling
guilty as hell that she was going to ditch me on Monday.

I'd been so tired last night I'd broken my own rule about unpacking your suitcase as soon as you reach your destination, so I gave everything an extra shake and filled the empty hangers in the closet with as many clothes as I could fit, doubling up some of them like a new twist on twinsets. I brought my clothes for the day into the bathroom with me so I could steam them while I showered. If that didn't work, maybe I could ask Chance to iron them for me.

The guest bath across the hall, with its faux marble Formica counter, avocado toilet, and gold brick linoleum floor, was irrefutable confirmation that the 1970s had, in fact, happened. At least it was clean and had decent water pressure. Always check the water pressure before you buy a house; nothing can ruin your day like an inadequate shower experience.

I showered quickly and blow-dried my hair while my clothes dewrinkled some more. I tiptoed into the kitchen and fired up the coffeemaker, then brought a cup back to my room.

I almost called Greg before I remembered I wasn't speaking to him. I called Denise instead.

"Good morning," she said. "How's my favorite thief doing?"

I'd totally forgotten about my heist. Not only was my whole world getting shakier by the minute, but I was also losing my memory on top of it. I wondered if that was a good thing or a bad thing. I took a moment to contemplate the headlines that might appear any moment in the local weekly, which tended to have so little real news that it wasn't above making up its own: Mother of Two Makes Passes at Reading Glasses. I'd Do It Again in the Blink of an Eye, Unrepentant Matron Cries from Jail Cell.

"Hello? You called me, remember?"

I took a quick sip of coffee. "Oh, sorry. You're not going to believe this. Shannon is going to Boston on Monday."

"For the day?"

"No, for the month. Or almost a month. I can't stay here—"

Denise burst out laughing. "With *Chance?* Of course you can stay alone in your daughter's house with your adorable son-in-law. You'll be the talk of Hotlanta."

I lowered my voice in case the ceiling wasn't properly insulated. "It's not that I don't like him. It's just that it's going to be awkward, since I don't really know him."

"So you'll get to know him."

"Okay, and he called me Mom again. It just seems to me that if someone hasn't given birth to you or adopted you, you should wait to be invited. Or not."

"If you don't like it, just tell him to knock it off."

"Yeah, that would go over well with Shannon." I loved Denise, but the fact that she didn't have kids sometimes gave her a limited perspective.

"It's all about setting limits and telling people how to treat you. Just say, Chance, I'd prefer it if you called me *Sahndra*, and in the meantime I'll call you, I don't know, Chuck? Buck? WhattheFuck?"

"Funny. I was thinking I might move into the hotel. How long is Josh staying?"

"Where?"

"At the hotel."

"What?"

"Who's on first?" I said.

Instead of *What's on second*, or even *WTF are you talking about*, there was dead silence on Denise's end.

"Josh is in Atlanta?" she finally said.

I had the oddest urge to backpedal, to say something like *oh, never mind, maybe I dreamed it.*

"You didn't know that?" I said instead.

"We're busy people. It's not like we tell each other every little thing."

I took another sip of coffee to give my brain a chance to catch up. "Oh, wait. He called you. Yesterday from the hotel. You were in a meeting. Or you must have been in a meeting."

"What time?" Denise said in her lawyer's voice.

"Five. P.M. Approximately. I think." I hadn't even done anything, and I was feeling guilty. I could only imagine how fast I'd cave when they came after me for the reading glasses.

"And I was in a meeting?"

"Yes. No. Wait. Okay, I think he said he called you and you must have been in a meeting because you didn't pick up."

Denise didn't say anything.

"Maybe the call didn't go through. It happens."

"So," Denise said. "How's the weather down there?"

ZUMBA TURNED OUT to be less intimidating than I expected. It was really just the choreographed aerobics of the 1980s with a Latin beat. And instead of the younger women baring their tights-covered butt cheeks on either side of a thong leotard, they showed off their naked abdominal muscles between their sports bras and yoga pants.

I wiped the sweat off my forehead and reached for my water bottle. The woman in front of me was wearing a pearl choker. When it came to workout attire, I shot for a clean T-shirt. I'd once read that body secretions are good for the luster of pearls. Maybe she was working on her luster while I worked on my cellulite.

The instructor searched for the next song. I watched a glowing Shannon jog effortlessly in place and took a moment to mourn the body I used to have. I wish I'd had more photos taken of it as proof that it had once existed, but the truth was I'd always dodged the camera.

If a camera had ever loved me, I'd missed the declaration. The only way I'd been able to appreciate my looks was in hindsight. If someone somehow managed to get a photo of me today, I'd probably think I'd looked pretty hot in that Zumba class when I got to be, say, eighty.

I didn't really want my old body back, exactly, if it meant I had to go through everything my daughter still had in front of her. But if they ever figured out a way you could store your real body and rent an avatar while you went through pregnancy and childbirth and toilet training and minivan driving and parent/teacher conferences and teenagers staying out late, and then pick it up again later when you could fully appreciate it, I would be totally pissed off that I'd missed it.

The sudden blast of what sounded like a kind of merengue/hip-hop hybrid made me jump. Given the size of the tiny speakers up by the ceiling, the volume was impressive. Either loud music had gotten louder since the 1980s or my ears had gotten more sensitive. I thought about tearing off pieces of tissue and stuffing them into my ears the way we'd stuffed bigger wads of tissue into our bras in junior high, but I didn't want to embarrass my daughter.

I marched in place with the rest of the class, rocking my hips to the quick one-two-three-four beat. We started traveling, four fast step-slide-togethers to the right and then to the left. The instructor had short hair the color of cherry cough syrup and a tattoo of a black rose on the back of her neck. Whether or not you agreed with her fashion choices, they certainly made her easy to follow.

The trick to Zumba, and probably everything else, is not to expect perfection right away. If you stay relaxed, anything you don't pick up right away will make more sense the next time it comes around. The only real obstacle I ran into was that my hips didn't work as quickly as they used to, but I solved that by just doing every other beat during the fastest parts.

Shannon caught my eye as we turned to repeat the steps to another wall. "Doing okay?" she mouthed.

"Of course," I said. "And you?"

When the song ended, the fifty or so women and two men clapped and hooted. I hit my stride on the next number, which seemed to be a combination of the flamenco and the cha-cha. We pretended to swirl big puffy dresses as we spun around the room and then did a front-back-cha-cha-cha to all four corners.

My muscles loosened up and I remembered how much I'd always loved to dance. I'd talked Greg into taking ballroom dance classes about a zillion years ago, and he'd hated it. The classes were held in an old community center basement with metal support posts scattered around the room. One day he rammed my back right into one while we were making a pitiful attempt at the fox-trot. He swore it was an accident, but I never really believed him. He'd also accused me of trying to lead, which was probably true, but in my defense, somebody had to.

I really did love to dance. I had rhythm. I had flair. The progressions of steps actually clicked in my head like the balanced equations that never made sense in math class. With the right partner, I could be tangoing my way across the country right now. I'd have a closet full of sexy dresses and a crazy collection of high-heeled dance shoes. I could spend a season on *Dancing with the Stars*, or at least *So You Think You Can Dance*.

Ah, the things you never thought to ask before you committed to a lifetime with another person. Will you get up with me to watch the sunrise, or will you snore the morning away? Will you write me poetry or take the easy way out with a Hallmark card for every occasion? Will you get the house ready to put on the market when I ask you to? *Can you dance?*

I flipped my imaginary flamenco skirt coquettishly. I made a quarter turn counterclockwise and flipped it again.

Shannon caught my eye on the next quarter turn.

"I can't stay there if you're not there," I mouthed.

"Of course you can," she mouthed.

I turned and flamencoed right into the woman next to me.

CHAPTER 21

"YOU SHOULD SEE THE OTHER WOMAN," SHANNON said to her pedicurist over the sound of the waves crashing in the foot soak spa.

I leaned back in my massage chair. "It was so embarrassing," I said to mine. "I can't believe they had to call an ambulance."

"She was only bruised," Shannon said. "The gym just didn't want to take a chance on getting sued."

I checked the lump on my forehead, then adjusted the instant ice pack they'd given me at the gym. "She was definitely at fault, so liability shouldn't be an issue."

Shannon laughed. "I'm pretty sure Zumba collisions are no-fault in this state."

Our pedicurists ignored us, completely and unapologetically, and yet my daughter and I continued to act as if this were a four-way conversation. I would also overtip for both of us, even if the pedicures were only so-so. There was something about the inequity of letting another person scrub my feet that really bothered me. And yet I had to admit a pedicure was a lot like having a salad served to you. It was simply better when you didn't have to do it yourself.

"You are so not going to make me feel guilty," Shannon said. "It's a great opportunity for you and Chance to get to know each other."

"Oh, puh-lease," I said. "It's going to be ridiculously awkward for both of us." I looked at my pedicurist for backup, but she was busy scrubbing the calluses on my right foot with a pumice stone.

Shannon rolled her eyes at the top of her pedicurist's head. "*His* mother treats me like a daughter."

"What's that supposed to mean?"

"Exactly what I said. You don't like him. Not that I care what you think, but you should at least come out and admit it."

"It's not that I don't like him. It's just that I don't know him very well yet."

"Mom, he's my *husband*."

"How did you get to be so grown up?" I said.

We watched our pedicurists in silence. Mine went to work on the calluses on my left foot.

"I think you're right about that balcony," Shannon said.

"Of course I am," I said. "Your kids won't be able to resist throwing things from it, or following each other off the edge, like lemmings."

"Thanks for the image, Mom."

Shannon pushed a button on the arm of her massage chair and leaned back. My chair had been pounding me in the same place since I'd pushed the big green On button, and it was starting to feel like a knife being stabbed repeatedly into my back. I squinted and tried to read the massage cycle options. It was all a big blur, so I closed one eye and then the other, which made no appreciable difference. I leaned sideways and tried to reach my reading glasses in my shoulder bag, but my arm wasn't quite long enough.

Being totally dependent on reading glasses to function in the world was the only thing that really drove me crazy about getting older. It was probably just a tiny bump for people who'd always worn glasses, but I hated how helpless no longer having twenty-twenty vision made me feel. I wish I'd taken a moment to appreciate my younger eyes while I had them.

"Can you read my chair for me?" I asked.

"God, I used to love it when you and Dad read to us," Shannon said. "*Papa, Please Get the Moon for Me, Pat the Bunny, Make Way for Ducklings.*"

"Never mind," I said. I pushed a random button. The rollers started moving outward and inward, catching hunks of my back between them. I yelped and hit another button. This cycle was better—kind of a kneading action that worked its way up both sides of my spine and back down.

"Okay," Shannon said. "How about this? You help Chance close in the balcony while I'm gone, and I'll kick Dad and Basement Brother's butts so the house gets on the market."

I was smarter than this. The first thing Shannon would say when she saw Greg and Luke would be, *Mom told me to kick your butts and get this house on the market.* Then it would be three against one. I'd be the bad guy, and I wouldn't even be there to defend myself.

"Dad and Luke are very responsible," I said. "I'm sure they've been working nonstop since I left."

"Chance will probably suggest it to you anyway. He loves to surprise me."

"Okay," I said. "A little casual direction might not be a bad thing. Just promise me you won't say it was my idea."

Shannon reached over to give me a high five. "Deal. Just make sure when you finish it doesn't look like a patch job."

"Trust me," I said. "I'm a professional."

"Oh, and can I have that antique trunk out in the garage for a coffee table? You never use it."

With my luck, all this kneading would make my back rise. I hit the big red Off button. "Are you going to show me the printouts saying the amount of furniture Dad and I have already given you is below the national average?"

Shannon pushed another button on her chair. "Ha. Don't think I couldn't."

Once our newly polished toes were dry, I took a moment to appreciate the fact that March in Atlanta was actually flip-flop weather. It was probably snowing back in Boston, and if we were getting pedicures there, we'd have to sit for a few extra cycles under the toenail dryer before we dared put on our boots.

"The weather here is amazing," I said.

"Talk to me in August," Shannon said, "when you're sitting on the beach enjoying a sea breeze and it's a million degrees here, but mostly it's great."

I paid and tipped. Someday I'd like to meet just one woman who went Dutch on dates with her daughter. Maybe once you moved into senior housing and started eating cat food, the tables would finally turn. Shannon pulled in gobs of money, as did her husband, and in my daughter's defense, she sent lovely, generous gifts on all gift-giving occasions. I wondered if even the mothers of millionaires still picked up the mother/daughter tab.

"Clothes or shoes?" I said.

Shannon shook her head. "I'm a new woman. If a store doesn't have *home* in its name, it's dead to me."

"Okay. HomeGoods or Home Depot? Wait. Do you want to swing by the hotel so you can check it out first? I'd love to hear your thoughts on where to start and take another peek around myself. Then I can keep an eye out for finds while we shop."

Shannon was already halfway out the door. "Absolutely. I can help you do a spreadsheet when we get back to my house."

"You might want to save that for your father and brother," I said.

Both Shannon and Luke were good drivers, but I had to admit I still got a little bit nervous when I was a passenger and they were driving. There was just something so unmotherly about giving up control like that. I soothed myself by air braking and pointing out potential accidents.

"Calm down, Mom. I know what I'm doing." Shannon drove the way she did everything, like she was on a mission.

"It's not you I'm worried about, honey. It's the rest of the crazy world."

"You're the one who's acting crazy. Relax." Shannon put on her blinker and swerved into the next lane.

I leaned back and tried to close my eyes. I couldn't do it. "Whoa, look out for that guy. He's on his cell, and he's way over the line."

Shannon shook her head. "Can't you call Dad or something? You know, just to keep yourself busy?"

In lots of ways your daughter can be like a girlfriend, even your biggest BFF in the whole wide world, no offense to Denise intended, but there's always that family line. A good mother doesn't step over it, and I really believe that no child, no matter how grown up, ever wants to hear her mother trash-talking her father, or vice versa. So I did what I always did—I bit my tongue and kept my mouth shut.

But what I really wanted to say was this: *I can't call your father because I'm not speaking to him. He's driving me crazy, and if I do call him all this not calling him will be for nothing because he'll think I don't really mean that I'm not coming back till he gets the house finished. Do you think I mean it? I really think I do, because the other thing I've been thinking about a lot is that maybe after all these years we've reached the point that we just want different things and maybe even different lives. There doesn't have to be any big drama, does there? I mean, you and Luke are too old to be traumatized, aren't you? Do you actually think I could just walk away like that? You know, leave him and start a new life? And if so, do you think he'd be okay? Would I?*

We pulled off the highway, and I gave Shannon the street address again.

She took a right. "Oh, I know where this is. There's a tapas place about two blocks away. Maybe we can grab something to eat after we see the hotel."

"Absolutely," I said. "I'm starving."

I twisted in my seat to look for landmarks. "If we see a parking spot, we should snag it. I think the hotel is just past the next intersection."

"Give me a heads-up if you see something before I do."

A couple was walking toward us past a long row of flowering Bradford pear trees, popping in and out of view as if they were playing peekaboo. They were both wearing jeans, and the man had his arm wrapped casually around the woman's shoulder. They were holding Starbucks coffee cups and laughing like they were in love. I wasn't sure why I was so drawn to them. Maybe they could have been Greg and me a long, long time ago.

They stepped into the gap between two trees. The man pulled the woman close.

I squinted at the man. It was Josh.

"Oh, boy," I said. I whipped my head around, partly so he couldn't see me and partly so I wouldn't have to watch. But it was like trying to turn away from a car wreck. I looked back just in time to get a glimpse of them kissing.

"Do you see anything?" Shannon asked.

"That's an understatement," I said.

I pulled my shoulder bag to my lap and started fumbling through the contents.

"Bummer," I said. "You're not going to believe this, but I think I forgot to bring the hotel key."

"Is there anybody there who could let us in?"

"Just a couple of rats," I said. "Come on, let's go get some lunch instead."

CHAPTER 22

NOT LONG AFTER WE MOVED INTO OUR NEW OLD house, Greg and I found the wooden steamer trunk at an estate sale and decided to give it to each other for our anniversary. It was in rough shape, with split leather straps and handles, and dented metal trim, so we got it for a song. But it fit the age of our house, and it still had its original long brass key. Plus we could also use it to store clothing. The house was big on charm, but short on closets.

We carried it right up to our bedroom and put it at the base of the bed. Greg sat down on it. "Great place to tie my sneakers."

"How romantic," I said. "Happy anniversary to you, too, honey."

He reached for me. "Hey, have I told you lately—"

Shannon and Luke raced in to sit on either side of Greg.

All four of us looked up as a shard of paint hit the floor. The clean white ceiling of our beautiful master bedroom sanctuary had begun bubbling like an angry rash. Then about a week ago it had begun to flake. Now every time we went into the room, we'd find new splinters of white paint on the bedspread or the floor.

Greg held up the paint chip. "Do not, I repeat, *do not*, put one of these in your mouth."

Shannon rolled her eyes.

Luke was two and spent most of his waking hours testing limits. He crawled from the trunk to our mattress and grabbed his own paint chip. He popped it into his mouth and waited to see what would happen.

I screamed.

Greg scooped him up, and we all ran to the bathroom.

We washed out Luke's mouth as best we could and put in a call to the pediatrician. Massachusetts law didn't prohibit the sale of properties containing lead paint or other potentially hazardous substances, and our Realtor had talked us into waiving our right to have the house inspected for lead. "It's an old house," she'd said. "Just don't let the kids gnaw on the windowsills."

I watched Luke's eyes for signs of brain damage while we waited for the pediatrician to call back. It turned out Dr. Murphy owned an old house, too, and he quickly diagnosed a calcimine ceiling.

Calcimine paint, sometimes called distemper paint, was a kind of inexpensive whitewash made with dried calcium carbonate, essentially chalk, that was popular in the nineteenth and early part of the twentieth century. Since coal and woodstoves heated the houses back then, calcimine was a quick fix for soot-stained walls, and especially ceilings. The good news for Luke's brain was that calcimine paint was lead-free. The bad news for us was that harder, stronger modern paints like the one we'd just used pulled it away from the ceiling.

Greg and I spent our anniversary carrying the trunk and all three mattresses down to the living room floor. We covered the dressers and the floor with cheap plastic drop cloths. We scraped the ceiling. We washed off as much of the calcimine as we could. We opened the windows wide. Greg went into our one semifunctioning bathroom to get cleaned up enough to go pick up the special calcimine coater paint we'd finally tracked down at a paint store almost an hour away.

I wove my way through the three mattresses on the floor of our former front parlor/new great room to the kitchen. I was too

exhausted to deal with the steak we'd splurged on for a late romantic dinner after the kids had fallen asleep, so I threw it into the
freezer and plopped two boxes of macaroni and cheese on the
kitchen counter.

The kids looked up from playing with their LEGOs.

Shannon crossed her arms over her chest. "This day is no fun,"
she said.

Luke crossed his arms over his chest. "Yeah," he growled.

I crossed mine, too. "Yeah."

We ended up piling the kids into the minivan and taking a
family trip to the paint store. We picked up pizza on the way home
and drove with it to the beach. We ate sitting on the edge of a seawall, the seagulls swooping around us, biding their time as they
eyed our crusts. After dinner Greg and the kids went out to the
yard to play. They picked a bouquet of mostly weeds to surprise me.

We finally crawled into bed, the kids' mattresses flanking ours
like bookends. A mattress on the floor had never felt so good. The
white paddle fan circled lazily above us in the dark room, and when
I squinted I could almost pretend it was the moon.

"So," I whispered. "Happy anniversary."

Beside me, Greg let out a long, ragged snore.

Decades of proper anniversary celebrations would follow: break-
fasts in an actual bed; dinners in fancy restaurants; weekend jaunts
to the Cape; a wild, childless week in the Caribbean. But whenever
we strolled down the memory lane of our anniversaries, this would
be the one we remembered first.

SHANNON REACHED FOR one of the tapas. "Are you okay? You
look like you've just had your identity stolen."

There was possibly more truth to that statement than my daughter intended, but I let it go. Then I thought for a moment about whether I should tell her about Josh and the woman, but I let that go, too. Somehow it felt like saying it out loud might make it more real.

I picked up a serving spoon and eyed my choices. "I was just thinking about Denise. Trying to figure out how to tell her the guy she's dating is an idiot. Ooh, what's that?"

Shannon scanned the little tapas map on the table between us. "It must be the Queso de Cabra. Baked goat cheese in tomato basil sauce."

I put a scoop on my little red plate and tasted it. "Mmm, to die for."

"So what else is new?" Shannon said. "All the men Denise falls for are assholes. She's probably connected the dots by now."

I'd never really thought of it that way. "Then why does she date them?"

"People choose what they think they deserve. Otherwise they'd drop that zero and get themselves a hero."

"I don't think it's that simple," I said.

"Of course it is," my daughter said. "Look at Whitney. Even when we were in high school, she always had to pick the one guy in the room things would never work out with. She thinks she can change them, they break her heart, she has high drama, her friends come to the rescue, and then she does it all over again. I have to tell you, it's getting old. I mean, she's twenty-six. Get your shit together."

I tried to remember the time in my life when I'd thought I had all the answers the way my daughter did.

"Remember when Luke ate the rabbit poop?" Shannon said.

"Don't remind me." I reached for my iced tea.

"I told him it was chocolate," Shannon said. "I have a lot of guilt about that."

"Oh, please," I said. "My brother asked me to hold his football while he practiced kicking field goals and broke my finger."

Shannon took a sip of her iced tea. "Totally different—that was an accident."

"It most certainly was not." I put on my reading glasses so I could identify the tapas. "Ooh, 'Artichoke rice cakes with Manchego, a tart melted cheese center made from sheep's milk.'"

We ate for a while in silence.

"So, if it bothers you," I said, "apologize to him."

"It doesn't bother me *that* much. He did plenty to me. He used to scare the shit out of me whenever you left us with a babysitter."

"Yeah, all three times."

"*What?* You guys went out all the time."

"That's ridiculous. We almost never went out. We were too busy chauffeuring you and Luke around."

"You're crazy."

"Right. And you fed your brother rabbit poop."

"You and Dad were the only parents I knew who even *wanted* to go out together. My friends used to think we were this freakishly perfect family."

"Sorry," I said. "You should have spoken up. We could have fought more or something."

Shannon put her fork down on her plate. "A trial separation would have really helped me out. I was the only one in my third-grade class who always knew where I was sleeping that night. I had such a low drama quotient."

We both reached for the last shrimp fritter.

"Take it," Shannon said.

I cut the fritter down the middle and gave Shannon the bigger half.

"Dad and I will try to make it up to you," I said.

Shannon speared her shrimp half with a fork and pointed it at me. "Don't even joke about it. Chance and I talk about you guys all the time. You're our model."

"What about Chance's parents?"

Shannon tucked her hair behind her ears and opened her eyes wide. "OMG, they hate each other. You know, that southern thing, where they're nice as pie in front of everybody, but they haven't slept in the same room for years. Chance thinks they just stay together because his dad's girlfriend doesn't cook, and his mom's boyfriend has cats and she's allergic."

"Really?" I said. "They seemed so crazy about each other when we met them."

Shannon dabbed her mouth, then put her napkin on the table. "Trust me, Mom, you're it. You and Dad are the last real marriage standing."

I twirled the straw around in my iced tea and tried to read my next move in the ice cubes. I took a deep breath.

I met my daughter's clear green eyes. "Your father and I aren't doing so great these days. I'm starting to think we might have reached our expiration date."

Shannon held my gaze for a moment, considering.

She let out a quick laugh and turned to look for the waiter. "You're just hormonal. Every relationship has its ups and downs. Come on, let's get some shopping in before it's too late."

CHAPTER 23

SHANNON WAS DRESSED TO TRAVEL IN TIGHT DE-
signer jeans, a crisp button-down blouse, and a pair of Ann
Roth heels. If I ever tried that, someone would have to cut off my
clothes at the end of the flight. If you're past your first bloom, allow
for the possibility of swelling when you travel. Think ballet flats or
flip-flops you can kick off. And yoga pants, or a bohemian skirt, or at
the very least some spandex threaded discreetly into the fabric
of your jeans. No one will even notice the rest of your outfit if you
wear nice earrings and throw a pashmina over your shoulders or
knot it around your neck as camouflage, the added bonus being
that you can use it as a travel blanket.

"Are you sure you don't want to take your GPS with you?" I asked
after we finished our good-bye hug. I'd offered to take Shannon to
the airport, but Chance wouldn't hear of it. So my plan was to make
a quick getaway to give the newlyweds a few minutes alone together.

Shannon rolled her eyes like she was still thirteen. "Mom, I
used to *live* there."

I used to live there, too, almost slipped out of my mouth, but I
caught it just in time.

My daughter reached for the coffeepot. "If you want to return
the rental, you can borrow my car."

"Thanks, but I'd much rather bill Denise's boyfriend than put
wear and tear on your car." I grabbed the rental keys from the back-
of-the-door organizer. "Okay, well, have a safe trip and, uh—"

"I know, kick Dad and Luke's butts for you."

Shannon unplugged her iPhone and its charger from the sleek black charging station on the kitchen counter. She'd given me one just like it for Christmas, and every time I looked at hers a little wave of homesickness broke over me.

By the way, if you don't have a charging station yet, you should get one. The design has come a long way, and you can even find them with stainless drawer pulls to match your appliances and a hidden surge protector power strip. Not only will its integrated drawers and slots help do away with clutter, but it will also eliminate the hassle of all the cords of your life getting tangled up like spaghetti.

Then all you'll need to do is find a way to separate the tangled cords on the inside of your life, the ones that don't show so much.

Chance strolled into the kitchen all dressed for work, with his damp hair freshly combed. If he harbored any resentment about the fact that Shannon wasn't taking me with her, he hid it well.

"Good morning," he said pleasantly.

"Beautiful day," I said.

"It sure is," he said.

He looked up from pouring a cup of coffee. "What time were you thinking about for dinner, Mom?"

I had a sudden vision of myself all tied up in that goofy apron, cooking three squares a day for my son-in-law.

"I wasn't," I said. "I was thinking I'd try to survive the day first." In case that sounded a bit prickly, I softened it with a smile.

"Love you," I said to Shannon on my way out the door. If Chance wanted to think he was included in the sentiment, *whatever*.

A morning chill almost made me feel like I was still in New England. But the trajectory of the day's heat was different here. At home, whatever warmth we'd get would hit its peak around noon. In Atlanta, the day would just keep getting warmer and warmer until the temperature reached its hottest point around 4:00 P.M. I pictured myself buying a little brick ranch with a pool down the street so I could jump in to cool off at the end of a busy day.

I hummed that old *Mister Rogers* song about it being such a beautiful day in the neighborhood as I plugged in the GPS and rolled backward down the long driveway. Shannon and Luke had loved that show, and I was sure Mister Rogers was a nice guy and all that, but something about the way he took that cardigan of his out of the closet always gave me the creeps. *Sesame Street* felt safer to me somehow, but who knew what twisted things went on behind closed puppet doors at that show either.

"The world's a tough place," I said out loud.

The GPS squawked awake. "Turn left onto Interstate 85."

"Not even close," I said. "Go back to sleep."

Why should I have to be the one to tell Denise her boyfriend was a two-timer, a snake in the grass, a sleaze bucket? In the code of female friendship, were you always honor bound to let your best friend know when you saw her significant other, or even her insignificant other, kissing another woman? And what if Denise already *knew* that this idiot saw other women? What if she accepted that as part of the dues of dating a cute, rich, hot, younger man? Maybe I should try to get an answer to that question before I jumped into the fray. *So, I could say, how's the weather up there? Oh, by the way, do you and Josh see other people? Just curious. Not that I'm prying or anything.*

No, wait. I'd make Josh tell Denise. That's what I'd do. It was only fair. And if he wouldn't tell her what a slimeball he was, I'd quit. And then I'd tell him exactly where he could put his stupid hotel. And then I'd . . . *what?* Go home? Put on that *Stepford Wives* apron and rustle up some grits for Chance? Tell Denise, so we could shoot Josh and run away together? Bali? Paris?

"You have reached your final destination," the GPS said.

Amazingly, we were in front of the hotel. "Right on the money," I said. "Good job."

I figured there must be some hotel parking around here somewhere, but I certainly couldn't find it. I should have thought to ask,
but, I mean, the least Josh could have done was to let me in on
something like that.

We pulled into a small lot down the street. I started to lock the
GPS in the glove compartment but decided it would be safer to
take her, I mean, *it* with me.

I stopped in at Starbucks for a nonfat latte. I wasn't really stalling. I just wanted to make sure I was sufficiently caffeinated for
confrontation.

As much as I loved Shannon's lush suburban neighborhood, I
could see myself living here in the city, too, in a town house or a
midrise condo with a nice view of the Atlanta skyline. I wouldn't
even bother to buy pots and pans. I'd just wander the streets and
graze. There were plenty of interesting restaurants, and I was pretty
sure I'd passed a Trader Joe's.

I'd find a gym and take some more Zumba classes. I reached up
and felt my forehead. There was just a small knot where the swelling had been. Next time I'd be more careful on those turns. Maybe
I'd even bring the GPS with me for navigational backup. *In eight
beats, please turn right. At your first opportunity, reverse direction and
execute a legal booty shake.*

A homeless woman was sitting on the ground, leaning against a
wall with a black garbage bag for a pillow and a handle-less ceramic
mug with a pittance of change inside. I averted my eyes, but not
before I saw that the mug said WORLD'S BEST MOM.

I kept walking. She might not even have any kids. She might
even use the money she panhandled to buy drugs. I'd seen an episode like that on *Addicted*. Or maybe it was *Intervention*. If I gave
her money, I'd probably just be enabling her.

It wasn't that I didn't care. My problem was that once I started
caring I didn't know how to turn it off. There was so much pain

and suffering in the world that sometimes it felt like if I stopped to let it in, the floodgates would open, and I'd be swept out to sea. I was the kind of person who couldn't just write a check to a disaster relief fund without wanting to jump on a plane and save the whole country. We'd adopted our family pets from animal shelters, and yet I could still see the faces of the ones we didn't take home with us.

It wasn't my job to mother the whole world. Every crying baby wasn't really calling out to me, and every homeless woman sitting on the sidewalk didn't have my name on her forehead. I'd paid my dues. It was my time now.

I'd given. I gave at the office, and I gave on the home front. I was always giving. Give, give, give. I'd spent the last two decades at it. I mean, did anyone in my family ever have a need I didn't meet? Was there ever a car pool I didn't drive, a committee I didn't serve on, a crisis I didn't try to solve?

It wasn't just our immediate family I'd mothered. I'd collected food for the local food pantry, shopped and wrapped for the Christmas toy drive, driven into Boston to drop off donations at Rosie's Place and Dress for Success, dragged two eye-rolling teenagers and one husband who would have rather been playing tennis to help build a Habitat for Humanity house.

Back when Luke was in elementary school, not one but two of his friends had spent a long string of overnights with us while their mothers had chemo. We'd registered and paid for one of Shannon's friends to take the SATs and helped her apply to colleges because her parents were embroiled in the first stages of a bitter divorce and refused to take responsibility for anything.

Done. Finished. Over it. If there were a pill for selfishness, I'd totally take it. I wanted to be one of those women who spent the whole day thinking *me, me, me*. I'd fill my days with massages, manicures, shopping, maybe even some minor plastic surgery.

I finished my latte and lobbed the cup into a barrel. I walked back to Starbucks and ordered a bacon, Gouda cheese, and egg white frittata on an artisan roll, and a Grande Caffè Mocha.

When I handed the homeless woman the bag and the take-out coffee cup, I couldn't quite look at her.

"Thank you," she whispered. She put the hot cup on the ground and kept one hand on the bag, as if I might change my mind and try to take it back.

"You're welcome," I said as I walked away.

I wasn't going to think about her anymore.

CHAPTER 24

I REVERSED DIRECTION AND WALKED PAST THE HOTEL. I picked up my pace and started swinging my arms as I practiced reading Josh the riot act in my head. Then I made a U-turn and marched straight to the hotel.

I turned the key in the lock and karate kicked the door open.

The lobby was empty.

Somehow I thought Josh would be standing there, that I'd catch him red-handed with the other woman in his arms.

Maybe they were still in bed. I pictured myself going from room to room, kicking open each door until I found them naked and quivering in fear. But I didn't know where the guest room keys were, and even at a glance I could tell the doors were too high quality to kick in on my own.

I perused the immediate area, looking for clues. Two snifters still perched on the bar, one dotted with sticky brown Kahlúa residue, and the other with about an inch of liquid in the bottom. Judging by the make of the glasses and their position on the bar, they appeared to be Josh's and mine from Friday.

But perhaps this was simply the spot where Josh lured all his women: *Hey, what's a nice girl like you doing in a place like this? Can I buy you a drink, baby? What sign are you? Would you like to come upstairs and see my etchings?*

I held the glass that may or may not have been mine up to what little light there was in the dark bar. I wasn't sure what telltale signs

I was looking for. A shade of lipstick that only a home-wrecking, boyfriend-stealing slut would wear? That wasn't fair. The poor woman probably thought he was unattached. I mean, Tiger Woods, Jesse James, or Josh, who's really at fault here? So what if the women aren't perfect—porn stars can be victims, too.

I shifted the snifter so the light would catch it, but I still came up clueless. Why hadn't I kept reading mysteries after I graduated from Nancy Drew?

"A little early, isn't it?" Josh's voice said behind me.

The snifter in my hand hit the concrete bar and shattered instantly, stale Kahlúa spattering my favorite denim jacket and white T-shirt like a zillion little freckles. As hip as they are, never ever put in concrete counters if you're the least bit attached to your glasses and dishes. They're simply unforgiving.

I started picking up the glass and then decided that, given the circumstances, my outfit was more important.

"Clean cloth and soda water," I said.

"Aye-aye," Josh said. He found a cloth behind the bar. When he pushed the button on the soda nozzle, it let out a blast of air. "Shall I try the Sprite?"

"Water," I said. "Unless that thing has OxiClean on tap."

Josh laughed, which I thought was unfair, since I hadn't intended to be funny. I made sure his fingers didn't graze mine when he handed me the dampened cloth. I couldn't even look at him, but out of the corner of my eye I could see he was wearing jeans and a Woodstock T-shirt. I mean, give me a break, he was probably too young to have even been born at Woodstock.

"Is that your mother's T-shirt?" slipped out of my mouth, possibly a result of overcaffeination.

Josh stopped picking up the shards of glass. "Excuse me?"

I looked him right in the eye. "I saw you. I saw you kissing a woman on the street."

Josh didn't look away. "And you're asking me if it was my mother?"

"Ick." This guy really was a sicko. "I'm not asking you anything. I'm telling you that I drove by over the weekend and saw you kissing another woman. In broad daylight. On the street. Between two Bradford pear trees."

He smiled. I wanted to kill him. Or at least ground him.

"They were flowering," I said randomly, as if this would prove that I'd been there and maybe even wipe that smirk off his face.

"You should have stopped," Josh said. "That was Melissa. We've been friends since college. We wandered around and then picked up pizza for her husband. And three kids."

I looked for signs of lying, perhaps a small twitch or a higher pitch to his voice. I'd read somewhere that women often lie to make others look good, while men are more likely to lie to make themselves look good. I'd also read that women think they look much worse than they actually do, and men think they look substantially better. I thought these two tidbits might be related, to each other and to this situation, and when I had the time to sit down and meditate about them at length, I hoped to come to some profound conclusion.

In the meantime I'd focus on the most important thing. "You didn't cheat on Denise with her?"

"Hardly." Josh took out his cell and flipped open the lid. "If you don't believe me, you can ask Melissa yourself."

"That's okay," I said quickly.

We looked at each other.

I looked away first. I bunched up the damp cloth and started wiping down the bar. "Don't tell Denise, okay?" I said. "She'll kill me."

Josh smiled. "Don't give it another thought. She's lucky to have you for a friend."

The phone in his hand let out the first few tinny notes of "Stairway to Heaven."

Josh pushed the Off button.

If you're ever trying to figure out if someone is lying to you, watch carefully. Are the answers to your questions delayed? Does the face become stiffer, the lips tighter? Are the palms balled into fists? Are the shoulders hunched? Is the potential liar pale? Breathing heavily?

I simply couldn't tell. But I was watching him.

I'D MET DAN THE HANDYMAN on the highway on Zebra Day. He showed up on time with a big truck and a couple of beefy sidekicks and got right to work. Josh and I figured out what would stay and what would go, marking the trash with big Xs made from a roll of orange plastic tape we'd found. When we finished, Josh headed out for sandwiches and coffee while I unpacked the sample paint colors I'd picked up over the weekend.

Chocolate walls were a no-brainer if we were going to call the hotel Hot Chocolate. They'd also give the hotel the feeling of relaxed sophistication I was going for. But it went beyond that. I'd once read that a blind person entering a red room actually feels warmer than when entering a white room. I wanted sightless and sighted visitors alike to feel the warm, decadent, comforting kiss of chocolate when they stayed in this hotel.

For a chocolate lover, there are four basic food groups: dark chocolate, milk chocolate, white chocolate, and chocolate martinis. My design plan was to hit them all.

I'd use the richest, deepest chocolate for the main public spaces and lighter flavors in the adjacent areas. Benjamin Moore Chocolate

Fondue was a real contender, but my gut was that Behr Iced Espresso was going to edge it out. Iced Espresso was a rich, sophisticated chocolate brown with black undertones. Back in the day, you might find a shade like this in a smoking room or a man's study. Repurposing a traditionally manly color had the added bonus of giving it kind of an illicit feel, the way women must have felt when they first traded in their whalebone corsets and petticoats for the comfort of pantaloons.

I painted large swatches of each color on several walls. I'd let them cure and deepen, and in forty-eight hours I'd know for sure.

I believed in keeping life and color palettes streamlined and simple. Since the life part was a little rocky right now, I'd redeem myself in the color department by sticking to the tried-and-true 60:30:10 rule. I'd use 60 percent of the deepest color, either Chocolate Fondue or Iced Espresso, then 30 percent of a lighter color like Behr's Cliff Rock or Sherwin-Williams Nomadic Desert on the ceilings and an occasional wall. The 10 percent would be our accent color, maybe a pop of fun turquoise or deep teal or even a spicy red. A warm white chocolate trim would bring it all together if I went with the red or teal. If I went with the turquoise, I'd go with a shade closer to whipped cream or the marshmallows you'd put in hot chocolate.

All these paint names were actually making my stomach growl. Oddly enough, I didn't really *feel* hungry. Maybe surrounding guests in the color of chocolate would make them feel as satisfied as actually eating it, the way flipping through an occasional cookbook satisfied any residual urge I still had to cook.

Josh kicked the front door open. He put a big white paper bag on the bar and began pulling out sandwiches and coffee.

He handed me a chocolate rose.

I kept my hands at my sides. "What's that?"

He laughed. "I just thought we should mark the occasion."

He put the rose in the empty snifter on the bar. "Never mind, I got peanut M&M's, too—all this chocolate talk is killing me."

I took a quick bite of a turkey sandwich and went back to painting.

"Soup's on," Josh yelled to Dan and his posse the next time they passed through.

I kept painting.

"Okay, well," Josh said. "I've got some work to catch up on, so if you don't need me for anything. . . ."

"Just a check," I said. I nodded at the three guys inhaling their sandwiches. "And I'll need a deposit for the electrician and the plumber, too."

Josh finished chewing a bite of sandwich. "How long do you think the whole thing will take?"

"Not a minute longer than it has to," I said.

He pointed to a paint sample. "I like that one."

He had a good eye. He'd picked the perfect contemporary accent for the chocolate walls and white chocolate trim.

"That's Million Dollar Red," I said.

"I like the sound of that." Josh popped a handful of M&M's in his mouth and held out the bag.

I tried to resist, but somehow I took the bag from him anyway. "Everybody does," I said. "I think we should use it on the front door, too. It's good feng shui."

Josh nodded. "So, what's next for you?"

My eyes teared up. "I have absolutely no idea."

As soon as the words came out of my mouth, I realized he meant the job. I looked up at the ceiling so my tears would drain back into my eyes.

"Paint fumes," I said, even though we were using zero-VOC paint so there really weren't any.

He didn't say anything.

I popped an M&M into my mouth. "Shopping. Shopping's next. What I meant was I'm not sure which store to start with, but I'll make a quick loop to see what's out there before the electrician and plumber get here."

I carefully counted out three more M&M's and handed the bag back to Josh.

"Want some company?" he said.

"I thought you had work to do."

"I can do it later."

I shrugged. "Suit yourself. But I'm driving."

Before we left I wrapped up the remaining half of my turkey sandwich and grabbed the chocolate rose off the bar.

Josh wrinkled his forehead. "I think there's still a bag of chips left."

I found them at the bottom of the big white bag.

"Is your daughter not feeding you?" Josh asked.

"I'll meet you outside," I said. I jogged the half block and dropped off lunch for the homeless woman. Her eyes were closed, so I just put the rose on her lap and the sandwich beside her.

I thought I heard her say thank you, but I was jogging away too quickly to be sure.

The hotel and restaurant surplus outlet was a huge flat-roofed mint green building in what appeared to be a sketchy part of the city.

"I don't know about this," Josh said. "I'm not sure we should even get out of the car here."

"Relax," I said. "I haven't lost a client yet."

"By the way," Josh said. "You're allowed to park in the hotel parking lot."

I took the keys out of the ignition. "As soon as I find it, I'm planning to."

The minute we got inside, I was in bargain-hunter's heaven. I found the padded and tufted chocolate Ultrasuede headboards first.

"I don't know," Josh said. "Are you sure they're even new?"

"At that price, of course they're not new," I said. "They're rejects from a five-star hotel somewhere. But what do we care? They're in great shape, and they'll take up most of the wall and make a huge statement."

Josh tilted his head. "They do sort of look like big Hershey bars."

The hotel had forty rooms, and there were exactly forty-one king-size headboards. "One for good luck," I said.

Josh still didn't look convinced. "Shouldn't we put two beds in some of the rooms?"

"I don't think so," I said. "If we're targeting solo female travelers, they're not going to be sharing a room. And I'm not sure we should even make that an option. We want to put a guest in each room, not pack 'em in like sardines."

"What do we do with the headboards we already have?"

"Sell them," I said. "I'm hoping we can get this place to load up what we don't want on the delivery truck."

Josh nodded. "Good thinking. Do you want me to do the negotiating?"

"Just smile and look pretty," I said. "I'll do the talking."

I found folding luggage racks for the suitcases to sit on. There were only twelve with animal print strapping, but there were lots with solid tan strapping, which would be almost as good. Nothing says boutique hotel room like folding luggage racks.

Everything else that looked good was in smaller lots, but in some ways, that was more fun. Five butterscotch leather chairs, four funky night tables, plenty of mismatched lamps. We'd keep the little desks and chairs we already had and replace the clunky armoires with more streamlined consoles.

"What about this?" Josh held up a crackle finish lamp that looked like a snowman wearing a lampshade.

"Good find," I said, partly because he looked so excited and partly because there was only one of them.

"It's like a scavenger hunt," he said. "I had no idea shopping could be fun."

"Who knows," I said. "Maybe you've just found your next profession."

He put the lamp down next to the headboard. I'd brought the roll of orange tape, and we were marking all our stuff with Xs so nobody else walked off with it.

Josh ran a hand through his hair and smiled his Johnny Depp smile. "I don't think so. It's the novelty I like—that's why I jump from project to project. I'm great in the beginning, but I suck at maintenance. I get bored easily. Always have."

He held out this flaw like a prize, or maybe a challenge. Once upon a time, I knew the thrill of the chase with guys like this. *What if you were the one who could change him? What if he never got bored with you?*

CHAPTER 25

"So," I said.

"So," Chance said.

Thus far, that was one of the high points of our conversation.

I'd thought about stopping to pick up something to assemble for dinner on the way home, but I didn't want to set a precedent. I mean, assembling a meal wasn't something I did for just anyone, and I wasn't sure a son-in-law with two perfectly good arms of his own qualified. Generations of women had fought hard for the right not to cook. The weight of their slaving over the stove was on my shoulders, so I didn't plan on entering into this decision lightly.

Chance's reasons for not throwing his hat into the dinner-making ring were his own. In any case, I'd just pulled into the driveway when my son-in-law rolled his white BMW SUV up beside me. It was dusted with an inch of yellow pollen like the rest of the cars in springtime Atlanta, so that made it a bit less pretentious. But it was still too flashy for my taste, and the fact that describing it required a double dip of acronyms really bugged me.

"Here we go," I said to the GPS as I unplugged it.

I stepped out of the comfort of my air-conditioned car and into the blazing Atlanta heat.

"Hot one," Chance and I said at the exact same time.

"Owe me a Coke," I said.

"Sure will," Chance said. "I think we might could have some. I'm a sweet tea man myself."

"Never mind," I said.

I waited for him to unlock the side door. He held it open and let me walk in first. After that the choreography fell apart, and we were like dance partners without a leader.

We walked across the family room toward the kitchen. His long lanky steps got him there before me, so he stood off to the side. I stopped and stood off to the other side, because I didn't quite get what he was doing. Just when I realized he was waiting for me to go up the three stairs to the little raised 1970s contemporary kitchen, he gave up waiting for me.

We hit the staircase at the same time and walked up awkwardly together, like a pair of Keystone Kops.

I started to open the refrigerator, then stopped in case it might seem presumptuous, given that it wasn't my refrigerator. Or worse, that it might send off some kind of a territorial signal, like a dog peeing on its turf. I sat down at the little breakfast table instead.

Chance stopped in the middle of the kitchen. "Can I get you a glass of wine? Oh, wait, you wanted a Coke."

"Oh, please," I said. "Wine."

He poured me a glass of wine and opened a beer for himself. He opened the freezer and stared into its depths, perhaps looking for a sign from the refrigerator gods. Then he closed it again.

I took a long sip. He took a big swig of beer, right from the bottle. Either my daughter's husband was beginning to relax around me, or he was smart enough to realize that I was probably not going to take over the dirty dishes department.

The awkwardness between us was almost palpable, filling the kitchen like the smell of burnt toast.

I decided not to rush in to fix it, because there was a more important issue at stake here. I reviewed the options in my head and still came up with only two: wait him out, or cook for him until Shannon got back.

I took another sip of my wine. Chance took another swig of beer. He sat down at the table.

We looked at each other.

"Thoughts?" he said.

"Not that I've noticed," I said.

"Mellow Mushroom delivers," my son-in-law said. "Oh, wait, the one near us doesn't deliver, but we can use Takeout Taxi."

"My treat," I said.

"My parents didn't raise me to let the guest pay," he said.

"Oh," I said. "How are your parents?"

"Just fine," he said. "Couldn't be happier."

Apparently I wasn't even going to get any good in-law dirt.

"My mama sure does love to cook," Chance said.

"Lucky you," I said.

"The only thing that beats her southern fried chicken is her Coca-Cola chicken."

"Interesting," I said. "Do you add it after it's already dead, or does the chicken drink the Coke first?"

Chance fired up his laptop and found the Mellow Mushroom menu. He slid his chair over so I could see, too.

"The spinach calzone looks good," I said.

"Love me some of that steak and cheese," Chance said.

"Bad for your heart," I said.

"Thanks for looking out for me, Mom," he said. It actually came out like a cross between *mom* and *ma'am*, perhaps some new hybrid created for a mother-in-law who not only has invaded one's house but also has no intention of caretaking.

Chance closed his laptop and reached for his cell. "I'll call it in."

I was already dialing.

"I think I'll go change out of my work clothes," I said when I finished placing the order, even though I was wearing jeans. At least I could soak my spotted T-shirt in the guest room sink.

We retreated to our respective bedrooms like prizefighters between rounds. I stayed in my corner until the doorbell rang.

I searched my wallet for a tip as I danced down the hallway. Chance sidestepped me and tried to hand some bills over first.

"I've got it," I said.

"I insist," Chance said.

The Takeout Taxi guy looked at his watch.

"You can get it next time," I said as I forced my money into the guy's hand.

Chance put the two paper plates that came with the order on the table. I found the plastic utensils and paper napkins at the bottom of the bag.

I wondered for a moment if I could get away with bringing my calzone into the guest room.

"Delicious," I said after my first bite of spinach calzone.

"Mmm-mmm," Chance said. He took a careful bite of his steak and cheese calzone.

"So," I said.

"So," he said.

"So," I said again. For the life of me I couldn't think of anything else to say. The seconds were sliding by so slowly that it felt like Chance and I had been sitting at this table for centuries.

I took another sip of wine. "Oh, I know. Can you get some of your friends over here so we can rip down that ugly balcony and drywall it over to surprise Shannon?"

Chance chewed and swallowed. He dabbed his mouth with a paper napkin and took a sip of beer.

"You think Shannon would be all right with that, mo'am?"

I burst out laughing. "Like I'd dare touch it if Shannon hadn't told me she hated it."

Relief practically bloomed on Chance's face. "She absolutely positively hates it?"

"Absolutely, positively, definitely," I said. "How about you?"

Chance shrugged. "A happy wife is a happy life."

"You and I are going to get along just fine, son," I said.

He grinned. His phone rang. He looked at me.

"Go ahead," I said.

"Hey, babe," he said. "Shannon," he mouthed.

"I hope so," I said.

"Just fine," Chance said. "She's right here." He nodded, then looked at me. "She says hey."

"Hey," I said.

I got up from the table to give them some privacy. Chance stood up at the exact same moment, so I sat back down. He did, too.

I held out my hand. "Stay," I said. I picked up my plate and headed for the guest room.

For a woman who has lived within the confines of a family for most of her life, there's something incredibly decadent about eating alone, and stretched out on a bed, no less. The calzone was doughy and comforting, with just the right ratio of cheese to garlic and onion-sauteed spinach.

It was huge, so I ate about half, then wrapped it up and put it on the bedside table. I found my cell and called Denise.

She answered on the first ring. "What's up?"

"Not much. How 'bout with you?"

"Same. How's the hotel coming?"

"Making progress," I said. "I've got the paint samples on the walls. The electrician came by, and as soon as I find the right fixtures, he'll be back to install them."

Denise didn't say anything.

"The plumber was a no-show, but what else is new? I've got another one coming by tomorrow. And I found the best chocolate candy bar–like Ultrasuede headboards. You'll love them."

"Great," Denise said.

"I mean, if you ever even bother to come down here to see the hotel."

"Right," Denise said.

Denise and I rarely had awkward conversations, but we were having one now. Josh was the elephant in the virtual telephone line. Technically, since he was Denise's boyfriend, I thought she should be the one to mention his name first.

"So," I said. "Can I tell you how awkward it is to be at Shannon's house when she's not here?"

"I bet. Listen, I'm still at the office, and I'll never get out of here if I don't get moving. I'll call you later in the week, okay?"

I stared at my phone for a while after we hung up. The thing about long-term best friendships is that you have to let them ebb and flow. That's why they last.

I swung my legs off the bed and picked up my calzone. I made as much noise as I could when I shut my door. I cleared my throat as I walked toward the kitchen. It seemed only fair to give Chance some warning just in case he was talking about me.

He was still on the phone, sitting at the table. I could tell it was still Shannon just by the way he was laughing. And because every other word out of his mouth was *babe*.

I walked past him and started opening drawers and cabinets, looking for some plastic wrap so the calzone wouldn't dry out. I put the calzone on the counter and opened another cabinet. The three Danish serving trays I'd mailed to Shannon were neatly stacked next to the monogrammed sterling silver baby mug and the Royal Doulton Winnie-the-Pooh birthday cereal bowl I'd mailed her the week before.

In front of them sat my favorite reading glasses.

CHAPTER 26

OKAY, SO I WAS LOOKING AT MY FAVORITE READ-
ing glasses, and my favorite reading glasses were also sitting
on top of my head. One plus one added up to my daughter being in
some serious trouble.

I gestured to Chance to hand me the phone.

"Babe," he said. "Mo'am wants to say hi."

"Mo'am?" Shannon said into my ear. "When did that start? Are
you being mean to him?"

"Shannon Elizabeth," I said.

"What'd I do?"

"I can't believe you didn't tell me I mailed my reading glasses
to you."

"Oh. Sorry."

"Sorry? That's all you have to say for yourself? Sorry?"

"Mom, what's the big deal? You have a gazillion pairs."

"Not like those I don't."

"Mom, no offense, but I've seen those glasses on you and they're
not that great. I think you need something more like the ones Tina
Fey wears."

"Honey, Tina Fey and I have completely different face shapes.
She's an oval and I'm a square."

"Tina Fey is a heart."

"You're missing the point."

"Come on, Mom, let me talk to Chance. I'm tired."

"Shannon, I broke the law because of those glasses. I stole an identical pair from the post office because I thought they were mine."

"OMG. Calm down, Mom. Have you ever considered medication? Oh, Dad and Luke say hi."

I handed the phone back to Chance.

Marlene Dietrich once said something about how it's the friends you can call at 4:00 A.M. that matter. Since I couldn't remember the last time I'd stayed up past ten-thirty, what mattered more to me was having a friend I could call back about four minutes after we'd hung up.

I went into the guest room and called Denise on my cell. It rang and then went to voice mail. I called her again, and the same thing happened.

The third time was the charm. "What," Denise said.

"You're not going to believe this," I said.

"Don't make me guess. I'm not in the mood."

It was a small guest room, but I did my best to pace anyway. "Those glasses I stole from the post office? They weren't mine. I mailed mine to Shannon, and she forgot to tell me."

"So?"

"So? So? I have absolutely no justification for stealing them now. I'm a common thief."

Denise let out a long-suffering sigh. "So, mail them back."

"I don't know. What if the pair I just found breaks? Then I won't have a backup pair."

"So, keep them."

"You make it sound so simple."

"Sandy, if this were the biggest problem I had in my life, I'd be a happy woman."

"Wait," I said. "It's almost your turn. Just help me think this through. Okay, I stole the glasses. But no one is coming after me. Right?"

"Right. I checked the weekly paper and even looked around the post office last time I was there. No wanted poster with your blurred videotaped face on it."

"But Ponytail Guy will remember me."

"So, make Greg pick up the mail from now on. That's what husbands are for."

"Good point. Okay, we're making progress."

I paced three steps in one direction then executed a legal turn.

"Moving on, Ponytail Guy is a jerk, and he probably scooped the readers from the Lost and Found anyway. If I give them back, it's not like they'll even make it to their rightful owner, so my giving them back will only serve to support his jerkdom."

"His *jerkdom?* Is that even a word?"

"Come on, Denise, stay on task here. Okay, so the only thing I can't get past is that, technically, I stole something, so I have to figure out some kind of—"

"Penance?" Denise laughed. "Whoa, those nuns really got to you. I'm so glad I skipped Sunday school. I mean CCD. Or OCD, or whatever it was."

"Ha," I said. "You know, I thought what I was looking for here was rationalization, but maybe it is penance. I just don't want to have to feel guilty. I hate that."

"Okay, I'll even save you a trip to confession. Say three Hail Marys and five Our Fathers—"

"Wow, your priest was much easier than my guy. Mine would have upped it to ten each, plus an Act of Contrition, and then told me to give the glasses back *and* light some candles at the altar, too."

It sounded like Denise had made it home from the office, since she took a long sip of something that sounded a lot like wine. "Okay, give a pair of reading glasses to someone who needs them and do three nice things for a stranger."

"Genius," I said. "I feel better already. Okay, your turn."

"Tell me the truth," Denise said. "Is Josh seeing another woman down there?"

"I'm not sure," I said.

Denise waited.

"At first I thought he might be," I said. "But now I don't think so."

"Then what's he doing in Atlanta?"

"I don't know," I said. "I think he's excited about his new hotel."

"That'll last about five minutes."

"I think even he knows that," I said.

"He's totally ADD. He's got the attention span of a tsetse fly."

"I thought tsetse flies caused sleeping sickness."

"Whatever. We can't even go to a movie theater because he can't sit through an entire movie without pausing it. He always needs to be moving—you know, on to the next thing."

"You have a lot of energy," I said. "So it's not like you can't keep up."

"That's not the point. The point is whether or not I want to."

Nobody said anything for a moment. I walked across the hall to check on my T-shirt. The Kahlúa freckles had faded but not disappeared. I held my cell in the crook of my neck while I scrubbed them with shampoo. If that didn't work I'd go see what Shannon had for stain removers, and maybe throw in a small load of laundry before things started to pile up.

"He didn't even tell me he was going to Atlanta," Denise said.

Let's just say that Denise and I had been down this road a few times before. The truth is you can pick your friends, but you can't pick your friends' boyfriends. And since you didn't have to date them either, essentially I believed you shouldn't get a very big vote here. Being a friend in these situations meant doing as much listening and giving as little advice as possible.

"Do you usually tell each other where you're going?" I said.

"Yes. No. I don't know. I mean, when we're with each other we have these periods of intensity where we tell each other everything, and then we retreat into our separate worlds, and the whole thing falls apart. And then time passes, and it's like it never happened, and then we do it all over again."

"How does that make you feel?" I said.

"What are you, my shrink?"

"Sorry. Maybe he's got a bit of a commitment phobia," I said, understating the obvious, like a best friend should.

"Ya think?" Denise said. "I'm doing it again, right?"

"It's a possibility," I said. "How much do you like him?"

"I don't know. How much do I like him?"

"Hard to say," I said. "It might just be that he's young, hot, and rich."

"Ha. And then there are the superficial things."

Since it was starting to look like we might be on the phone for a while, I began organizing my clothes for tomorrow. It had been a long day, and I was dying to crawl into bed. That way I could just turn out the light and go to sleep as soon as Denise finished talking. The only flaw in this plan was that even a best friend doesn't put up with you brushing your teeth while she's talking. So my best bet was to keep moving and get organized.

"I don't know," Denise said as I studied two taupe shirts with slightly different detailing, as if it mattered which one I picked. "When we're together it's good. We have so much in common, the sex is great, we laugh a lot."

"Nothing against great sex, but can he dance? Can he clean? Can he get the house on the market?"

Denise blew a puff of air through the phone line. "Come on, you had your turn."

"Sorry," I said. "Okay, so what is it you actually want from your relationship with Josh?"

Denise's voice exploded in my ear. "What do I want? What do I *want*? What kind of question is that? I want what everybody wants. I want someone who has my back. I want someone's name to put in the blank space after In an Emergency Please Call. I want someone who'll drink the other half of the bottle of wine so I don't, and someone to make it worth sitting down at an actual table to eat. I want someone who's dying to get home after a long day because I'm going to be there."

I cleared my throat. "Is this a bad time to point out that you've had this a few times already?"

I braced myself for another explosion, but when Denise finally spoke it was almost a whisper. "I want someone I'll still want eighteen months later."

I heard myself sigh. "Some of that is a choice you make."

"Well, maybe I'm finally ready to make it."

A good friend knows when to suspend her disbelief, because a big part of the job is being a cheerleader.

"Okay," I said, "if you want something more out of this relationship, you have to tell Josh. You can't expect him to read your mind. I know it's hard for you, but you have to put yourself out there."

"Do you think he's capable of something more?"

"Oh, puh-lease," I said. "We're all capable of exactly what we want to be capable of."

Denise didn't say anything. The low drone of the television coming from the living room ended abruptly, and I heard the creak of the stairs as Chance headed up to bed.

"Oh, God," Denise said. "I'm going to end up all by myself. I might as well start buying cats now. Or those yappy little dogs. Or maybe I should hire a companion and overpay her so she'll stay with me until I die, as long as I leave everything to her, which I might as well do, because who the hell else am I going to leave it to?"

I opened the door and started tiptoeing across to the bathroom. "You're overdramatizing. He's a nice guy. You're perfect for each other. Have you noticed that he looks a little bit like Johnny Depp around the mouth?"

Denise laughed. "Keep your hands off him."

"Ha." I gave my imaginary pom-poms another shake. "Trust me, it'll work out. I can feel it in my bones. I'll even be your matron of honor. Again."

CHAPTER 27

I FULLY EXPECTED THE HOMELESS WOMAN TO BE SITting in the same place, just waiting for me to drop by with the other half of my spinach calzone. Then I'd ask her if she wore reading glasses, and if she did, I'd give her the root beer pair with the tortoiseshell highlights I'd tried to give Ponytail Guy. If my eyes turned out to be in worse shape than hers, she could just hang on to the glasses until hers caught up to mine.

And then, *presto change-o*, I'd be three-quarters of the way finished with my Denise-imposed penance, and I could go back to learning to be selfish again. I'd have given away a pair of reading glasses and fulfilled two of the three nice things I was supposed to do for someone. Just in case counting the glasses twice was cheating, I could even add another nice thing to be sure, which would mean I was only half done, not three-quarters. And who said I sucked at math.

But there was no sign of her. I even circled the block to be sure. Then I pulled into the little lot and tucked the GPS into my bag.

It was practically the crack of dawn when I'd left the house this morning, partly because I woke up early and figured I might as well get an early start, and partly to give Chance and me both a break. If you can possibly avoid it, never face an in-law before your coffee has kicked in.

It's funny how something that didn't bother you all that much when it was said can double back in the middle of the night and hit

you like heartburn. Chance's mother's Coca-Cola chicken was piss-
ing me off big-time. I mean, secret family recipe, give me a break.
What does it take to pour a freakin' can of Coke over a pair of
chicken breasts?

It's not like I *couldn't* cook. I'd simply graduated from the cooking phase of my life and moved on. But I'd left a solid cooking leg-
acy in my wake, with my own secret family recipes, thank you very
much. I mean, Shannon had even served my own beef stew back to
me the first night I'd arrived, so clearly my cooking days had made
an impression. And honestly, that bottle of Guinness stout from
Chance's side of the family hadn't added much.

The street was still relatively empty, with only a few eager bea-
vers like me dashing down the sidewalks. It looked almost like the
set of a musical. Any minute Martha and the Vandellas' version of
"Dancing in the Street" might start blasting from hidden speakers.
If I had time I could choreograph a little dancing-to-work number
for us.

Lines were forming at the coffee shops already, so I decided I'd
delay my second cup and go straight to the hotel to check out the
coffee-making possibilities there.

Just as I was fumbling for the key, the front door of the hotel
swung out to greet me. I opened my mouth to say hi to Josh.

It was a woman. And it sure as hell looked like the same one
Josh had been kissing between two Bradford pear trees.

Perhaps you've never spent an unplanned night with a man only
to tiptoe out early the next morning. But if you have, you probably
didn't look so great the next morning either. The woman before me
had messy hair, wrinkly clothes, a smear of mascara under her right
eye. She looked past me, avoiding eye contact.

"Melissa?" I said.

For a minute I thought she might run. Just take off down the
sidewalk like a bat out of Luke's bat cave. Once, a long time ago, a

friend told me that her starter marriage had ended when her ex-husband walked into a restaurant with some colleagues and saw her sitting across the room with another man. She denied it—to his face later that night, to their marriage counselor the following week. *You're crazy*, she kept saying. *She must have just looked like me.*

This woman gave me the same kind of look, a look that said in a million years I am never going to admit to being named Melissa.

"How was your pizza the other night?" I asked sweetly. "Did your husband and three kids like it?"

She kept walking.

Apparently Josh didn't even have the class to walk her to the door, since he was nowhere to be found. I stomped through the lobby and into the kitchen. I put my leftover calzone in the refrigerator and found a big bag of coffee beans in the freezer. Always keep your coffee in the freezer if you have room. It stays fresh longer.

I found a big stainless steel Bunn restaurant espresso grinder with a cracked plastic hopper. I ground some coffee beans, pretending they were Josh's private parts. If there'd ever been an espresso maker to go with the grinder, it was long gone. Since I'd discovered where the keys were kept, I opened the first guest room I came to, borrowed the little coffeemaker, and set it up on the bar. I hated black coffee, and I hadn't thought to buy milk, so I grabbed a tub of Cool Whip out of the freezer to tide me over.

The only way I'd be sharing any coffee with Josh would be if he ended up wearing it, so I brewed just enough for one person. The Cool Whip–topped coffee was surprisingly good, but I drank it down so quickly I only noticed that on my last sip. What had I been *thinking*? Why hadn't I kept my mouth shut instead of cheering on Denise to pour her heart out to this clichéd creep?

The minute I got my hands on him, I'd make him call Denise and tell her. I'd hog-tie him if I had to. He was probably still upstairs in his room. Or maybe he'd slunk out the back door, lowlife that he was.

Then I'd quit. No, I wouldn't. I'd stay here and make him miserable. That's what I'd do. I'd finish the job, and then I'd bill him within an inch of his life. I could feel my hourly rate soaring already.

The second plumber I'd called actually showed up, or maybe he was the first and a day late. In any case, I got him to fix the rippled glass sinks in the lobby restrooms the old owners had tried unsuccessfully to take with them. Then I sent him to inspect each of the guest rooms for leaky faucets and running toilets, and any other potential plumbing problems.

The plumber must have flushed Josh out of his den of iniquity, because he came strolling into the bar. I'd set up my laptop on one of the round tables, and I was scrolling through Atlanta lighting stores, trying to decide where my best bet would be to find a chandelier for the entrance that was a perfect blend of funk and function.

I didn't even look up. "I'll need a check for the plumber," I said.

"Good morning to you, too. Any more of that coffee around?"

I kept my eyes on my computer screen. "It's your hotel. Look."

"Can I make you a cup, too?"

I glanced up. Josh was wearing fresh clothes and looked like he'd just stepped out of the shower.

"No," I said. "You can't. But I think it might have been a nice gesture to make one for Melissa before you sent her home to her husband and kids."

Josh walked away without answering. I couldn't imagine why.

A minute later I heard the roar of the coffee grinder.

He strolled back into the bar area. I ignored him.

"What did you use for a coffee filter?" he asked.

"A cocktail napkin," I said.

"Good thinking."

I ignored him. The coffee bubbled and spat into the little coffeepot. I took out a pen and a notebook and made a list of addresses for the best lighting bets.

Josh poured himself a cup of coffee.

"Not," he said, "that it's any of your business, but Melissa and I met for breakfast, and then I gave her a tour of the hotel."

"Right," I said. "And then you had to jump in the shower after all that exertion."

"Excuse me?"

I looked right at him. "There's no excuse for you."

Josh turned a chair around and sat so that the back was between us. "I didn't take you for the kind of person who can't understand friendships between men and women."

"I didn't take you for the kind of person who would mistake me for someone stupid."

Josh's eyes never left mine. "I'd have to be crazy to think I could get away with something like that."

"Not necessarily," I said. "But you'd certainly have to be a jerk."

"Why would I cheat on Denise?"

"I don't know," I said. "Why don't you give her a call, and maybe the two of you can figure it out together."

"Here's the thing," Josh said. "Nothing happened. Melissa had a big fight with her husband and needed someone to talk to. Period."

His eye contact was amazing. He was facing me full on rather than half twisting away. His palms were open. Even his feet were pointing in my direction. Every aspect of his body language read like an open book.

And I didn't believe him for a second.

CHAPTER 28

I PULLED INTO TRADER JOE'S ON MY WAY TO SHANNON and Chance's house. I couldn't help myself.

The GPS wasn't happy about it. "Reverse direction at the earliest opportunity," she pleaded.

I shook my head. "I know, I know. But I mean, come on, how would you like to be compared to a woman who cooks with *soda*? She probably thinks ketchup is a vegetable."

"Recalculating," the GPS said.

"Exactly," I said.

I was on a mission. I even grabbed a full-size grocery cart instead of one of those little plastic baskets with the handles. My first thought was to take Chance's mother's stupid Coca-Cola breasts up a notch. After all, there was precedent, since she'd embellished my beef stew with her completely unnecessary bottle of Guinness stout. Dr Pepper thighs? Mountain Dew wings? Whole roast chicken bathed in Fresca?

Of course, since this was Trader Joe's, I'd probably have to substitute Sparkling Clementine or maybe even Dry Rhubarb soda.

After some deliberation, I decided to play to my strengths instead. I knew I could assemble circles around that woman. And so I would.

I rolled my cart straight to the prepared food section. Everything looked great, but I was only here for inspiration. Buying a fully finished dish would be cheating. I had standards.

The tandoori chicken with butternut squash, spinach, and peppers in rice looked good, as did the mushroom tortellini with asparagus. But it was the pesto chicken that called out to me.

I banged a right and headed for the pesto in the refrigerator case. Then I hung a left and crossed over to the produce section for a carton of grape tomatoes. I tooled around the produce section until I found a box of prewashed baby mesclun lettuce.

I faced my first dilemma. On the one hand, nothing fakes homemade like a sprig of fresh basil garnishing each dinner plate. On the other hand, and probably a contributing factor to my swearing off actual cooking in the first place, nothing says guilt like trying to ignore an overpriced bunch of herbs as they decompose in your refrigerator.

I found a potted basil plant just to the side of the tomatoes. It was certainly a good alternative, but unfortunately one that required caretaking. I took a moment to remind myself that I was in one of those remarkable and rare free-pass phases of my life. Parents and pets dead and buried, kids flying mostly on their own, grandchildren still long range and conceptual. If it ever happens to you, don't screw it up by taking in stray houseplants.

I pinched off a stem of basil. It was getting leggy anyway, so you could look at it that I was actually helping the plant. I tucked it behind my ear like a hibiscus bloom.

The pasta surprised me by turning out to be right next to the pasta sauce. Trader Joe's is constantly moving everything around so you'll discover new items instead of getting stuck in a rut. At first it drove me crazy, but then I realized I was one of those people Trader Joe's was trying to save.

I heard the muffled strains of "Chapel of Love" from my shoulder bag.

I held my cell up to the ear not holding the basil. "Hi, honey."

"Just tell me, Mom, that you're not going to make Chance eat takeout every night you're there."

I lobbed a bag of bow tie pasta into the cart.

"How's the training going, honey?" I said.

"Don't try to change the subject."

"Why is this my responsibility? Doesn't Chance know how to cook?"

"Of course he does. He makes breakfast and sandwiches, and he mows the lawn."

"I don't think the lawn counts as cooking, Shannon. And, FYI, I paid for those calzones last night."

"TMI, Mom—I don't care who paid."

"I was simply pointing out that I contributed to dinner. In my own way."

"Can't you just fake it a little? For *me*?"

My daughter hung up on me. This was not a new experience. In fact, she'd been doing it fairly consistently since she'd turned thirteen. I almost called her back, mostly because I didn't want her to think my assembling for Chance had been her idea. I would have liked to establish that I'd already been in the grocery store of my own accord when her call came through.

I also would have liked to pump her at least a little. Were her father and brother making any progress on the house? Were they subsisting on takeout, or had someone picked up the cooking reins? Were they having fun? Did they miss me?

A bolt of sadness hit me like lightning. This might have been my last chance to be a foursome with my family, and I was missing it.

I shook it off. I was losing my groove. I was missing the big picture. It was all about focus and tenacity. And waiting them out. Once Greg knew I really meant it, he'd get his butt in gear, and we'd sell the house and ride off into a romantic sunset together. We'd talk to the kids often and see them on holidays.

Trader Joe's was getting crowded, so I picked up the pace. I hit the meat section for a package of grilled smoked boneless chicken breasts. They were even sliced into almost bite-size strips. I mean, how good does it get?

Biscuit sections are a helluva lot bigger in the South than they are in New England, so finding that was easy. Here's a trick for the next time you're assembling a meal. Buy a refrigerated tube of breadsticks. Pop it open and separate into strands. Loop each strand into a knot, then flare out the ends until they match your bow tie pasta. Place on a Pam-sprayed cookie sheet and sprinkle liberally with the Parmesan cheese that's probably been sitting in your fridge forever. *Woilà!* People will think you kneaded the dough yourself. Especially if you tell them that you did.

All that was left was dessert. I grabbed some brownies and a package of Trader Joe's Dark Chocolate Crisps, which, if you haven't tried them, are like deep cocoa Pringles. They didn't carry Cool Whip, so I settled for a guilt-free tub of Truwhip, which contains neither hydrogenated oils nor GMOs, whatever they are.

"Ma'am?" the cashier said.

I looked up from swiping my credit card. His silly Hawaiian shirt made me smile despite myself.

He pointed to the basil behind my ear.

"Oh, right," I said. "Thanks for reminding me."

He held up one finger. "I'll be right back. Don't go anywhere."

So much for my life of crime. At least I'd gotten away with the reading glasses.

The cashier reappeared. He grinned and held out another sprig of basil. "For the other ear."

If I were in charge of the world, Trader Joe's could be my assistant.

I'd left work early, and it seemed that Chance had worked as late as he possibly could. The combination of the two meant that when he got home the table was set and I'd had more than enough time to bury all incriminating evidence in one of the trash barrels out in the garage.

When my son-in-law walked into the kitchen, I was standing at the sink, wearing his wife's apron. He stopped. I turned and smiled. If we were in black and white, I might have passed for the star of *The Donna Reed Show*.

"Ha," he said.

"Can I get you a glass of sweet tea?" I said.

"Ha," he said again.

"Sit a spell," I said. "I'll bet you had yourself a long, hard day at work."

At the risk of sounding immodest, once I finally convinced Chance to sit down, dinner was a big hit.

"This is amazing, mo'am," he said.

I dabbed my mouth with a cloth napkin. "Thank you, son. It's a secret family recipe we've passed down through generations. We call it chicken pesto bow ties with halved grape tomatoes and coordinating hand-kneaded Parmesan bread bows."

Chance took another bite and closed his eyes while he swallowed.

"Mmm-mmm," he said.

I smiled. "Don't forget to save some room for dessert."

If you ever want to assemble a dessert that's sure to impress, get out your fanciest wineglasses. Spoon some Cool Whip, or Truwhip if you're feeling virtuous, into the bottom of each one. Crumble some brownies on top of that. Add more Cool Whip/Truwhip. Crush some Trader Joe's Dark Chocolate Crisps, or even a Heath bar, with a hammer and sprinkle it on. Continue layering until you reach the top, ending with a nice dollop of Cool Whip/Truwhip. Then grab a bottle of hazelnut liquor from your kids' liquor cabinet and douse the damn thing within an inch of its life. This might possibly negate the Truwhip benefits, but trust me, it's worth it.

"Unbelievable," Chance said. "Can you make this again for my friends when they come over?"

He sounded about twelve.

I patted him on the hand. "Of course I can, son."

I left Chance with the dishes and went in to call Denise. I'd been putting it off all day.

The muffled notes of Bette Midler's "Miss Otis Regrets" trilled from my shoulder bag.

"ESP," I said once I managed to unearth my cell. "I was just calling you."

"Guess what?"

I went with my most optimistic guess. "You met another guy?"

"Funny. No, don't tell Josh, but I'm flying in to surprise him this weekend. Can you pick me up at the airport? I'm thinking a pep talk on the way over might not be a bad idea."

"Does he know?"

"Of course he doesn't know. I just said it was a surprise, didn't I? I've been thinking it through, and the best way to do this is in person. Neither of us is really a phone person, but the minute we're actually together, things always click right back into place."

"When was the last time he called you?"

"I'm not even sure—I've been flat out all week."

Silence hung in the air like smog.

"Why are you doing this?" Denise finally said. "Putting myself out there was your idea in the first place."

I took a deep breath. "I think Josh *is* seeing someone else. He said she's an old college friend, but I'm not buying it."

"Oh, that's just Melissa. He talks about her all the time."

If a guy you're seeing talks about another woman all the time, it's never okay. Even if it's his mother.

"Denise," I said. "I don't have a good feeling about this."

CHAPTER 29

I'D FOUND THE PERFECT STATEMENT PIECE FOR THE lobby. It was a twelve-light contemporary chandelier with a clean geometric look. The crisp chrome finish was offset by square-cut crystals and silk shades, providing traditional pops on a modern frame. The shades were available in a deep chocolate color that would harmonize spectacularly with my staging plan.

The chandelier was even designed by Candice Olson of HGTV fame. The line also had smaller coordinating four-light chandeliers that would be perfect for the guest rooms, as well as matching wall sconces with single-drop crystals that would look amazing on either side of each bathroom mirror. I ordered them all from a wholesale online lighting supplier.

I hoped Candice Olson got a big percentage. Maybe she'd be so grateful that she'd invite me to appear on the show to help her transform a room. From there all it would take was a single brilliant appearance to land my own staging show. *All the World's a Stage with Sandra Sullivan? Sandy Sullivan Stages?* I mean, if HGTV gave me my own show, they could call me whatever they wanted.

A lot of HGTV show episodes seemed to be taped in Atlanta, so it wasn't even that much of a pipe dream. I knew my stuff. I had a sparkly personality. I could look pretty damn good for my age when I focused. And I'd recently read that one in four Americans had appeared on TV, so I was due.

I'd find a hip loft apartment, and when I wasn't too busy working on my next episode, I'd meet Shannon for lunch. Or even a Zumba class. I'd have to log a lot more Zumba hours if I were going to be on camera.

I had a small plastic container of chicken pesto bow ties with halved grape tomatoes beside me in the car, along with two Parmesan bow tie breadsticks wrapped in foil. If I saw the homeless woman today, I'd give them to her. Otherwise I'd eat them myself for lunch, the way I'd ended up eating the spinach calzone, and figure out another way to work off Denise's penance. I mean, you can only do what you can do.

I cruised down the block, half-looking for the homeless woman, half-looking for a parking space. Just past the hotel, I turned my head and saw a narrow alley I'd never noticed before.

A sign-less signpost marked the opening. I clicked my blinker and took a quick left. The alley was closely flanked by a brick wall on the hotel side and by a building on the other side.

I rolled the length of the alley and stopped. The alley opened to a hidden parking lot—small, square, and nondescript. A few weeds sprouted up through the cracks in the asphalt, and a single silver Corvette was parked in one space of the faded white parking grid. A little bit of weeding and some fresh paint on the parking spots would work wonders. And then I'd put two big chocolate pots filled with annuals on either side of the back entrance. I wondered if it led directly to the kitchen, or if guests could use the back door to access the hotel.

Three mismatched Dumpsters sat at the far end of the lot. They were a necessary evil, so there wasn't anything to be done about them. I hoped the flowerpots would be enough to distract the hotel guests from registering their unsightliness.

Just as my toe touched the accelerator again, I saw something move between the two Dumpsters closest to the hotel. I hit the brakes, bracing myself for a raccoon or even some southern varmint I'd yet to hear about. How big were possums?

A woman hoisted herself up. She picked up a big piece of cardboard and folded it carefully into neat sections, as if she were folding a quilt. When she was finished, she slid it under one of the Dumpsters. Then she leaned over and picked up a garbage bag.

The homeless woman.

She walked stiffly to the far end of the parking lot and cut between two buildings. After she disappeared from view, I just sat there. I put the rental car into park. I put my hands over my eyes.

It's not like I didn't know what homeless *meant*. I'd just never really taken the time to think about what it *entailed*.

Instead of passing her by, the way I'd passed so many homeless people in Boston and Atlanta, and well, just about every city I'd ever been to, I'd bought a homeless woman a cup of coffee and a breakfast sandwich. I felt better immediately. And she went back to sleeping between two Dumpsters.

I was spoiled and entitled, and my problems were so ridiculously insignificant. Maybe I even made them up just to have something to occupy my time as I lived my spoiled, entitled, ridiculous little life.

So my husband was dragging his feet about selling our big comfortable house. So my son wasn't quite ready to leave the bat cave. So my daughter hadn't stayed around to keep me company and had left me to cohabit with her perfectly nice husband in another comfortable house. So my best friend's boyfriend might be screwing around on her. They both had houses.

It's not like I'd missed the memo that homelessness was an epidemic. There was nothing new here. But I was crying anyway, hot tears streaming down my cheeks and racking sobs coming from someplace deep within. Maybe it was my soul. If I still had one.

Finally I pulled into a parking place.

"What were we thinking?" I said to the GPS before I unplugged her.

Then I went to find the homeless woman.

I found her sitting on the sidewalk, right in front of my eyes, yet blending into the scenery, as if she were invisible.

I handed her the chicken pesto and the bow ties. "How do you take your coffee?"

"Any way I can get it," she said.

Made you look, we used to say as kids when we tried to trick each other into turning to find something—a bird, a plane, a cute boy—that wasn't really there. Her comment took me by surprise and made me look at her for the first time—full on, instead of just over her head or off to the side of her face.

Given that she'd just crawled out from between two Dumpsters, she wasn't even that dirty. She looked about my age, with dry skin that could use a good moisturizer and gray springing from her once dark hair like the threads of a Brillo pad. Even without mascara, her eyes were her best feature: round and wide spaced, a lovely shade of green flecked with brown, undeniably clear and lucid.

"Thanks," she said when I handed her a latte.

I noticed she held one hand in front of her mouth when she spoke, the way I sometimes did when I'd eaten onions or garlic for lunch. I wondered if dropping off some toothpaste and a toothbrush for her would be a nice thing to do, or if it would be insulting.

I had to ask. "How do you manage to stay so clean?"

"There's an emergency shelter that lets me in to shower." She spoke in a crackly voice that sounded like it hadn't been used for a while. "I was sleeping there, but you can only stay for seven nights. So now I'm on a waiting list for a transitional shelter."

"Eat," I said. "You haven't even touched that." I sipped my latte and watched the people walking by while she ate the chicken and pasta. I guess I thought she might gobble, but she ate slowly and thoroughly, savoring each bite. Then she wiped the inside of the plastic container with the last piece of the breadstick bow tie and popped it into her mouth.

"Thank you," she said. "Did you make it?"

"I don't really cook anymore. I assemble. But I'll give you the recipe if you want."

Instead of answering, she put the top back on the plastic container and handed it to me.

"Sorry," I said. "That was stupid."

She shrugged.

We sipped our lattes in silence. It felt odd to be standing there hovering over her, but sitting next to her on the sidewalk didn't seem like quite the right thing to do either.

"Can I get you anything else?" I finally asked, as if I were a waiter at a sidewalk café.

She shook her head.

I took another sip of my latte. "Okay, well, I guess I'd better get to work."

She didn't say anything.

I turned to walk away. "Have a nice day" slipped out of my mouth before I could stop it.

CHAPTER 30

HAVE A NICE DAY? *HAVE A NICE DAY?* I MEET A homeless woman who has just crawled out from between two Dumpsters, and I tell her to have a nice day?

I flashed back to a long-forgotten day I'd spent with Denise and a bunch of other high school friends. We'd piled into somebody's old station wagon to drive the half hour from our suburban town to the nearest MBTA stop and take the subway to Boston.

The plan was to wander around Boston Common and then go shopping at Filene's Basement. It was a beautiful spring day, and we were all wearing bell-bottom dungarees and halter tops, as if they were uniforms. Fringed square-cut embroidered bags looped over our shoulders and bounced against our hips as we walked.

We flipped our hair and giggled whenever we passed boys who were even remotely cute.

"Yeah, so," one of us said.

"Buttons on ice cream, they don't stick," another one said.

Everybody else burst out laughing.

"Huh?" I said.

"*So* is really *sew,*" Denise whispered as we walked. "Buttons don't stick to ice cream, so you have to sew them on. Get it?"

"Not really," I said.

Denise rolled her eyes. "It's just something you say so it looks like you're talking, so guys don't think you're paying attention to them."

We followed the winding paths of the Common, dodging Frisbees as they sliced through the air. A couple of girls a few years older than us were blowing bubbles while a group of college guys made heroic leaps to pop them.

"Bubbles," Denise said. "Next time we have to remember to bring bubbles."

A man was sitting on the grass at the edge of the path. Street musicians were everywhere, but this was a different thing entirely. He had a cheap plastic guitar with two loose strings flapping in the breeze, and instead of an open guitar case for collecting money, he'd flipped over a ripped straw hat. His long hair was greasy and so were his jeans, and you could see the sole of one bare foot through a hole in his boot.

He was belting out a tuneless "Goodbye Yellow Brick Road" at the top of his lungs as he pounded the guitar. There was something so desperate about the sound of his voice that I stopped. I reached for my wallet, but I was afraid to move any closer to him, so I just stood there.

Up ahead, Denise turned around. "Come on," she yelled.

We went to Bailey's Ice Cream Parlor and sat in wire-backed chairs at button-topped tables. We all ordered identical hot fudge sundaes made with chocolate ribbon ice cream, Bailey's version of chocolate chip made with long thin slivers of dark chocolate.

And the whole time we ate I couldn't stop thinking about how I should have been brave enough to try to help that guy, even just a little.

JOSH WAS NOWHERE to be found, so I wandered around the hotel, looking at the paint samples that covered the walls like big chocolate stains. Then I made some to-do lists and wandered around some more. Finally I headed out to hit the flea markets and antique stores.

Bailey's Ice Cream Parlor had been closed for decades, but it was as if they'd shipped all their tables and chairs from Boston to Atlanta just this week. Everywhere I stopped I found another round glass-topped metal table or a pair of cute little chairs with heart-shaped twisted-wire backs.

I'd been thinking about something a bit more dramatic and Old World for the hotel patio. Bar-height tables and chairs that would be more comfortable to sit on and also more noticeable from the street. Elegantly curved steel legs. Maybe dark wood tabletops and distressed leather seats.

But the thing about staging is that you have to stay open to surprises, because they often turned out to be better than the things you planned. And you have to listen to the connections some mysterious part of your brain makes when you're not paying attention. Of course ice cream parlor tables and chairs made sense if we were going to name the hotel Hot Chocolate. How could I have missed it?

When all was said and done, this would be the thing people remembered. *Hot Chocolate*, they'd say, *you know that adorable boutique hotel in midtown with the patio that looks like an old ice cream parlor?*

I drove to Home Depot and rented a truck, then I retraced my route. By the time I got back to the hotel, I had eight slightly different glass-topped round tables and twenty-four mismatched chairs. I'd spray paint the table frames and chairs a rainbow of ice cream colors from mint green to orange sherbet.

I'd look for round wire Victorian plant stands, at least three feet high with lots of curlicues. And I'd keep the whole thing from getting too cutesy by placing tall square modern planters on either side of the door. Ooh, maybe I'd even splurge on some illuminated planters and tuck them into the corners. If you haven't seen them yet, they are amazing—tiny energy-efficient fluorescent bulbs make the whole pot glow from within, and the pots have reinforced fiberglass inner liners to handle the soil and water so nobody gets electrocuted.

I was glad I hadn't ordered the awning yet. I'd have to go back and look at the Sunbrella fabric samples again before I made a final decision about either the awning fabric or the paint colors for the tables and chairs.

I circled the block three times, trying to find an empty loading zone space in front of the hotel. I was careful not to look over at the spot where I'd last left the homeless woman. I had enough on my plate.

Fortunately the tables were small enough for me to carry by myself, but by the time I got everything onto the patio, my back and shoulders were screaming from the exertion.

Just as I was unloading the last chair from the truck, Josh pushed the front door of the hotel open.

"Your timing is impeccable," I said.

He reached for the chair I was carrying. I ignored him and kept walking.

He crossed his arms over his chest. "You could have called me."

I put the chair down. "Called you what?"

If he got it, he pretended he didn't. He scanned the jumble of tables and chairs. "Are those going to be safe out here overnight?"

"Probably not," I said. "We'll have to find a way to chain the tables to the patio, and the chairs will have to be stacked and brought in at night."

He reached for the door. "Let me prop this open, and I'll give you a hand."

"Knock yourself out," I said. And then I left it all to him and climbed into the truck.

After I returned the truck, I swung by Mellow Mushroom and picked up a pizza so I didn't have to get into another whose-turn-is-it-to-cook standoff. A note from Chance saying he had a meeting after work and would be home late was waiting for me on the kitchen counter.

I put two slices of pizza on a paper plate, poured a glass of milk, and carried them into the guest room.

When I woke up, fully clothed, I reached for my reading glasses and squinted at the bedside clock: 3:13 A.M.

I peeled off my clothes and pulled on a long T-shirt in the dark. I rolled back into bed and stared up at the ceiling. Finally I snapped on the light and fired up my laptop. I pulled out a paint brochure and my big fan deck of paint colors, too, since you never knew what kind of tricks your computer screen might play. While I loved all the bells and whistles of the paint company Web sites—the Benjamin Moore Personal Color Viewer even lets you upload a photo of a room and virtually change its colors with the click of a mouse—sometimes I just needed to make sure I was seeing accurate color representation.

The combination of a front door in Benjamin Moore's Million Dollar Red and tall chocolate ceramic pots would anchor the entrance. I'd pull the colors for the tables and chairs from the Gaston Seaglass–striped awning. I'd give everything a coat of Rust-Oleum rusty metal primer, and then start right in on the paint, spraying on two to three light coats a few minutes apart. Rust-Oleum had some great colors, too—Spa Blue would work for sure, as would Herbal Green, and maybe Grape and Teal. I'd buy only one can each of Candy Pink and Key Lime, just in case they veered past fun and into too much. As soon as I saw the colors on the chairs, I'd know.

The trick to using pops of a variety of accent colors is that each one needs to repeat in at least three different locations so it draws your eye around the space. So even though the arrangement of tables and chairs would look random, there would be a method to the cheerful madness.

Maybe I'd get the painters to do the spraying, or maybe I'd just borrow some drop cloths from them and do it myself out in the parking lot behind the hotel.

As soon as I thought of the parking lot, I remembered the Dumpsters. I closed my eyes, but I could still see the homeless woman crawling out from between them.

How could I have let her go back there?

But what could I have done? Dragged her to the transitional shelter and tried to talk them into letting her cut the line to get a bed? Taken her with me to a house that wasn't even mine and let her split the guest room with me? Shipped her back to Boston so that I'd have yet another person I couldn't get out of my house?

I crawled under the covers and turned off the light. I tossed and turned, trying to imagine what it would be like to try to sleep on a cardboard mattress between two rusty metal boxes. Would I be more afraid to go to sleep or to wake up and face the next day?

How had the homeless woman ended up homeless? Who had she been before that?

I stared at the nothingness of a pitch-black ceiling in a pitch-black room. Who was *I*? What did I want my life to be? What was my postmom mission?

CHAPTER 31

HER NAME WAS NAOMI. IT SEEMED LIKE THE WRONG name for a homeless woman, but maybe any name at all would have felt that way to me. Once she had a name, I couldn't look away.

I handed her a breakfast sandwich and a whole milk latte. I sipped my nonfat latte and watched the people passing by while she ate.

"WTF," I said finally. "How the hell did a nice woman like you end up in a place like this?"

She didn't say anything.

"What I meant is that I'd like to help you."

She seemed startlingly normal. But there was still a part of me that wondered if she might be bipolar, or psychotic, or even just plain old crazy. I mean, how else could she have ended up like this?

We found a vacant bench in a little park down the street. I wondered if anyone had ever spent the night sleeping on it. Maybe there was a waiting list for park benches, too.

I threw my empty latte cup into a trash barrel and then sat down on one side of the bench. Naomi sat on the other side. She squeezed her garbage bag firmly between her feet.

"So what happened?" I asked.

One thin, ring-less hand fluttered up to cover her mouth again. "My husband got sick. We were self-employed and our insurance company dropped him."

Her voice was so soft I had to strain to hear it over the sounds of the traffic and the birds.

"So we refinanced our bed-and-breakfast. And he didn't get better. The mortgage rate readjusted, and our payment tripled. The economy tanked, and suddenly I was running a sickroom instead of a business. We couldn't afford hospice. He died. Then the car died. The bank foreclosed a few months later. And I lived happily ever after."

"I am so, so sorry."

"Thank you," she whispered.

We sat some more. I don't know what she was thinking about, but I was racking my brain for a plan. I mean, what the hell was I going to do with her?

"Come on," I said. "Let's go shopping."

We put her garbage bag in the trunk of the rental car. I unlocked the car and held the passenger door open for her.

I climbed into the driver's side and checked my watch. "I'll be right back," I said. "I'm in the middle of a job, and I just have to get the painters going."

I thought for a moment, then I put my key into the ignition. I reached into my shoulder bag and took out the GPS and plugged her in. I picked up the unopened bottle of water that was sitting in the console cup holder and handed it to Naomi. Then I put the root beer readers with the tortoise highlights on the dashboard. I wrestled with my inner hoarder for a moment, then I exchanged them for Ponytail Guy's glasses.

A part of me might have been testing her trustworthiness. But another part could have been saying, Hey, *after all you've been through, if you've got somewhere to go and need to steal my rental car to get there, just do it. My GPS will keep an eye on you.* I'd wait forty-eight hours to report the car. *No idea,* I'd say to the cops. *Last time I saw it, it was just sitting in the parking lot, minding its own business.*

Denise would help me come up with a good explanation for the fact that I no longer had the car keys.

I'd hired the painting contractor with the middle bid, the best references, and the biggest crew. Behr's Iced Espresso had turned out to be a keeper, so we were ready to rock.

Of course, Josh was nowhere to be found, so I let the painters in myself.

"Good morning, ma'am," Harold the Painter said. "Looks like it's going to be a hot one."

In the South, even if you have a homeless woman sitting outside in your rental car, you can't just get down to business like you can in the North. You have to make small talk first.

"Sure does," I said. "How're you all doing today?"

The men all nodded and said witty things like "just fine, how about you, ma'am?"

I showed them the coffeepot on the bar and told them to help themselves. I'd given Harold the color numbers over the phone and marked the color I wanted on each wall with a big X, so this wasn't going to be rocket science.

"You sure about all this brown paint, ma'am?" Harold asked. "I only had 'em mix up five gallons at the paint store, just to be on the safe side."

I'd yet to meet a painter, North or South, who didn't think s/he was also a designer. You just had to nip it in the bud.

"The client's paying me to love it," I said. "So, yeah, I'm sure."

The crew snickered. "No worries," Harold said. "We've painted worse. And if the client shows, we'll back you up a hundred and ten percent."

"Thanks, guys," I said as I headed for the door. "Be back in a few."

"Still here, huh?" I said to Naomi when I got back to the car.

"If I had someplace to go, I'd already be there," she said.

On our way out to the highway we passed a group of homeless

men milling around a street corner. I glanced over at Naomi out of the corner of my eye, but she was staring straight ahead.

She reached for her water and unscrewed the top. "So what kind of a job is it?"

"What?"

"You said you had to let the painters in. I was just wondering what kind of work you do." She lowered her voice. "But I don't need to know."

"In point two miles, take ramp on right onto Route 285," the GPS said.

I leaned over and turned the volume down. "Don't be silly. I just wasn't following you. I'm a home stager."

"I've always wondered how that works."

My shoulders were so stiff from yesterday's heavy lifting that I could barely shrug. "Well, basically, you look at the big picture first. And next you clear away the unsightly parts. And then you focus on the things that get you the most bang for your buck."

When we got to Marshalls, we headed straight for the clearance rack. In my defense, I would have checked there first, even if I were shopping for myself.

"What size are you anyway?" I asked.

She shrugged. "I don't know anymore."

I flipped through a section of the rack I'd never fit into. "The good news/bad news, I guess."

Naomi put her hand in front of her mouth. "When my best friend was on her umpteenth round of chemo, everyone kept telling her how good she looked because she'd dropped so much weight. She said it was oddly flattering. 'Oddly flattering'—those were her exact words. Once when she was having a good day, I took her shopping, and she bought a whole new wardrobe."

"Did she make it?" I asked.

Naomi shook her head.

"Shit," I said. "Before or after your husband?"

"Before. She died just before he went into stage four."

I grabbed a nice pair of jeans, a pair of capris, and some T-shirts off the rack. "Here, try these on."

Naomi's hands were shaking. "Can we just get them? I don't think I can handle looking at myself."

She did try on a pair of Skechers, though. I grabbed some flip-flops and made her pick out a week's worth of underwear, a decent rolling suitcase, and a shoulder bag that doubled as a backpack.

"Okay," I said when we were back in the car. "Tell me the rest."

Naomi shrunk into her side of the seat, as if it could swallow her whole. "I met this guy online. It was a message board for people dealing with terminal illness. I had all these long hours to fill when my husband was dying, and he was such a good listener."

She pressed her cracked lips together. I handed her the bottle of water.

She took a small sip, maybe trying to make it last. "When everything fell apart, he was my lifeline. He'd check in maybe three, four times a day, and I'd tell him everything. When he found out I was losing the house, he asked me to move in with him. It seemed like a godsend. I didn't know what else to do. My kids flipped out—"

"Wait. You have kids?"

"Two. But they're just starting out, and they're both struggling financially, and I couldn't bring myself to tell them about the house. I don't know, I just thought I'd found the answer. And if it didn't work out, I'd get back on my feet and then figure out something."

"And your kids thought it was too soon, that you were betraying their dad?"

Naomi nodded. "They stopped talking to me."

"And the guy?"

Naomi was rocking softly now, like a mother trying to put a baby to sleep. "A total sicko. He had about eight different profiles, and he wanted me to cook for him while he spent all day reeling in women. It got worse and worse, and one day he asked me to do something I wouldn't, and he beat the shit out of me. Then he threw me out and locked all the doors. I hid in the woods behind the garage all night, and the minute he went out, I broke in and stole what I could."

"Oh, my God," I said. "Did you call your kids?"

"I didn't want them to see me like this," Naomi said.

She moved her hand away from her mouth and showed me what was left of her two front teeth.

CHAPTER 32

HERE'S THE THING. IF MOST OF YOUR TWO FRONT teeth are missing, it's not so easy to get a job. And if you don't have a place to live, you probably can't get one either. I mean, it's not like you can list the space between two Dumpsters as your mailing address.

We stopped at Atlanta Bread for sandwiches and so Naomi could change into some of her new clothes in the restroom.

I washed a bite of my Chicken Waldorf sandwich down with some seltzer. "Maybe we should give Dress for Success a call," I said when she came back. "They can give you some interview tips and help you get your skills up to speed. How comfortable are you on the computer?"

Naomi put her soupspoon down and covered her mouth. "I know Microsoft Word, Excel, and Outlook, plus Photoshop and Quicken. Oh, and Easy InnKeeping."

"Wow," I said. "Okay, so maybe they could hire you."

The GPS helped us find a walk-in dental clinic.

"Please don't tell them," Naomi said before we went inside.

Up until that second I'd planned on it. I'd go in, give the receptionist the whole song and dance, and get them to do the work for free. Or at least at a big discount.

"I'll pay you back," Naomi whispered.

"Damn right you will," I said. "I've wanted veneers for years."

It was a long wait, but even the temporary crowns made all the difference. "Smile," the dentist, who looked about twelve, said.

Naomi smiled.

"Wow," I said. "You're dazzling." And I wasn't even exaggerating.

I remembered Shannon mentioning that one of the hot bargains in Atlanta was New Talents, on West Paces Ferry, and that they had same-day service and did a great job. So that was our next stop.

"Don't worry," I said as the GPS and I searched for the address. "I'll go in with you and make sure they know what they're doing, but then I'm going to have to take off and check on the painters again while you're getting your color."

"A shampoo and a cut would be plenty," Naomi said. "More than enough."

"No way," I said. "After you get your life together, you can go gray if you want to. I might even do it with you. But there's enough ageism out there without putting up a gray flag, so for now, let's not take any chances."

"You're the expert." She was smiling like a pro now, as if she'd never stopped. "So tell me, is staging a person like staging a house?"

"Excuse me?"

"You know, look at the big picture, clear away the unsightly parts. Oh, and focus on the things that will get you the most bang for your buck?"

"Ha," I said. "You might have something there. Maybe I'll start a little side business."

Naomi turned Ponytail Guy's glasses over in her hands. "I can't decide whether I'm more grateful for the teeth or the reading glasses."

"Really?"

"You can't fill out a job application if you can't read it," she whispered.

As I drove, Naomi's words played over and over in my head. Without reading glasses, I'd be lost. Without a home, I'd be whatever was beyond lost. Homeless? Were there levels of homelessness, like Dante's levels of hell? Maybe Naomi didn't even think of herself as homeless so much as temporarily homeless. Were most of us only a paycheck or two and a couple of bad breaks away from being in the same boat?

BY THE TIME I got back to the hotel, some mysterious part of my brain had come up with an answer.

"You have reached your destination," the GPS said.

"Let's hope," I said.

The painters were still going at it, and Josh had actually materialized.

"Are you sure about these walls?" he said. Behind his back, Harold the Painter rolled his eyes.

"Absolutely," I said. "Have a seat. I've got some good news for you."

Josh chose a seat a few seats away from me at the bar, maybe wondering if it might be a trick.

"Coffee?" I said. "I keep forgetting to buy milk, but I have to tell you I found this amazing stuff called Truwhip. It's like Cool Whip for purists. I'm thinking we combine hot chocolate, Kahlúa, and vodka. Then we wipe the rim of a martini glass with Kahlúa and dip it in grated chocolate, we top it with Truwhip, and, *woilà*, we have our signature drink: Hot Chocolate Is the New Hotlanta."

"That's the good news?"

I put the coffeepot back. "I'm warming up to it. I think we should have a frozen signature drink, too. Maybe chocolate frozen yogurt and peppermint schnapps. We could call it Chocolate Chill."

Josh's pants pocket started to play "Stairway to Heaven." He pretended not to notice.

I raised my eyebrows. The tinny music stopped.

Josh stood up. "Sounds good. Okay, well, let me know if you need anything. I'll be . . . around."

I took a deep breath. "I can have the first-floor rooms completely staged by the end of the week. As soon as the paint dries, I think we need to start filling them. Nothing says success like a hotel full of guests."

"Whoa," Josh said. "I think we're getting ahead of ourselves here. Unless you're planning to move in and run the place yourself."

"Better than that," I said. "I found the perfect manager. Extensive bed-and-breakfast and inn experience, both as a manager and a former owner. Charming, reliable, detail-oriented. Up-to-date computer, reservations, and bookkeeping skills, cooking skills, the whole package. And, if we play our cards right, I think we can get her to move right into that efficiency next to the kitchen. We order her a computer and reconnect the phone lines, and we'll be up and running."

Josh tilted his head. "What's she looking for in terms of salary?"

"I don't have a figure," I said, "but essentially she'll be working round the clock, so she's not going to come cheap."

"I'm not going to pay her a cent over—"

And he named a figure that was double what I'd been thinking.

"Fine," I said. "But she'll need health care and a 401K. Matching."

Josh pursed his lips together and shook his head. "No way. It has to be contract. If she's still here and I haven't sold in six months, we'll talk."

I crossed my arms over my chest. "She has to have health care. It's nonnegotiable. Period."

Josh drained the rest of his coffee. "Done. Anything else?"

I gave him my most intimidating stare. "Yeah, her name is Naomi Hall, and if you hit on her, or so much as look at her cross-eyed, you and Denise and Melissa and her husband and I are going to have a nice long conversation, Mr. Stairway to Heaven. Got it?"

If he didn't gulp, he wanted to. "Got it," he said.

My eyes didn't tear up until he walked away and relief washed over me like a wave.

There are times when it makes sense to look at the big picture, and other times when you just have to look at one temporarily homeless woman at a time.

BEFORE I WENT BACK into the beauty school, I sat in the car and made some calls. I didn't want to keep Naomi waiting, but I just had to tell my family how much I loved them.

I dug my cell out of my shoulder bag and called the landline at home. It rang four times and went to voice mail. "I love you guys," I said after the beep. "I miss you and wish I were there with you. Whatever is or isn't happening with the house, I hope you're all having fun and just, I don't know, really appreciating each other. You know, having pizza and playing board games and all that good stuff. Anyway, call me when you get this."

I tried Greg's cell phone next. It went right to voice mail. "Hey, babe," I said. "Just want you to know I love you. I hope things are going well with the house, but even if they're not, I love you anyway. Call me when you get this, okay? I have so much to tell you. Did I say that I love you?"

I called Luke next. "Hey, sweetie," I said to his voice mail. "I love you. And I want you to know whatever you need from Dad and me, we're just totally there to support you. And I hope things are going well with your job and your girlfriend, and well, every-

thing, but even if they're not, I mean, that's okay, you have plenty
of time. Call me when you get this, okay?"

"Hi, honey," I said to Shannon's voice mail. "Hope your training is going well, and don't worry, I'll take good care of Chance.
Well, I won't do everything, but I'll definitely meet him halfway.
And even though it would be great if you can get Dad and Luke
moving, it's not the end of the world if you don't. Have some fun
with them, okay? I love you. Call me when you get this, okay,
honey?"

I sat for a minute, just drinking it in, feeling the love for my
family coursing through every ounce of my being. I wondered if
Naomi had ever taken the time to count her blessings, to appreciate her husband and her kids and her life before it all fell apart.
The world was such a terrifyingly fragile place.

"I guess we've just got to appreciate the good parts while they
last," I said to the GPS before I unplugged her. "And I want you to
know that I was pretty sure Naomi wasn't going to take you, but if
she did, the two of you would have had a nice life together."

Lucky I'd threatened Josh, because Naomi sure, as they say,
cleaned up good. Her chin-length hair was as shiny as a newly
stained mahogany floor, and when she turned her head, the highlights sparkled like a fresh coat of high-gloss polyurethane. As soon
as we hit CVS for some makeup, she'd be good to go.

She couldn't take her eyes off herself in the salon mirror.

I paid and tipped, and we headed for the car.

"I swear I'll find a way to pay you back every cent," Naomi said.

"Damn right you will," I said. "The first paycheck is all yours,
but after that, we'll set up a payment plan."

She stopped, one hand on the handle of the rental car. Her
pretty green eyes filled with tears. "It might take me a while to find
a job," she whispered. "I'm a little bit rusty."

"Don't be ridiculous," I said. "You start today."

I went over the details on the way back to the hotel.

"The weird thing is," Naomi said, "I actually think I can do this. And I'm okay with bartering it for a place to stay."

"Oh, puh-lease," I said. I told her the amount Josh had agreed to pay her.

"Dollars?" she said.

"Thousands," I said.

"Seriously?" she said.

"Seriously," I said.

Naomi closed her eyes. "OMG," she whispered.

CHAPTER 33

I COULDN'T BELIEVE HARTSFIELD-JACKSON INTERNA-
tional Airport let you park for the first half hour for free.

I reached over and grabbed my ticket from the machine. "Do
you hear that, Logan Airport?" I yelled as my window rolled up
again. "The world is not all about making a buck. A kind gesture
goes a long way."

The GPS crackled awake. "Continue point eight miles, then
turn left onto Airport Road."

"Nice try," I said, "but we're just about to park."

Denise was already waiting in the North baggage terminal when
I got there.

"Take your time, why don't you," she said when she saw me.

I shrugged. "So, next time call a taxi."

We gave each other a quick hug.

"How're you doing?" we both said at once.

"Owe me a Coke," we said as fast as we could.

"Tie," we said together.

"Two, two, two mints in one," I said.

"I wish we'd gotten to do one of those old Doublemint commer-
cials," Denise said. "We would have been brilliant."

"You look great," I said. I started rolling her carry-on toward the
exit. "Did you check anything?"

Denise reached in her bag for her iPhone. "Nope. You know me:
travel light, lighten up, don't be a lightweight."

Denise really did look fantastic. Great jeans, kick-ass boots, fresh blond highlights in her hair, and not a hint of regrowth at the roots. Her skin glowed like she was in love, possibly the result of a good chemical peel. She'd deny it, but she'd probably been prepping all week. I'd pretend I believed she'd just rolled out of Boston looking this good. That's what friends did for each other.

I had an odd urge to introduce her to the GPS when we got in the rental car, but I restrained myself.

"So," I said. "Have you talked to him?"

Denise put one hand behind her head and struck a glamour-puss pose. "Yes. I. Have."

"And?" I turned in my seat so I could back out of the parking spot without taking anyone out.

"And he lusts me, he really lusts me."

"Great," I said.

"Recalculating," the GPS said.

"You're not the one I'm worried about, honey," I said.

"What?" Denise said.

"Never mind," I said.

I slid my ticket into the machine. "Do you believe you don't have to pay for the first half hour here? It totally makes me want to move to Atlanta."

"It's still my turn," Denise said. "Okay, so our conversation went really well. Actually, I think Josh has been having some of the same feelings, and I'm okay with being the first to say it. I mean, I can understand that being in a committed relationship with me might be a little bit intimidating for him. I mean, I'm—"

"Older?" I said.

"Thanks. Anyway, we had such a great talk that I almost told him I was heading to Atlanta, but then I decided it would be more romantic if I surprised him."

We merged onto the highway. "The thing about surprises," I said, "is that you don't always get to pick the surprise."

Denise turned to look at me. "Did you really just say that?"

"In one mile, take ramp on right onto Interstate 85 North," the GPS said belatedly.

"Did she really just say that?" I said.

"Who?" Denise said.

"Hel-*lo*, we're already on 85. Listen," I said. "Josh is a cheater. It's all over him. I mean, what is he even doing in Atlanta?"

"Helping my best friend with the hotel?" Denise said.

"Not so I've noticed." I put on my blinker and managed to squeeze through the gridlock and over to a potentially faster lane.

Denise pitched her head forward and started fluffing her hair. "Okay, so he's not that helpful. Whatever."

"Denise, I'm ninety-nine percent positive he's here screwing around with his married college friend."

When Denise flipped her head back, her hair had tripled in volume. "I told you, that's just Melissa. Men and women really can just be friends, you know. We've evolved a lot as a species since *When Harry Met Sally*."

"We're not talking about men and women," I said. "We're talking about Josh."

Denise didn't say anything.

The car in front of us was covered in about six inches of pollen. Just looking at it made me want to sneeze. I wondered if the bees even bothered pollinating flowers in the South, or if they just sat back and said *whatever*. I mean, how could it miss?

"When I'm talking to him," I said, "his phone keeps ringing 'Stairway to Heaven' and he doesn't answer it."

"Big deal." Denise opened a bottle of water and took a long sip. "So it's her ring. Once they played it for twelve hours straight in college. That doesn't mean a thing."

"Reverse direction at the earliest opportunity," the GPS said.

"Good advice," I said. "Let's see if she takes it."

We drove for a while in silence.

"Shit," Denise said finally. "I did it again, didn't I?"

I exhaled. "I think so."

"But I wanna know-oh for sure," Denise sang.

"Don't worry, wild thing," I said. "We'll catch him—"

"And then we'll shoot him," Denise said.

"They'll never find us in Paris," I said.

BY THE TIME Chance pulled into the driveway, we were working on our second blender of Truwhip-topped brandied mint coolers, and Denise was just adding a big dollop of Truwhip to the strawberries, blueberries, and raspberries we'd layered in wineglasses.

"Genius," Denise said. "Who knew Truwhip was so versatile." She took a long sip of her drink. "Who even knew what Truwhip was."

"I know," I said. "It's the perfect counterpoint to whatever you're assembling. Hey, did I tell you yet that I did your penance?"

"Huh?"

"You know, do three nice things and give away a pair of reading glasses?" I took a sip of my drink. "Did you ever stop to think what it would be like to try to get through the day without your readers?"

Denise sat down at the table and gave me her lawyerly look. "Not having reading glasses is the biggest obstacle to disadvantaged people over forty reentering the workplace."

I shook my head. "How did I not know that?"

We heard the sound of a BMW SUV pulling into the driveway, and I dashed out to the garage to bury the assembled dinner evidence in the trash.

I made it to the door just in time to open it for Chance. "Hi, honey, you're home," I said sweetly.

Denise turned and struck a pose in the apron.

"Oh, boy," Chance said.

"Double trouble," Denise said.

"You remember Denise from the wedding," I said.

"Of course he does," Denise said.

I smiled my most persuasive smile. "You don't mind if she stays for a night or two, do you, son?"

My son-in-law stretched his mouth into a smile. "No, mo'am," he said.

Denise poured Chance a brandied mint cooler and topped it with an extra-large spoonful of Truwhip.

I pulled his chair out at the table. "Sit," I said. "We've been cooking for you for hours."

I finished assembling dinner while they chatted. I'd swung into Trader Joe's on the way home and picked up frozen grilled zucchini and eggplant, jarred bruschetta, shredded cheese, and a premade pizza shell. The whole meal will totally pass for homemade if you simply distress the edges of the pizza shell the way you might a mass-produced coffee table. Just whack the edges a few times with the back of a spoon. (With a table, it's better to use a ball-peen hammer.) Assemble a Trader Joe's Caesar salad kit, and you are good to go.

"Mmm-mmm," Chance said.

"Thanks, son," I said.

We watched Chance eat for a while.

Denise tilted her head back and polished off her mint cooler. "So tell me, Chance, why is it that men are such assholes?"

CHAPTER 34

"THAT SON-IN-LAW OF YOURS SURE DOES GO TO BED early," Denise said. "It wasn't even dark out."

"Ha."

"He's adorable. I didn't know it was possible to sigh with a southern accent. And those manners. To die for."

"I know. I think that's why Shannon fell for him. She said northern men are Neanderthals in comparison."

"I don't know, I love a good caveman."

We were each stretched out in one of the twin beds in the guest room, the covers pulled up to our chins. A single table lamp between the two beds made a circle of light on the ceiling.

Denise reached over and held her hand over the light.

I looked up at the ceiling. "Is that supposed to be a rabbit?"

"No, it's me giving Josh the finger."

"Got it. That's good though, right? I mean, if you're pissed, you're not feeling like a victim. I think you'll feel so much better after you confront him."

Denise made a fist with one hand and a peace sign with the other, then held both hands over the light. "That's a rabbit."

"Genius," I said.

"The thing is, I'm not even sure I should bother. Maybe I'll just block his calls. It kind of pales when you compare it to what you just told me about Naomi. God, I'm so superficial."

I put the backs of my wrists together and held them over the light. I flapped my fingers.

"True," I said. "But even superficial people have the right to be angry."

"Thank you. Is that a dog?"

"No, it's not a dog. It's a bird." I took one hand away. "And this is me giving you the bird."

Denise pulled her pillow out from behind her head and hugged it. "Do you think I'll ever get it right?"

"Sure, as soon as you pick someone who's not a loser."

"Thanks."

"I mean, you act like it's this great big secret, Denise, but the truth is nobody gets it completely right. You just pick someone who has your back and wants the same things as you do, and then you make it work."

We stared at the ceiling.

"I hope Naomi's doing okay," I said. "I'll get it fixed up, but that little efficiency she's staying in is kind of a dump."

"Ha, but it's not a Dumpster. God, can you imagine?"

"No. And wait till you meet her. She's so normal. You'd swear we went to high school with her or something."

I fluffed up my pillow and put it back behind my head. I loved Denise, but she'd definitely taken the better pillow while I was in the bathroom. She'd commandeered my mood ring, too.

"What if we're wrong?" Denise said. "What if he's not really seeing someone else?"

"See," I said. "That's why you get yourself in trouble. Even if we're wrong about this particular situation, which we're not, you shouldn't spend five minutes with someone you don't trust. You have to know that you're a team, that neither of you would ever betray each other. You just wouldn't."

"No offense," Denise said. "But you and your family are a tiny bit too perfect for my taste."

"Ha," I said. "Tell me that after one of them calls me back."

"What do you mean?"

I reached into the light and tried to make a rabbit. Maybe there was a certain developmental stage in your life when you moved from real pets to shadow pets. No vet bills, no poop or puke to clean up.

"It's just that I went through this big epiphany after Naomi told me her story, and I thought, *why am I making such a big deal about selling the house? I mean, it's a house. I have a great husband. What does it really matter where we live?*"

"He could get hit by a car tomorrow. Or you could."

"Thanks. So I called Greg and Luke and Shannon and left messages saying how much I loved them."

"That's so cute. It's like a Disney movie. What did they say when they called back? Or is it too gaggable?"

I pulled my pillow out again and gave it another punch. "That's the strange thing. They didn't call back."

"None of them?"

"Nope."

Denise hugged her pillow tighter. "How long ago did you call?"

"I don't know. Seven or eight hours."

"Ha. That's really funny."

"No, it's not."

"Maybe you've been such a bitch they're blocking your calls."

"Takes one to know one," I said.

"Wow, I haven't thought of that expression since high school. Remember: I'm rubber, you're glue, everything bounces off me and sticks to you?"

"Before I left, I told Greg not to call me until the house was ready to sell."

"So, big deal. He knows how you get."

"But what if something really did happen to him, and that's the last thing he remembers me saying before he dies?"

"Then he won't feel so bad about being dead."

"No wonder you're single. Who could live with you?"

Denise held her middle finger over the light.

"A one-eared rabbit?"

"Bingo." Denise sighed. "You know, if this were a movie, this would be the scene where we smoked a joint."

"Yeah, what's up with that anyway? I mean, they do it in every Boomer movie."

Denise held my mood ring under the light. "Look, the thought of good drugs makes me nostalgic."

"It makes us all nostalgic. It's the last time we can remember having any fun."

"Speak for yourself."

I gave my pathetic pillow another punch. "And then we'd have a pillow fight."

"No, first we'd eat everything in sight, and then we'd have a pillow fight."

"The munchies," I said. "I mean, how cool were the munchies." The pillow was still flat as a pancake, but I tucked it back behind my head anyway. "Drugs were different back then. It was a freer, gentler time."

"Oh, please," Denise said. "We were young and stupid."

"I read in an article that a significant number of Boomers said they'd start smoking pot again in their retirement, as long as they were in a safe place."

"Ha," Denise said. "You mean like a padded room?"

"Maybe that's why they put the master bedrooms on the first floor in those fifty-five-plus places," I said. "So you can get high and not break a hip falling down the stairs."

"The visiting nurse could come around and take your car keys."

"And stock your refrigerator."

"Mystic Mints," Denise said. "Remember those? I ate a whole box once."

"Frozen Snickers bars," I said. "And Twizzlers."

"Together? That's disgusting."

"No, first the Snickers. And then the Twizzlers. If you peeled them into strands, they tasted better. Like licorice hair."

"Ooh, that's heavy."

"Thank you. I'm really profound when I'm remembering being high."

"There's a whole cottage industry here," Denise said. "We could make a fortune. Hash brownies laced with Geritol . . ."

"Organic salad greens with walnuts, Gorgonzola, and sprouted marijuana seeds."

"We could chew on our hemp hospital gowns between drug deals. And get walkers with beeping lights so we don't accidentally run over anyone else in the nursing home when we're stoned."

"We'll make a fortune," I said. "We'll be in Paris in no time."

"But first we have to shoot Josh," Denise said. "It's the only way."

CHAPTER 35

CHANCE PROMISED TO TAKE US PAINTBALL SHOP-
ping, since he needed some new fishing lures anyway. I didn't
quite get the connection between the two, but I figured I'd have
plenty of time to figure it out. If you ever decide to remove a Juliet
balcony from your daughter's living room, be prepared for a long day.

Chance's friends started rolling in before our second cup of
coffee.

Denise pushed aside the bamboo blinds in the guest room. "You
know, somehow I'm feeling less depressed already."

I finished tying my sneakers. "Don't even think about it. Shannon will kill us both if you hit on one of Chance's friends."

"Don't worry. I'm all look but no touch. Hey, what are they doing out there?"

I joined Denise at the window. Three SUVs were parked in a
circle in the driveway with their backs facing and the rear doors
open. Chance's friends were sitting on their vehicles and drinking
coffee from take-out cups.

"It's called tailgating," I said. "It's huge in the South. Football
games, rock concerts, any time a zebra gets loose on the highway."

"What?"

"Never mind. Come on, I need some more caffeine."

I poured another cup of coffee, topped it with a spoonful of
Truwhip, then opened a cabinet and started piling things on the
kitchen counter.

"*What* are you doing?" Denise asked.

"Obviously," I said, "I'm assembling a coffee cake. I'm mixing instant maple and brown sugar oatmeal with walnuts and a tiny bit of butter, and then I'm going to sprinkle it over the top of this cinnamon thingy I bought at Trader Joe's and heat it till it's warm."

"It looks more like recycling than assembling to me."

"So, don't eat it."

It doesn't matter if you call it assembling, recycling, faux cooking, or cheating. I mean, potato, pohtahto, tomato, tomahto. But if you start a work session by serving hot fake-baked anything to men who are giving up a significant part of their weekend to help you with a project, you'll get on their good sides.

I cut whatever it was into squares and placed them on one of the Danish modern serving trays I'd mailed to Shannon.

"I'll do the honors," Denise said. She flipped the apron over her head.

I grabbed a handful of paper napkins and followed her out to the driveway.

"Mmm-mmm," Chance's friends said when they tried it.

"See," I said to Denise.

Every team needs a leader, and since it was Chance's house, I knew I had to give him the opportunity to assume the role.

Five minutes later, they were all still sitting around on their tailgates, drinking coffee.

"Looks like it's going to be a hot one," Billy, or maybe it was Hunter, said.

"Why, thank you," Denise said. She gave the ruffled hem of her apron a little shake.

"Time's up," I said. "Here's the plan. First we move out all the furniture, then we set up the scaffolding Chance borrowed. You remembered it, right?"

Chance jumped off the tailgate of his pollen-coated BMW SUV. "Yes'm, I did, but I'm thinking we might could use two step-ladders and just lay a big old board across them."

I shivered. "Every time I kill one of Shannon's husbands, she makes me find her a new one."

Chance's friends got a good laugh out of that one, and one of them even volunteered to be Shannon's next husband. But safety is key in any do-it-yourself project. You need to get a plan. You have to measure twice, or even three times, so you only have to cut once and so no one gets cut. And if you've taken the time to borrow some scaffolding from a painter friend, do me a favor and use it.

In no time, we had the living room cleared out and the furniture piled up in the other rooms. We covered the floor with drop cloths.

We all stood in the living room and looked up at the little balcony.

"Anybody want to do one last Juliet balcony soliloquy?" Denise said.

"Chance?" one of the guys suggested.

"Pass," Chance said.

"Come on," Denise said. She gave him a shove.

"Chance, Chance, Chance," his friends chanted.

Chance clomped up the stairs. The little wooden balcony shutters opened.

"Oh, Romeo, Romeo," Hunter, or maybe it was Billy, yelled. "Wherefore art thou Romeo?"

My tall, handsome son-in-law peered out over the living room, one hand held above his eyes like a visor.

"But soft," he said. "What light through yonder window breaks?"

Denise sighed. "Southern accents just slay me."

I elbowed her.

Chance switched hands and peered in the other direction. "It is the East, and Juliet is the sun."

He switched hands again. A sputtering noise came out of his mouth, like the sound of an old coffee percolator. He made a wave-like motion with one arm and then the other. "Yo, get up off your butt, start the day, make some hay, fair sun, and kill that envious moon."

Before Southern Shakespeare rap could take over the world, Chance's friends started peppering him with pillows from the sofa. He caught one and hurled it back, then closed the shutters and clomped back down the stairs.

"Moving right along," I said once he'd reentered the living room and finished bowing. "The balcony has to be screwed into the studs. So we just saw off the metal as close as we can, get rid of the balcony, figure out how to get the screws out, and take it from there."

"Piece of cake," Denise said.

Two hours and several saws later, Chance and one of his friends lowered the balcony down to the rest of us with a rope.

"Nice yard art," one of Chance's friends said.

"I don't think so," I said. "Let's bring it right out to the garage."

The Swiss chalet–like shutters on either side of the balcony opening had to go, so we took those down next and brought them out to the garage, too. Eventually we got all the metal screws unscrewed, both the big ones that had been holding the balcony and the smaller ones from the shutters.

"Okay," I said. "Now we close this sucker in."

Filling in a big hole with drywall is a bitch. It just is. First you have to cut a new section of drywall. Then you have to figure out how to make a support to screw it into. We finally managed to frame out some pieces of wood and get them to fit just right, without anyone falling out the hole in the second bedroom wall and ending up on the floor of the living room below.

If you don't want the drywall seams to show, you've got to match factory edge to factory edge and cut edge to cut edge. Then you screw them into place, apply drywall tape, and follow with mud. You sand and repeat as necessary until the wall is perfect.

We finished the bedroom side first, then went downstairs and climbed up on the scaffolding. Since only two of us could fit, somewhere along the line, Denise and Chance's friends disappeared. Loud music blasted out, and some really bad singing followed.

"Is that 'Good Vibrations'?" I said. "A barely recognizable karaoke version of 'Good Vibrations'?"

I kept one hand on the wall for stability. I wasn't a big fan of heights.

Chance stopped sanding. "Sounds about right. That's not karaoke, though. Shannon bought me Rock Band 3 for my birthday. You should see the guitar that came with it."

"Now that's a good wife." I took half a step back to assess our progress. "She is going to be crazy happy when she sees this."

Chance's face lit up. "I sure do hope so, mo'am. She's not always so easy to please."

"She gets that from her father's side of the family. Don't worry, you'll get used to it. Come on, let's give this some time to dry, then we can prime and paint."

Chance and I got in on the next round of Rock Band. My guitar playing wasn't much better than my voice, but I kicked butt when it came to choreographing the backup singers.

"Come on, follow me," I said as "Get Up, Stand Up" blared from the speaker and Denise butchered the guitar chords. "Your hands are going like this, and it's just step-touch forward and step-touch back."

Eventually Chance made a pizza run, and everybody else headed outside to do some more tailgating.

I tiptoed into the guest room and closed the door. I found my cell and checked for messages. Not a one.

I took the pillow off Denise's bed and tucked both pillows between my head and my headboard. I called Greg.

It went right to voice mail.

"I can't believe you haven't called me back," I said. Then I hung up.

THE GUYS ALL JUMPED into Chance's SUV, and Denise and I followed them to a store by the side of the highway. A huge yellow sign with a big-mouthed fish on it proclaimed BASS PRO SHOPS in red letters. I'd always thought that fishing was the most boring thing in the entire world, but it turned out there was something even worse: shopping for fishing stuff.

Chance and his friends cruised the aisles as if they were strolling through heaven. Chance held up a buggy-looking hairy thing that must have been a fishing lure. "Sweet," he said. "Listen to this: 'Drives bass wild with high-action round rubber legs, unique body styles, pulsating hand-tied hackles, and water-piercing colors.'"

"Hey," Denise said. "Enough with the fishing porn. Remember? You guys were going to help us go paintball shopping?"

Nobody even looked up.

I grabbed Denise by the arm.

We found the paintball section. Denise put on a big black Darth Vader–esque helmet with an attached visor and padded mouthpiece. She handed an identical one to me.

I slid it down over my reading glasses. "'If your mask fogs up,'" I read out loud, "'call yourself out, and ask for a referee to escort you to the deadbox.'"

"Who knew paintball would be so complicated?" Denise said.

"Well, I definitely think we want the pink paintballs," I said.

"I agree," Denise said. "The green ones aren't nearly as eye-catching."

I flipped to the next page of the instructions. "OMG. It says we need barrel condoms to protect against unintentional firing."

Denise put two in our shopping cart. "Of course we do. Accidental discharge is nothing to sneeze at. There are enough little paintballs running around unsupervised without us adding to the epidemic."

"'Do not overshoot people,'" I read. "'Overshooting occurs when you shoot someone more times than is technically necessary.'"

"Duh," Denise said.

I picked up a rifle. "I don't know," I said. "I thought they were going to be cuter than this."

I put the rifle down again. My readers were fogging up, so I handed the instructions to Denise.

"'Before shooting,'" she read, "'have your tank inspected. The valve of a CO_2 tank holds up to forty-five hundred pounds per square inch of pressure. If you accidentally unscrew it, it will become a dangerous rocket that might become airborne and kill people. This is serious and has resulted in the deaths of several unfortunate players and the occasional innocent bystander.'"

"Okay, that's it." I started taking the stuff out of our cart.

"Bummer," Denise said. "It was such a good fantasy. It got me through some really rough stuff over the years."

I shook my head. "They sure know how to take the fun out of violence."

We pushed our cart to the next aisle.

"Nerf guns are cute," Denise said. She unhooked one that looked just like a sniper rifle, except that it was bright yellow and purple.

"We wouldn't even have to go into the hotel," I said. "We could just set up on a rooftop across the street."

Denise hooked it back on the display. "We have to be careful. I think this one might violate the Geneva Convention."

I grabbed a Super Soaker off the shelf. "Luke used to have one just like this. Actually, he probably still does."

Denise picked up a hot pink plastic gun. "Aww," Denise said. "A bubble gun."

"That'll get their attention," I said.

She put the bubble gun back and picked up three plastic jars of bubbles.

"Is that it?" the woman at the register asked.

Denise handed her a credit card. "What else could we possibly need?"

CHAPTER 36

W E WERE SITTING IN THE HOTEL PARKING LOT, and Denise was blowing bubbles out the passenger window. She'd been doing this nonstop since we'd left Bass Pro Shops, leaving a trail of bubbles in our wake as we drove across Atlanta. My only hope was that she'd run out of bubbles before she started hyperventilating.

I turned the key in the ignition and lowered the window on my side.

"You okay?" I asked.

There was just enough light to see her shrug. "I should have bought that bubble gun. It had a nice heft to it."

She put her bubbles in the cup holder and opened the car door.

About a million stars lit up a sky that was the color of my mood ring on a bad day. I kept time with Denise as she walked a lap around the parking lot in sandals designed for neither speed nor distance.

She stopped at the Dumpsters. "This is where she was sleeping?"

"Yeah," I said.

I bent down and slid out a corner of Naomi's cardboard mattress.

"I kind of want to know what it feels like," Denise said. "I mean, can you imagine being out here all by yourself? And trying to sleep?"

Out on the street a horn beeped, cutting into the dull crunch of traffic.

I unfolded one flap of the cardboard.

Denise took a step back. "Careful. These sandals were really expensive."

I didn't say anything.

"God, I am so going to rot in hell for that."

"Okay," I said, "send Naomi a pair of the same sandals. And say three Hail Marys."

"Done."

I slid the cardboard back. We walked through the alleyway and out to the street.

"So," I said, "what's the plan? Once we have a plan, you'll feel so much better."

Denise turned and started walking away from the hotel. "Okay, new fantasy. We score some pot."

"Ha," I said. "Right."

Denise's heels clicked along the sidewalk. "I'm serious. You just have to go up to the first people we pass who look high and ask them if they know where we can get some."

"Me? Why do I have to ask?"

"Because I'm a lawyer. I could get into a lot of trouble."

"And I couldn't?"

"You're in a creative field. It's expected."

"But you can represent yourself. Come on, you're stalling." I grabbed Denise by the arm. We executed a legal U-turn and headed in the direction of the hotel.

"And then," Denise said, "once we're high as kites, we just march right into the hotel and start knocking on doors until we find them."

"Right," I said. "What do we say when we knock?"

"Candygram," Denise said in a fake voice.

I totally cracked up at the old *Saturday Night Live* reference. So did Denise. We laughed and laughed, in that hysterical way we all used to laugh in high school. A couple crossed the street to avoid walking by us. We leaned against the corner of the hotel for support. When one of us would start to wind down, the other would rev us up again.

"ROTGLMAO," Denise said. "No wait, I think it's ROT-GAMLO."

"That's ridiculous," I said. "How can you ass your laugh off?"

That set us off again.

"Cleaning woman," Denise said in the same fake voice.

I gasped for breath. "OMG, I think I just peed my pants."

"God, what else did they used to say in those *SNL* skits?" Denise said. "Oh, I know."

She knocked on the air in front of us. "Fire Department."

"Open up," I said in a low voice. "There's been a complaint that sparks are flying in this room."

Denise stopped laughing.

"Sorry," I said. "Sorry, sorry, sorry."

"Come on," Denise said. "Let's just get out of here. We can go pretend we have the munchies or something."

I looped my arm through hers. "You have to confront him. You'll feel so much better once you get it over with. And besides, I want you to meet Naomi."

Naomi peered over Ponytail Guy's glasses as she opened the door for us. I had to admit they looked better on her than they did on Ponytail Guy. Or me.

I introduced her to Denise. Denise gave her some bubbles.

"Thank you," Naomi said. She hugged the jar of bubbles to her chest.

There were only two chairs at the small round table, so I sat on the edge of the bed.

"How's it going?" I asked.

Naomi pushed the glasses up to the top of her head. "I'm getting there. I'm hoping we'll be ready to start taking reservations sometime next week."

"I don't mean that. I mean you."

She crossed her arms over her chest. "I think it's all just hitting me."

Denise reached over and put a hand on Naomi's forearm. "You have to call your kids."

"Sorry," I said. "I should have asked you before I told Denise."

"That's okay," Naomi said. "I used to tell my best friend everything, too." She closed her eyes. "I know I have to call them. I just want to get on my feet first."

Denise's hand was still on Naomi's arm. "Listen, I'm a lawyer. I specialize in family practice. I'll make the first contact for you and explain what happened. It'll make it easier on both sides."

Naomi looked over at me, then back at Denise. "Really?"

"Absolutely," Denise said.

"I'll pay you," Naomi said. "It might take me a little while, but I'll definitely pay you."

"Not necessary," Denise said. "You'll do a favor for me one day. Or you'll do something nice for someone else."

Naomi's eyes filled. "Thank you."

"Do you know if Josh is here?" I asked.

Naomi nodded. "I think I heard him come in about an hour ago."

"Was anyone with him?"

Naomi shrugged. "I heard a woman laughing."

"Perfect," I said. I pushed myself off the bed. "Come on, I'll go with you."

Naomi held the door open for us.

"Be right back," I said.

"Yeah," Denise said. "This won't take long."

Denise and I walked silently through the hallway.

Just as we reached the elevator, the door opened, and Melissa walked out.

CHAPTER 37

"CUT IT OUT," DENISE SAID. "I CAN'T BELIEVE HE TOLD you I was just his lawyer."

"Oh, wait, he also said he was your son's godfather," Melissa said.

"My son." Denise shook her head. "Like I'd let him near my son if I had one. What a snake in the grass."

Standing across from Denise, Melissa looked like a younger, blonder version of her. They were even wearing almost the same outfit. Skinny jeans. Nice jackets. Funky scarves. Edgy sandals. What was up with men dating the same physical type? Did they lack imagination, or was it encoded in their DNA that a woman with a certain height/build/hair and eye color was potential mate material? If something happened to me, would Greg grieve for an appropriate length of time and then go looking for Replacement Me?

A wave of anxiety rolled over me. I reached for my BlackBerry. In the night-light of midtown, I could see my lack of messages without even putting on my readers.

I tucked the BlackBerry back into my shoulder bag. "He didn't have pizza with you and your husband and your three kids last week?" I asked.

Melissa shook her head. "I'm divorced. Josh has never even met my kids. My life's a mess right now, but I'm not stupid."

"How long have you been seeing him?" Denise asked.

"Ha," Melissa said. "Which time? Josh has this eerie way of knowing when I'm vulnerable enough to sleep with him again, but not quite available. Does that make sense? I mean, we've been through this like eight times since college. The minute I want more, he's gone."

Nobody said anything.

"I would have stayed away if I knew he was involved with you," Melissa said.

"Thank you," Denise said. "But you're not the problem."

"Thank you," Melissa said. "I think he just makes me feel young."

"That's funny," Denise said. "He makes me feel old."

"I don't know," I said. "He makes me feel just right."

Melissa whipped her head around.

"Kidding," I said. "Sorry."

We strolled our way back to the parking lot.

"So now what?" Denise said.

"We could cowrite a blog about him," Melissa said.

Denise shook her head. "Too much work. And he'd probably love the attention. We could send out his obituary. At least that's just a one-shot deal."

"I know," I said. "Call him and say you both want to sleep with him. And then you handcuff him to the bed and give him a full body wax."

"You should have thought of that while we were out shopping," Denise said. "No way am I going to another store at this hour."

"We could sneak in and replace his shampoo with Nair," Melissa said. "He has this thing about his full head of hair."

"More shopping," Denise said.

I pointed to Josh's silver Corvette. "That's his rental car. I'm just saying."

Denise and Melissa were already rifling through their bags.

What they lacked in artistry, they made up for in energy. I held Melissa's key chain flashlight so they could see what they were writing.

I'VE GOT YOUR NUMBER: 0 Denise wrote in red across the windshield.

"Wow," I said. "That's the thickest lipstick I've ever seen."

"It's actually a Sephora rouge stick," Denise said. "Great for traveling."

I DO <u>NOT</u> HAVE PMS, I'M JUST OVER YOU Melissa scrawled in liquid eyeliner on the passenger window.

"OMG," Denise said. "Don't you hate when men attribute real issues to hormone levels?" YOU SUCK she wrote in Sharpie on the roof.

Melissa drew an arrow on the windshield. THIS HORN BLOWS AND SO DOES THE DRIVER she wrote in a really nice shade of lipstick.

I put on my readers with the hand not holding the flashlight and leaned closer to the windshield. "Ooh, what color is that? I love it."

Melissa turned it over to read the label. "Laura Mercier Amaretto. It's a little more money, but it's worth it."

NO, WE DON'T NEED TO TALK Denise wrote on the back windshield. WE NEVER NEED TO TALK AGAIN.

I HAVE THE RIGHT TO REMAIN SILENT. ANYTHING YOU SAY WILL BE USED AGAINST YOU she wrote beside it.

STUPID IS AS STUPID DOES AND YOU DID she scrawled.

She moved around to one of the back passenger windows. OH, THE FUN YOU'RE GOING TO MISS.

She put her rouge stick away. She took out a tube of mascara and drew a goopy picture of a hand with the middle finger extended.

Melissa and I looked at each other.

I put my arm around Denise. "Come on, let's just hair mousse his door handle and get out of here. There's a great tapas bar down the street."

Denise handed me the mascara and wiped her eyes with the back of her hands. "Good plan. Revenge makes me thirsty."

"Wait right here," I said. "I just want to invite Naomi to come with us."

"**THAT WAS FUN**," Denise said. "Well, not the most fun I've ever had in my life, but I mean, fun given the circumstances."

I put on my blinker and moved over a lane. "Josh might be an idiot, but I have to say he's got good taste in women."

"Yeah, I was hoping to hate her, but I liked Melissa a lot. And she was awesome when she called him from the tapas bar." Denise lowered her voice to a sexy drawl that sounded just like Melissa. "'Hey, sugah. Just wanted to let you know your girlfriend Denise and I are waiting for you in the parking lot. *Naked.*'"

"Ha," I said. "I bet that got him out there. I probably should have submitted my staging bill first, though."

"Don't worry," Denise said. "He'll pay. He knows who your lawyer is."

"Oh, wait. Maybe I should be more worried about Naomi. You don't think he'll take the car trashing out on her, do you?"

Denise picked up her bubbles and put them down again. "No way. She's probably the only woman in Atlanta still speaking to him. And it's not like he'll want to sell the hotel until the market turns, so my guess is he'll just pack up and move on to the next thing. We'll keep in close touch with her to be sure. Melissa said she'd call her, too."

Once the graffiti party was over, I'd had to fight to keep my thoughts from drifting. I wanted to be there for Denise, for Naomi, even for Melissa. But a part of my brain seemed to have plans of its own. At the tapas bar, I'd kept my BlackBerry on the booth beside me like a date, and twice I thought I heard the first notes of "Do You Want to Dance?"

It was just incomprehensible to me that my family hadn't called me back. Especially Greg. I couldn't wait to get home and check in with Chance to find out what was going on. He and Shannon were probably on the phone right now.

"I'm so glad I finally got Naomi to give me that creep's screen name," Denise said.

"In point three miles, take ramp on left," the GPS said.

I shook my head to bring myself back to the car. "Just be careful, okay? Naomi doesn't need any more trouble."

"Don't worry, he'll never know what hit him. I'll reel him in, toy with him mercilessly, and then figure out the best agency to turn him over to."

"It's so scary," I said. "I mean, who knows how many other women he's stringing along."

"And then there's Josh," Denise said.

I kept my eyes on the road.

"Next time," I said. "You'll get it right."

She didn't say anything.

"Are you okay?" I finally said.

Denise made a sound that was almost a laugh. "Yeah, I mean what are my choices? And it's not like a part of me didn't see it coming. I don't know, maybe it was the whole devil-you-know thing with Josh. The thought of going through it all again with another person feels pretty daunting right now. Do you think I'm too old to adopt?"

"A boyfriend?"

"Ha." She let out a long sigh. "You know, sometimes your life makes me feel so lonely."

I took my eyes off the road for just a second. "Sometimes your life makes me feel like I'm suffocating in mine. And other times it makes me feel lucky to have what I have."

CHAPTER 38

CHANCE HAD LEFT A NOTE FOR US ON THE KITCHEN counter: GONE FISHING. MAKE YOURSELVES AT HOME.

"Was it something we said?" Denise asked.

I dialed Greg's cell. It went right to voice mail. "Call me," I said. "Call me the second you get this."

I grabbed the iron railing and jogged down the three little steps to the living room, then back up to the kitchen.

"Something's wrong," I said. "Something's really, really wrong."

Denise opened the refrigerator and handed me a bottle of water. "What are you talking about?"

"Nobody has called me back. Nobody."

Denise took a long sip of water. "So? It could be lots of things."

"Like what?"

"I don't know. Maybe they're already in bed. Maybe they forgot to charge their cell phones."

I realized I was rocking. I crossed my arms and grabbed my elbows to stop myself. "I tried our landline, too. Maybe they're at the hospital. Maybe there was an accident. Maybe Greg had a stroke."

"Stop," Denise said. "Come on, it's late. They're probably asleep. You can call again in the morning."

"Something's wrong. I can feel it in my bones."

Long after Denise had fallen asleep, I stared up at nothingness. Finally I fumbled around on the bedside table in the dark until I found my mood ring. I slipped it on. I closed my eyes and tried to will myself to sleep. I kept them closed for as long as I could take it, then I opened them again.

I was so exhausted that when I finally grabbed my readers and went into the bathroom to check my mood ring under the light, for a moment I flashed back and thought I was on my way to read a pregnancy test.

I sat on the closed toilet seat and watched as my mood ring turned from an uncertain amber to a seriously stressed black.

I tiptoed back into the guest room and brought my BlackBerry out to the hallway.

Amazingly, the Missed Call icon was now lit up. I clicked on it.

Greg had called. Two days before. And there was no message.

ONE DAY NOT LONG AFTER we'd moved into our new old house and the kids and I were home alone, there was a knock on the door. Luke was napping, and Shannon and I had been waiting for one of Shannon's friends to get dropped off for an after-school play-date.

I didn't think twice. The heavy oak door creaked as I swung it open.

A guy was standing there. He was small and wiry with pale skin and a really bad haircut that made his hair stick out in little patches. He was wearing a white T-shirt and shiny blue work pants. He had a homemade tattoo on his forearm, something swirly and snakelike.

I pushed Shannon back behind me. "Can I help you?"

"Where's the bed?"

I shoved the door as hard as I could.

He moved his foot in to stop it, like a salesman selling encyclo-pedias in an old movie. Something about his eyes wasn't right.

"You live here?" he asked.

Come home, Greg, I thought. *Please come home now.*

"Yes, my husband and I bought it a few months ago." I put extra emphasis on the word *husband*. "He should be home any minute," I lied.

The guy inched his foot forward a fraction of an inch. He was wearing an ancient pair of Docksiders. Not work boots, but those boat shoes with little leather ties.

I could feel the warmth of Shannon's body pressing against me. Why hadn't we rehearsed this? *If a strange man comes to the door, go get your brother. Run across the street to the neighbors' as fast as you can and tell them to call the police.*

"Where's the bed?" he asked again. He turned sideways and did a ninja leap into the foyer.

If I grabbed Shannon and ran out the front door, I'd leave Luke upstairs in his bed.

I gave Shannon a nudge toward the door. "Go wait on the swings for Katie."

She dug her fingers into my thigh. "I don't want to," she said.

The guy peered up the long central staircase, then turned and sprinted through the hallway and out to the mudroom. I heard the door to the mudroom scrape open, followed by the *thud-thud-thud* of feet on the stairs up to the secret room. Their rhythm matched the beat of my heart.

I grabbed Shannon by the arm and raced up the stairs to Luke's bedroom.

"Cowabunga," he growled when he saw us.

Luke was getting too heavy to carry, but I scooped him up from his big-boy bed like he was a newborn.

"Mom?" Shannon said. When I saw the look on her face, my eyes filled with tears.

"Run," I said. "Just run."

We clomped down the stairs.

The guy took a long step into the foyer and crossed his arms over his chest.

I bit my tongue so I wouldn't scream.

"You didn't find no water bed up there in that room over the garage?"

"No," I said.

"Where'd they go?"

"Vermont," I said.

He scratched a patch of hair. "Well, that's too far to go for a fuckin' bed."

And then he walked out. Just like that.

And in the blink of an eye we had our old life back.

All of our lives hang by a thread. Anything can happen, and sometimes it does.

It was the randomness that was staggering. You could do everything right, cross your *t*'s and dot your *i*'s, and still that lightning bolt could head straight for you, and not for the people who didn't even bother to take their vitamins. The ones who, face it, barely even watched their kids.

What if that drunk gets into the car, just as we're heading home, all buckled into our minivan, snug as a bug in a rug? What if something happens to one of the kids? What if that lump on Greg's knee turns out to be, you know, something? What if the crazy guy comes back again? What if he has friends?

For the rest of my life, I'd never again open a door without thinking about what could be on the other side.

CHAPTER 39

I UNHOOKED MY SEAT BELT WHILE DENISE WAS STILL pulling into my driveway.

"Thank you," I said. "And sorry to make you get up so early."

Denise yawned. "It's not like there was anything to hang around for. And I need to go makeup shopping anyway."

I tried to laugh, but it came out like a croak.

Denise gave me a shove. "Go. Call me later."

We'd left so early that even the Atlanta streets were deserted. When we dropped off my rental car, the sleepy guy at the desk offered to drive us to the nearest MARTA station.

At the airport, I overpaid for a ticket while Denise paid the standby fee to get on the earlier flight.

She handed me her receipt. "Bill him. For both of us."

The flight was only half full. I tapped my toes and tried not to think, but every single horror story I'd absorbed over the years flashed through my head: entire families murdered in burglaries gone bad, gas explosions, accidental poisonings, heart attacks. I should have planned better, checked in more, said I love you a zillion extra times to each member of my family.

The outside house lights twinkled in the morning sun. The shades were still down.

I opened the mudroom door and stepped over a pair of sneakers. I slid my key into the lock that opened the door to the kitchen.

A towering pile of pizza boxes greeted me from the kitchen

counter. Shannon's Bedazzler shared the granite island with Mouse Trap, three empty beer bottles, a glass half full of milk, a Diet Coke can.

The kitchen cabinets were still doorless.

I couldn't believe it.

I dropped my carry-on to the floor and plunked my shoulder bag on the counter. I jogged across the great room to the center staircase.

"Somebody better be hurt," I yelled.

The bathroom door creaked open. "Hey," Greg said as he jogged down the stairs. "What are you doing home?"

"What happened?" I said.

Greg tilted his head. "Shannon didn't tell you, did she?"

He leaned in for a kiss. I took a step back. "Where are they? What happened? Just tell me."

"Relax," Greg said. "Everything's fine. The kids went out for a jog. They tried keeping up with me yesterday, and I blew them both out of the water. So now they're in training."

I wondered if coming back early for no reason to a house that was not only not ready to go on the market but a total disaster was grounds for divorce. I fought for control. "Why didn't you call me back?"

Greg smiled. "I tried once. But then I wanted to surprise you, and I had to wait till I was sure."

"What the hell are you talking about?" I said. I might have even screamed it.

"The house," Greg said. "We sold the house."

I could see his lips moving and even hear the words, but I couldn't wrap my brain around what he was saying.

"What?" I said.

"We sold the house. I mentioned it to the tennis guys a couple weeks ago, and I guess one of them knew somebody who knew somebody who was looking. Anyway, we were out in the side yard playing badminton—Shannon and me against Luke and Raven— and this couple just pulled into the driveway. So I let them in and they loved it."

"You let them in? Please tell me the house didn't look like this."

Greg shrugged. "Who cares? They made us an offer we couldn't refuse. I called a real estate lawyer from my gym, and he drew up the purchase and sales. As soon as you sign, we'll be in escrow. Shannon offered to forge your signature if we didn't have time to FedEx it to you. She said she perfected it in high school."

I sat down on the stairs. "You let them see the kitchen without the cabinet doors?"

Greg sat down beside me and put his arm around my shoulders. "Hon, you're missing the point."

I shook my head. "Just tell me you didn't let them open the drawers. Or the closets."

Greg kissed me on top of the head.

"Wait," I said. "We don't want to give it away. Fully staged houses always get more money. How much did they offer?"

He told me.

"Seriously?" I said.

"Seriously," he said.

"Do they know the housing market is in a slump?"

Greg wiggled his eyebrows. "It didn't seem like the best time to bring it up."

I closed my eyes and leaned against my husband as the full weight of seller's remorse kicked in. "It's just that there are so many memories in this house."

Greg squeezed my shoulder. "We'll pack them up and take them with us. Plus, now we don't have any choice. The kids split up most of our furniture. The new owners want to close in thirty days. Luke found a place, so we can crash on his sofa if we have to. Actually, I guess that would be our sofa. But I'm thinking we pay off our debt, put what's left of our stuff in storage, and do a little traveling."

I looked at my husband of almost three decades. "I'm speech-less."

I'd almost forgotten how much I loved Greg's laugh. "Well, that's a first," he said.

"I don't know," I said. "It's like the messy guys won or some-thing."

"I'm a good winner," Greg said. "I won't gloat."

I shook my head. "This would never fly on HGTV."

"It doesn't have to."

I just sat there and tried to let it all sink in. My house wasn't perfect, and neither was my life. And there's an emotional cost to new beginnings, a scary kind of letting go and heading into the unknown that fights with the part of me that wants to believe all the world can and should be staged.

But WTF.

I held out my hand and watched my mood ring turn blue. Not the pale blue of a cloudless sky at noon. But the rich deep indigo of the ocean blending into the sky under the light of a full beach moon.

CHAPTER 40

"ACTION," SHANNON SAID.

Luke pushed a button on the video camera.

"Shouldn't we make a sign for the opening credits?" I asked. "I think there's still some poster board out in the garage."

"Mo-om," they said.

"Owe me a Coke," they both said at once.

"We'll do the titles in iMovie after we finish," Luke said. "We can even add a theme song at the beginning."

Greg looked up from the box he was packing. "How about Tom Rush's 'Remember Song'? You know, the one about not being able to remember anything? It's got a nice Boomer vibe."

"I think we'd have to get permission for that," I said.

"Like he'd remember whether he gave it to you," Greg said.

Shannon looked over at the living room clock. "Come on, you guys. Chance is waiting for me to call."

"Yeah," Luke said. "Raven's going to be here in like ten minutes."

"Okay," I said. I gave my hair a quick fluff. "I'm Sandra Sullivan, and this is my audition tape for HGTV's *Design Star*. Actually, my plan is to expand the show by creating a spin-off. I'm calling it *Design Star Midlife*."

I looked straight at the camera.

"Because here's the thing: midlife women should have their own show. We've been around the block a few times. We know what we want, and we're not afraid to go after it. We've got great taste and the courage of our convictions. And face it, we pretty much rule the world."

I reached for my first prop. "Which is not to say that we don't have an Achilles' heel." I held up an empty gallon paint can filled with reading glasses. "The only thing that really sucks about midlife is that your eyes go."

"I don't think you should say *suck*, Mom," Shannon said. "Your demographic might find it offensive."

I let out a puff of air. "Shit. Does that mean I have to start over?"

"No," Luke said. "We can edit it out. Just pick up where you left off."

"Okay," I said. "The only thing that really *stinks* about midlife is that your eyes go. So if my show is chosen, I mean, *when* my show is chosen, a part of our outreach will be to collect reading glasses through Readers for Readers. You might not know this, but the biggest obstacle to disadvantaged people over forty reentering the workplace is that they can't afford readers."

I looked dramatically at the camera. "You can't fill out a job application if you can't see it."

I switched the paint bucket full of reading glasses for a full gallon of paint. I flipped the lid off with a flamboyant twist of a flathead screwdriver.

"Okay, here's my first tip." I took off a big rubber band I'd circled around my wrist like a bracelet and looped it over the paint can vertically so it bisected the opening evenly.

"Do you make a big, goopy mess every time you paint? Well, instead of wiping the excess paint on the side of the can and letting it drip down the edge and onto your drop cloth or even your freshly washed floor . . ."

I dipped a fresh paintbrush into the paint, and then ran the full length of the bristles along the taut rubber band. The excess paint dropped neatly into the center of the paint can.

I flipped my hair out of my face and smiled at the camera.

"It's genius. Oh, and this amazing paint color? Why, that's Million Dollar Red. Trust me, you'll love it. Everybody does. Anyway, you'll love my show, too. I'll share exclusive decorating and staging tricks and tips. We'll take a field trip to see a boutique hotel in Atlanta I just finished staging, and while we're in the area, I'll show you how to remove a Juliet balcony and turn it into a feature wall. And I'll even share some footage of me packing up my own personal home and deciding what to keep and what to pawn off on my kids."

Shannon and Luke rolled their eyes.

I ignored them. "And then you can follow my husband and me as we head off into our next chapter together."

I gave the camera my most dazzling smile and hit it out of the park. "Buckle up, everybody—it's going to be a wild midlife ride."

Go to **ClaireCook.com** and click on **Readers for Readers**
to find out how your outgrown reading glasses can
help someone else find a foreseeable future.

SANDRA SULLIVAN'S BEST STAGING TIPS

DE-CLUTTER, DE-CLUTTER, DE-CLUTTER.
You have too much stuff. Admit it. Get rid of it.

DUST, RUB, SWEEP, SCRUB. Clean till it gleams.
Make your world sparkle.

UP AGAINST THE WALL. If that's where your furniture
is, move some of it out entirely and float the rest of it in the
center of the room in cozy conversational groupings.

SHAKE IT UP. CHANGE IT OUT. Pile some books
on a table and top with a lamp. Bring in some accent pillows
in vibrant colors and interesting patterns. Rotate your accessories, which are the crown jewels of your home.

LET THE SUNSHINE IN. Ditch the heavy drapes.
Think sheer, airy curtains, with privacy blinds that disappear
during the daytime.

LIGHT UP YOUR LIFE. A dark house is a depressing house, so let there be light. Add under-cabinet kitchen lights. Tuck uplights behind potted plants or hide them in corners. Increase the wattage in your lamp bulbs to make your home a brighter prospect for buyers. (Switch to energy-saving bulbs and you'll still come out ahead on the eco front.)

MIRROR, MIRROR ON THE WALLS.
Think statement frames and bounce that light around.

WARM AND NEUTRAL IS THE WAY TO GO.
And paint is the way to get there.

DROP THOSE FRAMES. Hanging too high is the biggest rookie mistake going. Approximately sixty to sixty-five inches from the floor to the center of the piece of art is the rule of thumb. Think how low you can go and adjust as needed.

THREE'S THE CHARM. Three candles, three baskets, three seashells. Group your accessories in threes. If it looks too skimpy, you can up it to five, but keep it odd.

ALSO BY CLAIRE COOK

WWW.CLAIRECOOK.COM

voice